# The Return of Elliott Eastman
## A.K.A. The Occupy Wall Street Manifesto

by

Ignatius Ryan

TELEMACHUS PRESS

Cover Designed by Telemachus Press, LLC

Cover Art:
Copyright © ThinkStock Photos #101514776/Business Man Portrait on White Background/Hemera Technologies
Copyright © ThinkStock Photos #111939282/South Façade of White House with Cherry Blossoms/iStockPhoto
Copyright © ThinkStock Photos #92045098/Beauty Pinup/iStockPhoto
Copyright © ThinkStock Photos #95784195/Sheriff Badge on Blue Background/iStockPhoto
Copyright © ThinkStock Photos #87567816/PhotoObjects.net/Hemera Technologies/Getty Images

Published by Telemachus Press, LLC
http://www.telemachuspress.com

ISBN# 978-1-937698-35-5 (eBook)
ISBN# 978-1-937698-36-2 (paperback)

Version 2012.03.26

Printed in the United States of America

10  9  8  7  6  5  4  3  2  1

## To Elliott.

I hope you're out there.
We need you.

# The Return of Elliott Eastman

A.K.A The Occupy Wall Street Manifesto

# Chapter One

DR. PAUL YATES' cell phone rang. Lifting it from the end table and setting down the medical journal he'd been reading, he studied the number for a moment.

"Hmm," he murmured, recognizing the number as that of his radiologist, Ellen Hartmann.

"Why would she be calling so late?" he muttered to himself as he pressed the miniscule green button on his phone and said, "Hello, Ellen."

"I'm sorry to bother you at this late hour, but I thought you would want to know. Is your computer on? I can e-mail the x-rays to you."

"I can turn it on, but why the urgency? What's going on?"

Ellen hesitated, then spoke in a leaden tone, knowing the impact her words would have on the esteemed surgeon. "It's Elliott Eastman. I thought you would want to see them for yourself."

"Oh, yes, please send them over right away."

Dr. Paul Yates rushed to his computer. Five minutes later he was struggling to stifle a sob, staring horrified at the images on the screen.

Immediately he picked up his phone. He hesitated for a moment to be sure he could phrase this properly, then pressed the speed dial button.

A moment later a voice said, "Master Eastman's residence, how may I help you?"

Dr. Yates recognized the deep bass tones of Maurice, Elliott's butler and said, "Maurice, its Paul Yates. Is Elliott home?"

"Why yes he is Dr. Yates. Would you like me to inform him you are on the line?"

"No, no Maurice. Just tell him I'm on my way over."

"Yes, Dr. Yates."

As the Doctor drove, struggling to stay under the speed limit, he brushed the occasional tear from his eyes, recalling the first time he'd seen Elliott Eastman. The tough Master Sergeant had been hit by a road side bomb, fought for an hour and a half against the Afghani insurgents who had ambushed his command, then been rushed by medivac helicopter to the field hospital. When the soldiers brought him in on a stretcher and laid him on the table, the good doctor had carefully removed the bloody bandages, taken one glance at the wound and said, "That leg has to come off, right above the ankle."

Elliott looked up and said calmly, "I thought so. I'll flip a coin. Heads, you take it off, tails I do."

"Relax soldier. That's my job. You just enjoy the pain pills."

"No pills," Elliott growled. "We're still too close to the kill zone. They reduce my awareness of our surroundings."

For a moment the doctor studied the camouflage painted face with the piercing green eyes, the stubble of beard and the close cropped black hair. A trickle of blood, probably from a flying rock, dribbled from his right temple. "Whatever you say Sergeant," the doctor quipped.

"No pills."

At the time the young Dr. Yates thought the comment strange. He assumed the moment the saw touched his leg the soldier would cry out in pain demanding relief, but he'd not made a sound as the leg was removed just above the ankle. During the ensuing months of recuperation, the doctor had gotten to know Elliott Eastman and realized there were few people in the world like him. That was over 35 years ago. Since then, Elliott's parents had died leaving him quite well off, but he'd taken that money, invested it in a software company and tripled it. He'd then started his own global investment firm and over the years become one of the one hundred richest men in the world. He'd never married. In spite of his wealth he'd stayed in touch with the men of his platoon, helping them with financial or family issues when needed. They were his family, and they adored him.

As Dr. Yates drove through the enormous gates, over the quarter mile long gravel drive and up to the sprawling French provincial style mansion, he steeled himself to the news he must deliver. He promised himself he wouldn't break down while performing this hideous task.

Maurice, the butler answered the door and with a sweeping bow allowed Dr. Yates to pass through.

"Please follow me, sir. He's in the study."

Dr. Yates followed the servant past an enormous dining hall with twenty foot ceilings and a fireplace as big as a rail car. The winding hallway led alongside a cavernous living room towards the study, which was yet another huge room with floor to ceiling book shelves, a river rock fire place with a roaring fire and a twelve foot long desk stacked high with papers and manuscripts.

"Paul," Elliott greeted his old friend warmly, extending a hand and then gripping the doctors out stretched hand in both of his.

"Have a seat. Can I get you a drink? This is later than I generally receive guests, but as I have often said, my door is always open to you."

"I'll take a brandy if you have some," Dr. Yates replied softly, wondering how he was going to break the news.

"How about a 30 year old Napoleon brandy?"

"Sounds perfect."

"I believe I'll join you."

"How's the leg?" the doctor asked.

"Still missing," Elliott replied over his shoulder.

Dr. Yates smiled.

As Elliott moved over towards the glass shelving of the bar, the doctor studied him. Despite his prostheses he held himself perfectly straight and moved with a certain grace. The shock of white hair atop his head framed the rugged and deeply tanned face. It was hard to imagine this towering powerful figure of a man, a master sergeant, two-time United States Senator from Colorado and champion for the poor and for peace, did not know the future he faced.

With a brandy snifter in each hand Elliott turned from the bar and crossed the several paces of plush carpeting to where the doctor was seated. As he handed him the glass he said, "So, to what do I owe the pleasure? It can't be chess. The last time we played you vowed never to play me again."

Paul allowed himself a brief smile and decided to get right to the point. That was what Elliott would do if their roles were reversed.

"No Elliott, I'm afraid it's not chess. As you know, you were in for a check up a week or so ago. I received a phone call from my radiologist earlier this evening and, well I'm afraid the news is not good."

"How so?" Elliott replied, thoughtfully sipping his drink and sitting down on a rust colored over-stuffed leather chair.

"It's primarily pancreatic, but it's metastasized. It's wide spread and probably moving quickly throughout your body."

Elliott did not respond. Not even a shadow crossed his face, so the doctor continued.

"I probably didn't say that as properly as I might have. We can do dye tests, remove the tumors in the pancreas, and they have the radiation injection that can stop the damn stuff right in its tracks."

"You've never been a good liar, Paul. I can tell by the look in your eyes you don't believe a word you just said."

Paul studied the floor and whispered, "You've got six to eight months, maybe a year at the most. I'm sorry Elliott. I wish I had better news."

"Oh hell, let's look on the bright side of things. Not too many men get the chance to know the date of their death," Elliott said gruffly, standing and turning towards the fireplace. Paul stood as well. "Look, we can fight this thing. There are experimental drugs ..."

Paul fell silent once he noted Elliott's upraised hand.

"Do you believe I'm the type to be bedridden for a few months, watching myself slowly waste away and then die in delirium from a morphine drip?"

The two men fell silent for a moment.

"What will you do?" Paul asked. "You have no heirs. You never married. You have no children and your parents are gone."

"Do? Oh, there's a lot I can do. More than you know. There is something I've wanted to do for a long time. And as for heirs, maybe I've got a few hundred million heirs right here in the good old USA."

Dr. Yates was puzzled by the statement, but decided not to press the issue.

"I'm going to consult with some specialists over the next few days and we'll come up with a treatment plan," he said as he stood and shook Elliott's hand.

"Good, thanks Paul. I'll wait to hear from you."


Once the good doctor left, Elliott turned back to the fire and sipped his drink. He sat staring into the fire for a long time. There was so much he still wished to do with his life, but now he must pare down the list. Near midnight Maurice entered the room. "Sir is there anything else I can do for you before I retire?"

"Yes, as a matter of fact there is Maurice," Elliott replied moving over to the mahogany desk. "Please come and sit down."

Maurice complied with this strange request and took a seat on the edge of the chair.

"Maurice, you will not be in my employ much longer. As my way of saying thanks I'm going to provide you with some money, but before I let you go I would like you to do a couple of things for me."

"Is there something wrong?" Maurice asked, his voice tightening. "My service has always been prompt and discrete, hasn't it? We've been together for more than twenty years. I don't know what I'll do."

Elliott looked up to see the fear in his faithful servant's eyes.

"Maurice, you have been my friend for more than twenty five years. Did you think this is the way it would end, with a summary judgment and swift boot out the door in the middle of the night?"

Maurice smiled. "I don't know. I've seen you hand out some pretty swift justice to some pretty tough customers."

Elliott laughed, "True, but we won't let that story leave this room."

As Master Elliott spoke he was writing in his check ledger. When he was done writing, he tore out a check and presented it to his trusted friend. "I want you to take this one million dollar check. Take it down and open an account in your name at Dallas National Bank. If there are any questions, talk to Jim Arnold and tell him he's welcome to call me. In return I want you to accept stewardship of this estate until the time of your death when you will see that it is deeded to St. Jude's Hospital. Thirdly, I want you to mail these twenty envelopes first thing in the morning."

Elliott handed the butler a packet of faded letters held together by ancient rubber bands.

"What's wrong sir? Are you feeling alright? I can't accept this."

"I feel fine. I'm thinking very clearly."

"What are you going to do?"

"As far as you're to know I'm going to live out the last of my days at the ranch in Colorado, my friend. Now stand up and give your old boss a hug."

Both men stood and embraced for more than a minute. Then without a word, Maurice strode from the room.

# Chapter Two

ONCE HE COMPLETED his daily three-mile run, Eddie Kelley checked his mail around three in the afternoon. As he walked up the driveway to his ranch house flipping through the bills he noted a postmark from Dallas, Texas with the return address to one 'Elliott Eastman.'

Sitting on the front stoop he swiftly tore open the letter. The writing was clean and crisp.

Dear Eddie,

Your presence is requested at 1958 Eastman Road, Fairplay, Colorado on May 5th, 2018. Your travel expenses are covered. It's time for Operation Anvil.

Sincerely, Your Friend,
Elliott Eastman

'That's three days from now,' Eddie thought. Marching into the family room where his wife sat reading a book he announced. "The Master Sergeant has called a meeting in Colorado in three days. I'll be packing and leaving in the morning."

She knew when the Master Sergeant sent word there was no discussing the matter. He had helped Eddie on many an occasion, both financially and otherwise.

"Are you driving?" his wife asked.

"Yes, it's a little over a days drive from here."

"When will you be back?"

"A few days, no more."

"Let me wash up some clothes to take and I'll pack some snacks for the drive," she said, setting down the book.

The following morning she kissed him on the cheek and said, "Have a safe trip."

Nineteen other men received the same letter.

# Chapter Three

THE MEETING WAS held in the great hall of the main house at the sprawling Eastman ranch on the slopes of the Rocky Mountains. Wagon wheel chandeliers hung suspended from thick hand hewn pine trusses thirty feet above the floor. An enormous Kodiak bear head snarled down from where it was mounted on a floor to ceiling river rock fireplace. Along the rear wall, a series of French doors with clerestory windows above them gave the guests a panoramic view of the snow-covered Rockies. There was laughter and friendly ribbing between the men who had all served together under the Master Sergeant in Afghanistan and Iraq, but hadn't seen each other in many years.

The double doors from the hallway opened and the long-term ranch hand, Greer Jackson, dressed in white tuxedo, stood aside as Elliott Eastman strode into the room. The river rock walls and the heavy hand hewn beams twenty-four feet above shook to the thunderous ovation he received from his former men-in-arms. After a series of heartfelt hugs and firm hand shakes the men were seated and Elliott spoke.

"I'm sure all of you remember the raucous debates we had around the campfires back in Afghanistan when we were going to change the world. When we vowed more young men would not fight and die to fill the coffers of the Malliburtons and the Blackwaters of the world. When we vowed to make the world a better place by the sacrifices we made in the service of our country."

Elliott paused for a moment and studied the somber faces. "As you know, I was a Senator for a number of years representing the great state of Colorado. I saw the workings of our government at every level. I think it is safe to say our nation is in dire straights. It is not better off than it was when we left Afghanistan those many years ago. The economy is on the ropes, we're hemorrhaging jobs, the number of families falling below the poverty level has been increasing for years, and urban slums are cropping up everywhere. Money has a death grip on the government. It's obvious our beloved nation is headed in the wrong direction and has been for a long time; yet our corporate leaders grow ever wealthier with each passing day."

Again Elliott paused. "James," he said turning to a heavy set man with deep brown eyes and a neatly trimmed beard, "I know you had some issues with your son being unable to find work and resorting to petty theft. I helped you get him released after one year of incarceration when he was facing fifteen years in prison for stealing a bicycle under the three strikes law.

"Nine years ago I helped you Rick, when your daughter graduated from college with $60,000 in student loans at 19% interest. She was unable to find work, falling behind in payments and the interest rates and penalties were eating her alive. She was contemplating suicide as I recall, and you were very scared."

"Sallie Mae, the bastards had her trapped in debt before she even had a chance to start her life," Rick Wheeler replied through gritted teeth. "They had no qualms about ruining her life."

The other men in the room could feel the rage seething within Rick, the former sharp shooter.

"I could go on, but I think it's plain to all of us that the system is broken."

Elliott knew he might lose some of the men with what he was about to say, but he would test their mettle and go with the plan he was about to outline regardless.

"Look around you gentlemen. Life has been good, more than I've deserved really, but it is time for me to give back. So I ask you, how do we make a change in the direction our once great nation has taken? Do we write letters to our representatives? Do you believe that will change anything? The answer is, 'No.' I'm sure many of you will remember sitting around the campfires in Iraq lamenting our lack of Kevlar vests, flak jackets, or at least heavier armor for our Humvees. We all saw friends die over there for want of a few inexpensive items the government simply couldn't procure. We didn't understand it at the time. There were times when our anger was immense, and we hoped one of our beloved representatives would ride along with us just once."

"Here, here," Eddie growled, and a murmur of agreement rolled through the room. Many of the men were recalling those memories of bewilderment and anger at the lack of concern for their well being by those in power.

"We spoke those many years ago about an Operation Anvil; A way to bring about change in a swift and meaningful way. As I recall it was Eddie who said, 'we need a way to awaken the powers that be that simply could not be ignored, like dropping an anvil on their toes.'

"I can tell you from first hand experience that we are never going to change the way Congress works by going through the usual channels. They are awash in corporate money up there, both Democrats and Republicans. They are not going to reform themselves, and the public has no chance of reforming them. They aren't removable en mass as that would require a revolution, and you know me better than to think I would even remotely consider such a course of action. So how do we go about making change in this country, change of the magnitude we need, playing by the rules? The answer is we can't. I think it might be time to use a little friendly persuasion on our esteemed legislators."

The men all laughed and some huzzahs rang through the assembly. They all knew when the Master Sergeant suggested a little 'friendly persuasion' he usually was about to start kicking butt.

"I'm going to lay some ideas on the table, some goals if you will, and we can kick them around and share some thoughts on how we might achieve them. And remember, we need not worry about the money required to execute any plan we come up with because I can secure funding."

"One goal near and dear to my heart is to have credit card rates set at 7%. Where did the banks gain the right to charge 18, 24, even 29%? They got that right by funneling millions of dollars into the right lobbyists' hands. What better way to free up capital and spur the economy than relieving our fellow citizens from usurious debt? And Sallie Mae charges exorbitant rates on student loans, plunging our children into years and years of debt before their lives have even begun and leaves them facing a virtual debtors' prison if they were to miss a payment."

"I back you all the way on that one, Sarge," Rick said.

"And why should we pay trillions of dollars a year to support over 1,100 military bases across the world? Many of those bases are in countries where the local populace despises us. We could cut that number in half and bring that money home to hire teachers, build schools and repair bridges."

"I'm on board for that," one of the former army rangers in the back of the room said.

"Now the center piece comes from a very strong belief that the hole we have dug in terms of our national debt is far too huge to be dealt with by cutting a little here and increasing some taxes there. We can adopt a Financial Transaction Fee that will be charged on all stock, commodities, futures and derivatives contracts. These types of contracts have grown enormously in recent years and are now over $703 trillion annually. We can bring this plan to fruition, and once our national debt is eliminated we can apply the almost 600 billion a year we will save in interest payments on the debt to other worthy goals. There have been proposals of this nature on many an occasion, but they have always been shot down by the government. When Europe was in dire straights back in 2011 the Europeans were pushing hard for a Financial Transaction Fee, but Treasury Secretary Tim Guttner ..."

"Don't you mean Tim Gutless," one of the men shouted from the back of the room.

Elliott smiled. "Gutless would have none of it. I believe if he had stepped up, Europe might not have suffered the way it has since then."

James stood and said, "And for profit prisons must go. We imprison more people per capita than any other country in the world. Huge numbers of men and women enter our prison system for the smallest of crimes, turn into hardened criminals and become the huge profit engine that is our prison system."

"Hang on James. Let's not get carried away," Elliott said. "I don't want to try for too much. Just like in Iraq, the more complicated a plan is the more room for error. We can talk about the prison system when we break up into groups in a few minutes. If you gather enough support for a sound plan, I might consider it."

"Fair enough," James said and sat down.

Elliott continued. "To achieve these worthy goals we'll place a small transaction fee on stock trades, futures, commodities, derivatives and foreign exchange trades. Ten dollars on trades over one thousand, one hundred dollars on trades over one hundred thousand and one thousand dollars on trades over one million. I'm going to approach the people I know in Congress and the President with a proposal for a bill called the "War on the Deficit". I've done the calculations. We can pay off the eighteen trillion in debt in less than seven years. But in conjunction with this approach we must achieve deficit reduction. This will be initiated by the base closures, which by conservative estimates will generate 400 to 500 billion a year in savings. And lastly, the reduction in credit card rates will generate a consumer-spending boom. Remember when President Rush, back in 2006, gave every family six hundred dollars? It didn't do much. People paid their credit cards down. Now imagine if they, along with the reduction in Sallie Mae rates for our kids, were given six hundred or a thousand dollars a month more to spend for the next thirty six months rather than paying it to the banks. This is what the reduction in credit card rates will do. We'll have this economy back on its feet in no time, and it doesn't cost the government a dime."

"You'll never get the banks to reduce their rates," someone said.

"We'll see about that," Elliott replied, and held up his glass of wine. "Here is to Operation Anvil."

"To Operation Anvil," the men cried out as one and raised their glasses.

Following the conclusion of Elliott's speech the men broke up into small groups and discussed various ways of executing the ideas Elliott had put forth. The meeting went on well into the night. Brandy and cigars were consumed in great quantities. Morning light was beginning to filter through the huge arched windows of the hall when the meeting finally broke up.

Over the course of the next three days a plan of action was hammered out. Two man teams would contact the CEO's of Sallie Mae, Bank of America and Capital One. Richard 'Rick' Wheeler would head up the team to open discussions with Kenny Borel, the head of Sallie Mae. Another group led by James Lally would deal with the prison system in daring fashion. Elliott wasn't wild about the prison aspect of the plan and actually excluded it, but James felt so strongly about it that Elliott relented. James maneuvered himself to a quiet table with Elliott and pressed his case.

"I never told you none of this, but my boy was going to be locked up for a long time. He wrote letters to his mother begging her to smuggle rope into the prison so he could hang himself. It was killing her. He was going to be another one of the revolving door prisoners that never got out of the system. It wasn't right what they we're doing to him. It's not what this country is about."

James grew quiet and reached across the table and clutched Elliott's hand saying, "I can't thank you enough for all you did Sarge."

Elliott looked across the table at James Lally. James was older now but still broad across the shoulders and his red hair had grayed some, but he was still a handsome giant. He knew this man to be a fearless fighter. He'd gone into firefights to save his buddies when even Elliott might have hesitated, but Elliott had also seen James sobbing over the broken body of a little Afghani girl killed by mistake in a night raid. His was a heart of gold. "How is Martin now?" Elliott asked.

"He's doing great. He's married, got a baby on the way and a good job," James replied with pride.

"Good," Elliott said, "Listen James. I'll move forward with funding for your prison scheme, but it is not part of Operation Anvil. You're your own man on this one, and I'll only fund it under the caveat that not one solitary soul is to be injured. That means none of ours and none of the opposition. If anyone is hurt, I'll pull the funding instantly."

"Thanks Sarge. Thank you so much," James replied. "You won't regret it."

Meanwhile Elliott himself would enlist the help of retired General Robert Gates, one of the most esteemed Generals to ever wear the uniform, to open discussions with the Secretary of Defense Bruce Holland regarding base closures.

Also Elliott would have his team of lawyers, along with some legislative specialists, draft wording for a bill creating the Financial Transaction Fee and set up a meeting with the Securities and Exchange Commissioner to discuss it. Elliott felt if he could get the backing of the SEC, then he'd have an easier time getting a member of the House of Representatives to sponsor the bill in Congress.

# Chapter Four

THE JET-BLACK eighteen-wheeler raced through the night like an orca whale surging toward its victim. Two army drones armed with three stinger missiles each, rested comfortably in the cargo hold awaiting their mission. Eddie Kelley softly whistled an old Beatles tune under his breath as they neared Huntsville, Alabama. Six other two-man teams, similarly armed, neared their destinations as well.

At dawn the following day the big rig pulled off a lonely byway into the shadows beneath a towering stand of cottonwoods. They were about fifteen miles from Huntsville and its sprawling prison yard. At exactly nine a.m., during the prisoners' morning break, the drones were wheeled from the rear of the rig. Moments later they were whirling on their way. Each of the drones took out a guard tower with rubber bullets. Elliott's explicit instructions were that there was to be no loss of life. Eddie couldn't let the guards open fire on the prisoners once the attack was under way so he had to take them out, but do it in bloodless fashion. He smiled in satisfaction as the mini-cameras mounted on the wings of the drones showed the guards falling to the wooden floors of their towers unharmed, but out of the fight. Next, Eddie's laptop screen showed the drones' missiles striking the base of the compound walls in several locations.

Once the dust settled the cameras revealed gaping eight-foot wide holes in the walls and prisoners streaming through the openings. As the sirens began to wail the drones returned to the big rig and were quickly wheeled inside and the rear doors closed. Eddie drove a mile and a half to an overpass near the freeway, pulled underneath, and with the help of James pulled the thin film of black plastic from the sides of the rig. This exposed the slightly sun-faded lettering which read, 'Safeway' with the grocery company logo just below it.

As the two men pulled onto the highway they listened to the local police chatter on a short wave radio. Complete chaos was the only way to describe it. Guesstimates of more than one thousand prisoners escaping were commonplace. When he and his team were thirty miles away they switched the laptop on and turned to CNN. They took in the surreal sight of more than a half dozen of the biggest prisons nationwide, all minimum security with enormous craters where walls had stood and prisoners pouring through them.

"Even though this little trick went off even better than planned, I still have my doubts," Eddie said.

"How so?" asked James.

"Not all those men are mister Goody Two-Shoes locked up by some miscarriage of justice."

"Elliott ran the numbers. Almost 78 percent of them are not a threat to society, and the really bad guys are not allowed in the yard with the rest of the convicts," James explained.

"Still, some of these guys are going to hurt people. We'll just have to watch it play out."

# Chapter Five

RICK WHEELER TRIED to suppress a smile as he and his companion, Gordon Harrison, climbed out of the golf cart and dutifully watched Kenny Borel miss his four foot putt and curse soundly. The president and CEO of Sallie Mae walked towards the golf carts with his three golfing buddies following not far behind.

When the golfers neared the carts Rick stepped forward. He was dressed in a black three piece suit and wearing dark glasses. He held one hand in his coat pocket where he gripped a stun gun.

"Mr. Borel?"

"Yes," replied the short heavy-set man with the shock of graying black hair.

"I'm special agent Rick Wheeler with the Internal Revenue Service. We'd like you to come with us," Rick said discreetly, so only the CEO could hear.

"I'll do no such thing," Kenny replied, his voice laced with alarm.

"Is something wrong," one of the other golfers asked and stepped forward.

Gordon Harrison, Rick's partner on this mission, moved three paces forward and slipped his hand towards the inside pocket of his coat. "Stay right there, sir. This is none of your affair."

The man stopped in his tracks while Rick leaned closer to Sallie Mae's head man and said, "I'm afraid I'm going to have to insist."

"What is this all about?" Kenny asked, his alarm growing.

"Do we really want to discuss this here?" Rick asked nodding in the direction of a growing number of gawkers. "Please just come with us."

"Show me your license."

Rick flashed his badge and Kenny said to his friends, "You guys finish the round. A bit of an emergency has developed. I'll be in touch."

A few minutes later Kenny climbed into the back seat of the limousine with Gordon right beside him while Rick took the wheel. They drove three miles to a secluded single story ranch house where Kenny was led inside to the darkened living room.

"Take a seat," Rick said, indicating a single wooden chair in the center of the room.

"Now see here. This is enough. I demand to know what this is about or I'll be forced to call my attorney," Kenny said indignantly.

Rick spun around and savagely backhanded the CEO across the mouth, sending him to the floor. "Now sit in the damn chair and shut your face."

Kenny didn't say a word. Dabbing at his bleeding lips he sat down heavily in the chair.

"Upload ready?"

"Yep, pull down the Hi Def screen."

Gordon ran a cable from his computer to the four-foot by five-foot high definition television screen attached to the wall.

A moment later the first You Tube video sprang onto the screen. "My name is Rachel Ramirez. If you're seeing this it means I'm dead already."

The young face on the screen began to crumble into tears. "I don't want to die, but I feel like I'm dead already. I've got $90,000 in student loans and I've worked to pay them off. I've worked two jobs for almost three years. I've worked really hard, but I missed some payments and there are fines and late fees and the loans have gotten bigger. I've talked to the lender, but they won't listen to me. I can't go on. I'm living for these loans."

Again the woman started to sob. Finally all that could be seen was the top of her head and the shaking of her shoulders as she broke down completely. The screen went dark.

"Oh my god," Kenny said.

"Shut the hell up," Rick hurled the words like a dagger at the cowering CEO. The next video popped up on the screen. Together the three men watched two hours of people in distress because of student loans. One young man even slit his wrists on screen. To his credit, Kenny recoiled in horror at the scene. The final video was a group of cheerleaders all wearing Yale sweaters. The camera zoomed in and stopped on a man sitting in the bleachers. The man waved. It was Rick.

"Is that you in the stands?" Kenny almost shouted and started to stand up.

Rick shoved him back down, almost upsetting the chair. "Yes, it's me in the stands. Your daughter Amanda is a cheerleader at Yale, correct?"

Kenney nodded.

"I'll bet she doesn't have any student loans."

"You wouldn't," Kenny whispered.

"I'll stop at nothing," Rick replied. "You want to see more? I'll show you a video of me crossing the street right behind her. One jab with a needle and she's gone. Not dead mind you, but a vegetable for the next fifty years. A constant reminder of the choice you didn't make."

Kenny slumped in the chair. "What do you want?"

"You will lower the rates on all student loans to 7% effective tomorrow. You will make the announcement outside Sallie Mae's offices with local news crews at hand. You will become a spokesperson against the level of personal debt in this country. You're the one who is going to step up and make a difference."

"I've got investors to answer to."

"You've got a nation of students to answer to. How do you justify owning a private golf course on the backs of starving students? What do you want to say to people who are killing themselves because of your lending policies?"

"I don't know what to say," the CEO said in barely audible tones.

"You say it stops here and it stops now."

The room fell into a deep silence and then Rick concluded. "We're going to leave here now. You'll never know who we are but know this, we'll be watching, and if anything happens to us there will be others. You control your daughter's life, yours, and your wife's too if it comes to that. Do the right thing."

Kenny looked up. Rick swung a right upper cut that came from the floor and lifted the chubby CEO out of the chair. He fell in a crumpled heap on the floor.

"Sorry about that last bit," Rick said to Gordon. "I've wanted to do that for a long time."

"Not a problem. Let's load up our gear, wipe everything down and clear out," Gordon responded.

"Do you think we got to him?" Rick asked.

"Oh yeah, we got to him big time."

# Chapter Six

HALFWAY AROUND THE world, about the time that
Kenney Borel was being lifted out of the chair by Rick's mighty blow,
another team was at work.

President and CEO of Bank of America, Wilfred Blankenship,
was enjoying a cool drink surrounded by family and friends in the
grand ball room of his private yacht moored at a plush resort on the
French Riviera. Little did he know, despite extensive security
measures including two armed body guards, two divers were at that
moment hovering weightless beneath his magnificent yacht. As
bedtime arrived he begged off his guests, and he and the wife retired
to his private stateroom. The 'sweet suite', as his wife called it, was all
of nine hundred square feet complete with luxury bath, sitting room,
wet bar and private balcony. It was the balcony that proved to be its
weak point. With the guards located three floors up, bored and
fearing nothing, the divers, using suction cup devices climbed the
side of the ship and slipped over the railing to land softly on Mr.
Blankenship's private balcony. It took but a moment to jimmy the
French doors and step inside where they froze for a moment and
listened to the sound of calm, even breathing. Jim Buckner and
Michael Conrad padded softly across the room, their strategy refined

step by step over several nights of planning, and placed a hand carefully over the mouths of husband and wife simultaneously. The pen lights clicked on and revealed frightened eyes.

"We're not going to hurt you," each man said in a soft voice designed to quell their fears. "We just want to talk."

Blankenship nodded.

"When I remove my hand from your mouth, if you or your wife shout or scream, I'll be forced to silence you which will not be pleasant. Do you understand?"

Husband and wife nodded.

As soon as he was free to speak, the CEO started in with a tirade. "Now see here. What is the meaning of this? Do you know who I am?"

Jim slapped him squarely across the mouth and spoke in a harsh whisper, "Shut up. We know exactly who you are."

Michael pulled a laptop computer from the Dry Pak on his back and set it on the bed. He fired it up and whispered, "Watch the video."

The short movies, provided by a private firm employed by Elliott Eastman, were similar to those that Kenny Borel had witnessed. Testimonials by people who'd lost their homes, lost their livelihoods and been driven into poverty by Bank of America. People questioning the right of Bank of America and the interest rates on their credit cards of 24% plus. The clincher was a manager at a Bank of America branch in Los Angeles who testified regarding mortgage origination practices. "The orders from on high were to push our home buyers into adjustable loans, even though mortgage rates were the lowest they'd been in almost forty years, because we would make more money on adjustable loans than on a fixed rate. Then if we could slip in a high margin between the starting rate and the index, say maybe three or four percent over the index, we could be paid a bonus of upwards of ten thousand dollars per loan. We were paid to cheat our clients."

"You know this to be true, don't you?" Jim asked.

Blankenship nodded.

"Do you believe this is right?"

Blankenship shook his head no.

"What should you do to make this right? I'll tell you. You're going to go before the American people and tell them that temporarily, just for the next three years, you're going to reduce interest rates on your credit cards to 7% across the board. This will stimulate spending and reduce the amount of pain you've inflicted on your fellow citizens. Now understand that we found you, entered your inner sanctum, and could have killed you. Do you agree to go before the American people and make this proposal? And don't, lie because we will find you again."

Michael hit another button and the screen filled with a scene from a party showing Blankenship dancing with his wife. Another showed husband and wife walking on the beach hand in hand. The last one depicted shadows moving against a thin set of sheers. It was the Blankenship's bedroom window.

Blankenship's eyes widened in recognition of the locations.

"I can't, our stock price will fall like a rock. Our stock holders will scream."

"My friend here is an expert marksman and obviously, based on the video, we can find you almost anywhere. But think about it for a moment. With all the extra spending power produced by reducing the rates the economy will sky rocket and most people will run their balances up."

This statement gave the CEO reason to pause for a moment as he contemplated this possibility.

"I'll need to think about this," Blankenship replied.

"No time. And part of our agreement is that you convince your cronies at JP Morgan, Goldman Sachs, Morgan Stanley, Wells Fargo and all the other credit companies to drop their rates as well."

"I can't guarantee their agreement!" Blankenship almost shouted.

Jim back handed him across the mouth knocking out a tooth. He seethed between gritted teeth, "Keep your voice down scum and give me a straight 'yes' or 'no'!"

"The other banks might follow our lead. I'll do the best I can," Blankenship mumbled through bleeding lips.

"I said 'yes' or 'no'," Jim hissed, his face just inches from the cowering CEO.

Blankenship whispered, "Yes."

# Chapter Seven

SAMUEL GOLDMAN, THE Chairman of the Securities and Exchange Commission, gazed uneasily at the three attorneys who seated themselves across the vast expansive desk top from him. This was a highly unusual meeting, he thought, but when Elliott Eastman requested something one was better off complying, as it would probably come to pass anyway.

"I'm Robert Dale, and these are Paul Cranston and Bryan Banks, attorneys representing the interests of Mr. Elliott Eastman. He extends his personal thanks for taking the time out of your busy day to meet with us. He wished to be here, but unfortunately he had pressing business to attend to in Washington."

"My pleasure," Samuel Goldman replied, extending a hand shake to each man while still eyeing them with a degree of suspicion.

"Mr. Eastman respects your opinion greatly and wished you might render an opinion once you have read this one page document," Attorney Dale explained, opening his brief case and sliding a single sheet of paper across the desk. "He has also asked that any reference to this meeting and his name not leave this room."

Attorney Dale gazed sharp eyed at Goldman and the other members of the commission which were seated there.

"Agreed," Goldman replied brusquely and bent to the document at hand.

Goldman read it carefully. When he was finished he looked up and smiled. "It's bold and shows imagination, but why would Mr. Eastman be interested in forwarding such a proposal?"

"He feels this country has been very good to him and is concerned with the direction it has taken in the last few years. He believes such a proposal, a small transaction fee on stock trades, commodities, futures and derivatives, is painless and eliminates our growing deficit, which he feels is the single greatest threat to our nation. He also believes that with the explosion of various financial instruments in the last few years, the income stream will be quite substantial."

"I might agree with him, but it is pointless to discuss this any further. You'll never get Congress to agree. The banks have enormous sway over them. They'll not even get the bills written."

"Could you kindly identify the members of Congress who would most strenuously oppose such a bill?" Attorney Dale asked softly.

Goldman scratched his chin. "You'd have everyone on the Senate Banking Committee, Coryn, Graham, and Lanting against it. You'd probably have trouble with Bainer and Whitback over at the House Ways and Means Committee, and of course the House Speaker Cobbings will side with them. And that's just to name a few."

Attorney Dale swiftly wrote the names down on a note pad.

"If this bill were to be written, Mr. Eastman has argued it must be done with great care so as not to allow Congress to merely spend the monies. He also wants to be clear that this is not to apply to the savings and checking account transactions of the general public. He expressed a desire that the bill be very specific. It would require a division of the SEC to manage the monies and secure a lock box style of accounting, so not a single penny is misplaced. He'd like you to manage that division, under the SEC, and imagines there will be a sizable pay raise for this new staff, something in the six figure range for you as well as a spot on the national stage. The SEC would be the natural governmental body to oversea such a fee arrangement, as they would be on the front line of collections anyway. You have three years left in your term. You would be the inaugural General in the 'War on the Deficit.'"

Dale could see the lights glimmering in Goldman's eyes as he imagined himself on the cover of TIME magazine.

Attorney Dale continued. "If Senator, I mean the former Senator Mr. Eastman, can get the bill to the floor he would respectfully hope you would endorse it, and he means strongly endorse it. He believes your endorsement would go a long way toward getting the bill passed."

"Of course. I'd have no problem with that," Goldman swiftly replied. "But with the powerful lobbyists that every major corporation has at their command, there is not the proverbial snowballs chance in hell of such a thing happening."

"But if it was to take place, do we have your word that you would strongly endorse such a bill?" Dale pressed the chairman.

"Yes, you do."

"Thank you for your time Mr. Chairman."

# Chapter Eight

ELLIOTT EASTMAN PACED softly across the thick carpeting of the Oval Office with his hands folded behind his back. The sun was just rising to the east of the White House, slowly spreading thin fingers of sunlight across the Rose Garden. Elliott was humming softly. The door swung open and in walked President White with a big smile on his face. He greeted the former senator warmly, grasping the proffered hand saying, "It's been awhile, Elliott. It's so good to see you again. Can I offer you some coffee or tea?"

"No thank you. You're looking well, Samuel. The presidency must agree with you."

"Agree? Other than a constant headache and a couple dozen bleeding ulcers, I'm just peachy," the President laughed heartily.

"Please tell me you're kidding."

"Yes, it is a marathon everyday, but we're doing okay. The poll numbers are still lower than they were, but they seemed to have stabilized and the team has high hopes I'll win a second term."

"Is it too early for congratulations?"

"Well the election is still a year away Elliott, so I'd say it's a tad early."

"Let's sit and talk. I've got two ideas that, when linked together, I think might just win you a second, and possibly a third term," Elliott suggested.

Paul smiled. "A third term? You're a better salesman than I gave you credit for. I got your message … something about 'problem solved.' Intriguing to say the least. Talk to me."

"I know you're pressed for time. Here are the ideas in a nutshell. We cannot grow, cut or tax our way out of our debt issues. We are facing the same fate that Greece, Spain, Italy, Portugal and Ireland suffered a few years ago. We need a new income stream. It's the only answer. I've had some of my people do the math. There are approximately 985 million trades each day on various US stock exchanges and two sides, buyer and seller, to each trade. By the way, that 985 million is tapes A, B, and C. The Nasdaq, the New York and the Euronext exchanges. It doesn't include commodities, futures or derivatives contracts. In any event, tapes A, B, and C reflect approximately 1.8 billion trades. We should place a nominal fee; a flat fee so easy to understand even a child could grasp it, on each trade. Say ten dollars on trades over one thousand, one hundred dollars on trades over one hundred thousand and one thousand dollars on trades over one million. We calculate that this will generate in the range of forty million dollars a day, or two hundred billion a year on the stock trades alone. If we throw in a similar fee structure on the commodities, futures and derivative contracts, you know, the more exotic financial instruments this could generate another trillion a year in fees. I'll give you a little background. The derivatives market back in 1997 was $17 trillion a year. In 2005 it was $125 trillion, whereas today it is estimated to be $703 trillion a year. To put that into perspective, it's about forty times the Gross National Product of the entire country. Also, the gentlemen that run some of these hedge funds earn quite a bit." Elliott paused flipping through his notes. "Jean Simmons of Renaissance Technologies earned 2.5 billion dollars last year and David Tepperson of Appaloosa Management made over 4 billion, so it would seem this is a very lucrative business. I would suggest even a modest fee on these transactions would generate something in the neighborhood of $1.5 trillion dollars a year. We've tried to take a conservative approach. In previous experiments with these fee arrangements business has gone to other countries, but they want our dollars and they want our business. If they threaten to leave, we counter by denying them access to our market. Problem solved. The experts I hired believe we could pay off our national debt in seven and a half years."

President White started to speak, but Elliot held up his hand.

"And that's only part of it Paul. We must cut defense spending as well, and overseas bases are the low hanging fruit. We calculate we could save a minimum of $350 billion a year by closing just six hundred bases."

The President was about to beg off, but Elliott pressed on.

"Look at it Paul. It's beautiful. We can generate something in the neighborhood of two trillion dollars a year and not have to cut social programs or any other important safety nets. Once the debt is extinguished we could fund education, infrastructure and social security; all the things we've been trying to address for years. Polls show the deficit as the fourth item on the fear factor list in the minds of the American public. What they don't show you is that it was eighth on the list just five years ago. People are rapidly becoming aware of the risks posed by the deficit. Secondly, it's really their future they are expressing concern for in these polls. What better way to address their fears than addressing social security. It appeals to the aging baby boomers and the younger generations who are expressing growing resentment at their obligation to pay for their parents' retirements. And look where the tax comes from; trades. Only thirty percent of the American population own stock, and none own derivatives, so the tax is avoided by most of our population. The funding of this program sits squarely on the financial speculation industry. We tax gamblers, don't we? That's all these outfits are, gamblers. And most importantly, it's just a temporary tax, only for a few years. You're going to appeal to the young new voters in this country and draw generations of voters into the democratic fold. At the same time you're solving the biggest headache for our retirees wondering if their money will last the remainder of their lives. You'll win all their votes. Your legacy could be the president who tamed the deficit."

President White took a moment to comment. "Initially I must confess I like it, but as you know I'm going to have to run it by my re-election team. I can see one possible pitfall. The corporations that trade most of the stock and hedge funds and their lobbyists will fund any candidate who opposes it. The results could be disastrous for my campaign, but I'll let you know what my team recommends."

"Paul, we've known each other for a long time and I know your aim to get re-elected is paramount to you, but I must ask you something. It was the question I found myself asking quite often in my last years in office. What about the American people? What happens to their interests when we leaders of the nation must bow to the wishes of Big Money? I kept coming to the conclusion that they deserved better. At some point we politicians need to do what's right by the American people."

"I understand the sentiment Elliott, but I can't let those types of thoughts get in the way of my re-election."

"Paul," Elliott said softly, a measure of sadness evident in his voice. "These problems are real. A trillion dollar a year deficit is unsustainable. At some point we will bankrupt the nation, if we haven't done so already. We'll go to the media with the names of the corporations that oppose this bill. Any corporation that doesn't support the new 'War on the Deficit' will be blacklisted and their products avoided. We can win this battle. Does your team have any proposals on the table to deal with it?"

"Nothing concrete yet, but it is something we're keeping an eye on," the President replied while glancing at his watch. "I've got another meeting to go to in about ten minutes regarding the Israelis, and I need to be briefed on the latest events."

"In complete honesty, allow me to digress for a moment. I would also like to see a Value Added Tax. We're the only advanced democratic nation in the world that doesn't have one. And perhaps a National Sales Tax enacted for two or three years to further destroy our common enemy, the deficit, but that is for another day and time. I didn't want to reach too far and those two proposals affect the average American worker, so I much prefer this approach. So I'll close by making this promise to you, Mr. President."

The President noted Elliott's change in tone and looked over at the former congressman, but at that moment Elliott chose to gaze at the table in front of him collecting his thoughts. He was losing the President. The leader of the free world wasn't listening.

The President looked away again until Elliott spoke more forcefully.

"Listen to me Paul. The time is now. If we can get this into bill form and on the floor of Congress, I will personally write a ten million dollar check to your re-election campaign."

The President was in the process of glancing down at his watch for a second time when his head shot back up. He stared intently into Elliott's face for a moment to be sure the former senator was not joking.

"I'll even have my team of lawyers help with drawing up the bill, but we need your backing," Elliott added.

"That is very generous, Elliott. Are you sure about that?"

"I'll put it in writing if you wish."

"That's not necessary. Your word is good enough for me."

Elliott stood and said in a very direct and formal manner, "Thank you for taking the time to chat with me Mr. President. I'll await word on your decision."

# Chapter Nine

EDDIE KELLEY CLIMBED from the shower, quickly dried off, and studied his sturdy figure in the mirror. The angry pink scars from the hail of shrapnel he'd endured dotted his physique. For a moment he thought back to his years chasing the Taliban around Afghanistan.

"For what?" he asked for probably the hundredth time.

James Lally called from the living room of their rented suite at the Comfort Inn in New Braunfels, Texas, "Dude, you gotta get out here and see this. It's all over the evening news. Maria Baritromo just said upwards of ten thousand prisoners have escaped."

Eddie strolled from the bathroom with a towel around his waist, grabbed a beer from the fridge and stood in front of the television.

"Is it just me or is Maria Baritromo hot as hell?" Eddie asked.

"Yeah, yeah. Look at that hole in the prison wall in Phoenix! Did those guys use a Patriot missile or something?"

"Sub-standard construction," Eddie replied. "They saved a few pennies on concrete by not filling the voids in the center of each cinder block."

"Let's see what they've got on another channel."

"No, not my Maria."

"Sorry."

"Damn, good-bye Maria."

The CNN news anchor was stating in shrill tones, "Local police forces are overwhelmed. Governments are calling in the National Guard. There are rumors the feds may send in the army. There are upwards of twenty thousand criminals released on the streets of our cities."

"Wow, the number of escapees just doubled," Eddie said.

James switched the channel again. Bill Maher was laughing with the other members of his guest panel.

"I don't see the big issue. Calling in the National Guard? Nonsense. Let me ask you a question? If you were a prisoner who just got a get of jail free pass, what are you going to do? I'll tell you what you'll do. You'll buy a six pack and find the nearest street walker. After that you go visit mom, and after that you get another six pack and find the nearest … ! Anyway you get the picture. I don't think these guys are the threat they're being made out to be."

The show goers burst into laughter.

James laughed as well saying, "I love Bill Maher. He's always so right on."

"He does have a unique view. I'm bushed. I'm going to hit the hay. If Elliott calls wake me."

"Sure thing. Good night."

"Good night."

# Chapter Ten

STEVE CRAWFORD AND Silas Woodford, two of Elliott's long time warriors, waited patiently inside a forest green Ford Expedition watching for any movement outside an enormous walled and gated mansion that overlooked the Hudson River.

"Place looks like a fortress," Silas commented.

"Did you expect something less? Don't forget this guy is the CEO of Capital One."

"Yeah, yeah, big deal. I'm just saying it looks like more than a two-man job."

"Piece of cake," Steve replied lowering the pair of field glasses from his eyes. "From what I'm able to see it looks like one guard with a dog is all that patrols the grounds, and the electronic surveillance system was disabled this morning by a fake UPS delivery man."

"We're a quarter mile away and it's starting to get dark. Are you sure that's all we're up against?" countered Silas.

Steve gave him a withering look and said, "When I say I'm sure, I'm sure. Have you got the iPad 12?"

Silas patted a back pack in front of him resting on the floor of the vehicle.

"We'd better get moving," Steve continued. "The intelligence we were given indicates George Hearthstone is a creature of habit. He always pours himself a double scotch at exactly 5:30 and sits out on the patio reading the Wall Street Journal."

Exiting the vehicle the two men set their watches. Steve shouldered a heavy rifle case while Silas checked the batteries on the iPad 12 for the third time in the last two hours.

Fifteen minutes later they were kneeling in the shadows of a towering Black Oak against the ivy covered wall of the palatial mansion.

"Okay," Steve whispered handing Silas a rifle with silencer and scope. "You've got four darts. Take out the guard first and then the dog. This stuff isn't lethal. It's a combination tranquilizer and muscle relaxer. It will take them down instantly but leave them still able to see and hear. Don't miss. Take your shot at exactly 5:36 and I'll take care of the main target at the same time. Hop the wall and meet me at the rear porch. And take care not to damage the iPad 12."

"Roger that. No one else around?"

"No, his wife is at a private jewelry auction in Manhattan and will stay at their townhouse in the city. Hearthstone's lady friend doesn't arrive here until 8:30. Let's move."

A few minutes later Silas, peered over the wall to find the guard and dog a hundred yards away across a vast expanse of lawn, strolling leisurely along a garden path. He checked his watch and eighty eight seconds later, with a sound like a human exhaling, sent two darts at the targets. The guard fell heavily into a rose bush while the dog staggered a few paces and fell on the lawn. Instantly Silas was over the wall and moving like a shadow across the grass.

Meanwhile, Steve sighted carefully and squeezed the trigger. The dart struck George Hearthstone in the center of his back. He spilled his drink and slumped heavily to one side of his chair. The two attackers met at the rear patio of the mansion and lowered

Hearthstone from his chair until he was lying on his back looking up at them. What the CEO saw was two men gazing down at him dressed in army camouflage suits and black stocking cap hoods. The fear, evident in the CEO's eyes, became even more palpable when he lost control of his bladder.

"Pretty tough guy when he's charging little old ladies 27% interest, but a little different when his world is violated," Crawford whispered.

"That's a shame," Silas chimed in. "You probably ruined your nice seersucker suit."

Silas pulled the iPad 12 from his knapsack and pressed the on button while Crawford continued speaking.

"You're George Hearthstone," he said removing a photo from his pocket and comparing it with the face of the man lying on the patio.

"Yep. Now we're going to show you some photos on our neat little tablet computer here."

Silas leaned over and held the iPad 12 about a foot from the terrified face. As he pressed down on a button at the end of a cable that extended from the computer, a picture flashed on the screen.

"This is you having dinner with a friend at the Saint Marks Hotel in San Francisco," Silas commented. "You probably told your wife it was a business trip. Nice looking dish too, I might add."

George Hearthstone's eyes widened.

Silas pressed down on the clicker.

"This is you and the dish heading upstairs to your room."

The clicker sounded again.

"This is you and the dish tearing at each others' clothes in the hotel room. Yes, it's the wonder of modern technology. Slip a little eye ball camera under the door and you've instantly got an X-rated movie."

Silas hit the clicker again.

"This is you having breakfast the next morning, and that's me sitting at the table next to you."

Again the clicker sounded.

"That's you leaving your office, and that's me cruising by you on the moped. I hate those damn things. Not a motorcycle or a bike, don't you agree?"

Silas fell silent for a moment while Crawford tucked the handheld back in his knapsack.

"The point is Mr. Hearthstone," Silas continued, "you're going to give a speech to your board explaining how you've gotten wind of the fact that other credit card companies are going to reduce their rates to 7%. They're going to steal millions and millions of customers away from you unless you act first. You will do this, correct?"

Crawford reached down, grasped the CEO by his hair and nodded his head up and down for him.

"Great, I thought you'd agree. You're going to do right by the American people and stop charging them usurious rates. If you don't, then these and many other photos are going to be sent anonymously to your wife. If that doesn't work, you will see me again. It doesn't matter where. Maybe on a moped in the street or in the lobby of an office building or maybe we'll have breakfast together again. The point is I can get close to you. Then all it takes is a slight pin prick, something you'll hardly even feel, and you'll be dead in thirty seconds. Do you understand?"

"Settle down tiger," Crawford said. "Remember he can't move."

Silas stood for a moment looking down at the CEO while Steve Crawford moved off across the lawn. "I'm tempted to give you a few broken ribs, but I won't kick a man when he's down. Remember, if you don't do as you've been told you're a dead man, and that's a guarantee."

# Chapter Eleven

ELLIOTT'S CHAUFFER HELD the door for him as he climbed in.

"Where to sir?" the immaculately attired chauffer asked.

"Ninety nine eighty eight Fort Hunt Road, Alexandria, the home of General Bob Gates."

"Yes sir."

Elliott leaned back in his seat as the limousine eased away from the curb and thought about the meeting with the President. It had been thorough and clear cut. Elliott knew the President. He was a consummate politician and he wanted desperately to be re-elected. If he refused the proposal it would mean he was held under the sway of the banking industry to a greater degree than Elliott believed. On the other hand, if he agreed to the proposal it was tantamount to declaring war on the banking industry. Elliott sighed. He was glad he wasn't the President. On the other hand, if Paul White chose the proper course, Elliott stood ready to throw his considerable weight behind him. Elliott felt he knew Paul well. They had come up through the congressional ranks together and had fought very similar battles on the way up. Paul was a good man whose conscience often weighed heavily in his decision making. Elliott hoped such was the case again.

Suddenly a sharp stab of pain pierced the Master Sergeant's lower right side. He winced and gasped in pain. The chauffer noted the contorted expression on the former senator's face and asked, "Is everything okay sir?"

"Yes," Elliott replied weakly, "it's just indigestion."

Twenty minutes later the limo pulled up in front of a large stately two story colonial home with a fine view of the Potomac. A widow's walk ran across the length of the roof and a covered balcony stood over the front door. The home had been built during World War I to house Naval Commander Admiral Fightin' Joe Johnson and his family. After Joe's death his heirs neglected it, and the grand mansion had fallen into a state of disrepair. Then Robert Gates bought the property and began a project to lovingly restore the building to its former grandeur.

The front door opened and General Robert Gates stepped out, briefcase in hand and a heavy coat over one arm. A stiff breeze blew in from the sea.

Once seated inside the car the old friends shook hands, greeting each other warmly.

"Good to see you again Bob," Elliott said. "Ready to go to war again?"

"Yes, from what you mentioned over the phone I must admit I'm quite intrigued."

The two men had often sided together, with Bob Gates as the Secretary of Defense and Elliott as a ranking member of the Senate, to fight military cost overruns and waste as well as attempting to eliminate costly and outdated military programs.

"This time were going to go for the whole enchilada," Elliott said. "Along with other efforts that have been initiated, we could have this country back on track in no time."

"Any read on how Secretary of Defense Holland might respond to what you're going to propose?" Bob asked.

"I'm not sure but I'm hoping a little pressure in the right places, especially from the most respected former Secretary of Defense in history like you and an old senate war horse like me, will make him listen."

"You're too generous," Robert Gates replied. "I merely did my job."

"And shook up the whole war department like no one has in the last fifty years."

"From what I know of Bruce Holland he seems to be a thoughtful, concerned and well meaning gentleman," General Gates observed.

"My thoughts exactly, which is why I think the time is right for us to approach him with these ideas. What have we got to lose? Think about it Bob. We're just a couple of old men. How much time do you think we have left? Ten, maybe fifteen years before we're just sitting in our rocking chairs at the old folk's home. We have a chance to change the course and fate of this country. I've had a team of nine of the best economists I could find put together a very detailed outline. I think with a little persuasion Bruce Holland will see the light."

The limo stopped at the guard entrance to the pentagon where a soldier inspected the ID's and passes of the two men. A moment later, he saluted them briskly and they were allowed entry into the most secure military base in the world.

A short while later they were seated at a table in the private office of the Secretary of Defense, Bruce Holland.

"Good to see you Bruce," Bob Gates said as they shook hands.

"Thank you for taking the time to speak with us, Mr. Secretary," Elliott said.

"The pleasure is mine gentlemen," Bruce responded. "Based on our initial conversation I've asked Dick Henghold to sit in. He is the acting director of the Office of Management and Budget."

The men shook hands.

"Now, how can I help you?" Bruce asked.

Elliot studied the man for a moment. He was young for the position, just in his mid-fifties, but a polished war veteran who understood the nature of command as well as the plight of the men on the ground. He had a reputation as a thoughtful decision maker. He wore his uniform well and was a credit to the armed services.

"Would you be so kind as to brief the general?" Bob said nodding in Elliott's direction.

Elliott dove right in. "As you know General Holland, the economy is in shambles, unemployment is fifteen percent, foreclosures are at a record pace and personal bankruptcies are soaring. The average Joe is hurting and has been for some time. It's time for those of us that have the vision and the power to bring about change. I want you to know that what we're about to put forth to you is not a single proposal. This is a multi-pronged attack. It's what I like to call the 'War on the Deficit'. I have it from a very trusted source that all the major banks are going to lower the interest rates on their credit cards to 7% for the next three years, thus providing a source of badly needed stimulus to the economy."

"Really," Bruce said. "That must have taken some arm twisting."

"Arm twisting and then some," Elliott replied with a smile. "Also a team of lawyers, at my behest, has approached the SEC with a proposal for a new source of tax revenue that should generate trillions of dollars in a few years. Sam Goldman, the Chairman of the SEC backs the idea enthusiastically."

"Could you expand on that please?" General Holland asked leaning forward in his chair.

"It's a small fee imposed on stock, commodities, futures and derivatives contracts. The experts figure it could generate 1.8 billion dollars a day and will fall most heavily on speculators and flash traders. Just the people we want to hit rather than the average Joe. But there is another aspect to this campaign against the deficit, and that's where you come in. I've asked some experts to compile some data. It's only a dozen pages or so, and I must admit it's some very boring reading. I'll summarize it for you. Out of 1,100 military bases we have around the world there are upwards of 400 to 600 bases that could be shut down at a savings of 600 billion dollars a year. For instance, one base in Saudi Arabia, one in Diego Garcia, one in the Philippines, along with our carrier fleets in the region are more than sufficient to protect our interests in the Indian Ocean theatre. Yet we have over a hundred and fifty bases and two hundred thousand men and women of our armed forces and contractors deployed there. We send $500 million dollars a year to Pakistan, $1.8 billion to Egypt and another one billion to the Saudi's. It's all detailed in the summary here. All told, the savings could be approximately 400 billion dollars a year."

Dick Henghold laughed. "You'll never get Congress to pass cuts of that size."

Elliott gave the director of the Office of Management and Budget a nod.

"True, but let me continue. I've heard it said that certain people, off the record of course, feel the war on the Taliban is a joke."

Elliott stared pointedly at the Secretary of Defense for a moment.

"The figures I've seen, which are also compiled here, indicate there are maybe 5,000 Taliban fighters, maybe a few more when the harvesting is over. They don't have planes, missiles, or anything in the way of modern weaponry and yet we are supposed to believe they pose a threat to our national security?"

"I argued the same point ten years ago," Robert Gates interjected.

"The expenses far outweigh any gains we have in fighting a war against them. All the facts and figures are here," Elliott concluded.

"I still say you'll never get it passed through Congress," Dick argued. "The military lobbyists will be all over them."

"Which is why I've waited to tell you the other half of the plan; the two of you labor in relative obscurity. The average American will know the starting lineups and slugging percentage of the home team, but know nothing of you or what you do. That's because what you do, at least in their perception, has no impact on their lives. I'm proposing to change that starting today if I can get your agreement to spearhead this approach. I will take out full page ads in the Washington Post, The New York Times and The USA Today with a photo spread of the two of you, Bob here, and the head of the SEC touting you as the leaders of the War on the Deficit. The article will outline the plan of attack and the proposed dollar amounts we are saving. You will be instantly vaulted to celebrity status and you will become household names. Who knows where it might lead your careers? President, vice president, hell Ron Reagan was a spokesperson for General Electric or something before he became president. But more importantly I'm hoping to educate the public in a big way, and in doing so counteract the influence of the corporations."

Elliott took a breath.

"Seriously, you will be spearheading the single most important effort in the history of this country, aside from perhaps D-Day. Our national debt is the single greatest threat our nation has faced, and it is largely being addressed with aimless drivel by our leaders. You gentlemen are in a position to save our nation. If the opposition is too strong in Congress I'll post more articles. I have a team of free lance writers who are ready to go to work on this, naming names of those lobbyists and members of Congress who would stand in our way. Lastly, if it appears Congress is to stand in our way, I will personally fund a national referendum so that the American people can vote directly on these measures. We cannot let corruption in high places ruin our chances here."

As Elliott ceased speaking the room fell into an eerie silence. The two men seated opposite him were quit literally stunned. Neither had been sure exactly what this meeting was to accomplish and had merely agreed to meet out of respect for Senator Eastman and General Gates. What had been voiced was nothing short of mind numbing.

Finally General Holland collected the brief and stood up. "Obviously a proposal of this magnitude will take some time to consider. I must confess I find it somewhat interesting."

"My thoughts exactly," Dick Henghold agreed, his face looking a little flushed as he stood as well.

"There are a number of players in other facets of this plan. I don't want to push you, but I'll need an answer as to whether you can back this or not in the next forty-eight hours," Elliott softly explained.

"I'll need to run this by the President," General Holland advised.

"I've already spoken to him. I think he's on our side," Elliott responded. "But do as you see fit. You know how to reach us. Good day."

Elliott strode from the room with General Robert Gates beside him.

Once they were in the corridor Gates couldn't suppress his enthusiasm. "Good lord Elliott. You blew them away. Hell, you blew me away. That plan would change the world as we know it."

"I think it will. It's really nothing new. Most of the plan has been kicked around in various forms for years."

"A tax on derivatives, commodities and futures transactions, I've never heard of such a thing. I say it's brilliant!"

"Actually, England has had a half percent tax on her stock transactions for years," Elliott added, "and it generates about 40 billion a year in revenue."

"Oh, still, it was a master stroke. And a National Referendum?"

"Actually, we can't initiate a National Referendum without an approval from Congress, but there are about 29 states that already have approved state referendums over the years."

"Still, just the threat of a National Referendum will start them shaking in their boots on Capitol Hill. It's the perfect approach. The power is with the people, or so the constitution would have us believe, so let them vote directly on the issue."

"It's just a dream at the moment Bob, but perhaps someday. I'll be honest with you, I don't like the way both Holland and Henghold backed off so quickly. It was as if they were worried someone might have been listening in," Elliott replied as he climbed into the limo again. "It was as if they were suddenly handed a hot potato and wanted nothing to do with it."

"I think you're reading too much into it. I think they were just dumb struck by the scope and boldness of the plan."

"You know, with Twitter and texting I wonder if maybe the time has come for a National Referendum," Elliott mused out loud.

General Gates laughed. "Don't go pushing your luck there kiddo. They would have to work out some way of verifying the votes were legit, rather than one kid sending in a couple thousand text messages an hour."

Elliott smiled. "I think you may be right. We're a couple of years ahead of ourselves, but I could see a text message or e-mail including a PIN number to vote becoming a reality in a few years. Thanks for helping out."

"It's the least I can do," the General responded, glancing at Elliott as he climbed out of the limo. "You don't look so hot."

"I don't feel so hot either. I'm just tired. Very, very tired."

# Chapter Twelve

IT WAS LATE afternoon when Elliott let himself into the Colorado ranch house and laid his car keys on the vestibule table. Slowly he walked over to the bar in the living room and poured a stiff double shot of scotch. The pain in his side came and went, but seemed to be lingering longer each time. Elliott pressed a speed dial button on his phone and then hung up.

A moment later, the longtime ranch hand Greer knocked discreetly on the den door.

"Come in."

Greer stepped into the room, removed his cowboy hat and lowered it hesitantly to chest level. Elliott studied the sun bronzed wiry old man for a moment. Many years ago Elliott's father had found Greer as a young boy sleeping in the hay loft. Greer claimed he was hungry and had no money or home. Elliott's father liked the boy's forthright manner. When he got the boy a change of clothes he noted the deep bruises that covered his body and the fact that he was rail thin. He suspected what the boy's home life was like and why he had run away. Right there and then Elliott's father had taken him in and decided to teach him the ways of ranching. The young boy and old man working together had helped frame the enormous new ranch house and overseen the layout of the pond and orchard. As the work progressed over the course of many months, the two had grown very fond of one another. When Elliott's father passed away Greer had simply stayed on. He'd been a fixture at the ranch for as long as Elliott could remember.

"Greer, how long have you worked here?"

The old ranch hand reached up and scratched his head. "I don't rightly know sir. I reckon it's gotta be close to forty years."

"Closer to fifty. I have a proposal for you Greer. I'm not sure how much longer I'm going to be around. I've asked my attorney to draw up papers and have them recorded at the county offices. I'm going to split off twenty acres along with the original house down by the creek and deed them to you."

"You don't need to do that Mr. Elliott. I like sleeping in the bunk house just fine," the ramrod protested.

"I'm not through. Remember I said this was a proposal. Your part of the bargain is to be sure my parents' graves are properly tended to, they are never to look neglected."

Greer smiled. "Heck Mr. Elliott, I been doing that for years anyhow. Wait, maybe you think they don't look so well cared for, is that it?"

"No, no, I think they look just fine, but I want to be sure they are kept that way."

"Say, what's going on here? Are you going away somewheres?" Greer asked, suddenly squinty-eyed suspicious.

"Nothing lasts forever," Elliott replied, "including me. I want to be sure we get this done right. You've been very loyal to me and my family. You deserve this."

"I don't rightly know what to say sir," Greer replied softly. "It's a mighty fine house and it's way too big for the likes of me."

"Greer, I plan on leaving the other seventeen hundred acres, this ranch house, the barns, corrals, bunkhouse, and everything but the old ranch house and your twenty acres to the state of Colorado as a park."

"That there is a mighty big gift. I wonder if your pa would approve. He loved this ranch and all."

"Oh I think he's looking down on us and smiling right now. Why have the ranch locked up? Let's let young city people come on down here and go riding. Let them learn to love the land like we did."

"When you put it that way I guess it does sound pretty good."

"And I know my father would want to be sure you are well cared for. The old ranch house along with some money set aside should do you very well."

"I still don't know sir."

"I know, Greer. Do you ever just know when something is the right thing to do? I mean really know it from deep down inside?"

"Sure, I reckon I do sir."

"Good, then it's settled. If you'll go saddle up Dusty I think I'll go for a ride before it's too dark."

"Yes sir, right away sir."

Dusty was a golden bay stallion with white mane and tail. He was getting up there in years, but still loved to run flat out. At the sight of Elliott he whinnied with pleasure. The senator approached him, gave him a sugar cube and talked in low tones to the big horse. He took him out through the big barn doors. Greer stood aside as he mounted up.

"I'll be back in an hour," Elliott said.

Greer nodded and watched him ride out of the yard. The old cowboy knew where he was going and smiled when he saw Elliott turn off the road and head for a little known hanging valley. The beautiful little valley was another thousand feet higher than the ranch. It consisted of about ninety pine-clad acres and had a small creek flowing out of the mountains with a lush meadow and small three acre lake right in the middle of it. Several spires of granite marked the entrance where a narrow hint of a trail wound its way up the last few hundred yards.

Greer shook his head.

"Going up to where he always used to take Miss Stephanie," he said to himself as he turned back for the barn.

Climbing higher, horse and rider topped out on a hogback ridge and saw the entrance to the valley in the distance. One would never suspect that a few boulders and a thick stand of pine could hide such a perfect patch of heaven. Riding around a house-sized rock outcropping and ducking low beneath the pine boughs they covered the last few yards to where the trail ended. The basin lay before them with the small pond in its center surrounded by a scattering of ancient pine and spruce. Suddenly a horse whinnied. Elliott, and Dusty, with his ears primed, turned in the direction of the sound. There, on the far side of the water, stood a pure white mare. She flicked her tail and whinnied again. Dusty snorted and stepped a few paces closer. They had seen her several times before, always alone in the valley, and she always seemed to brazenly study Dusty. Elliott laid his hand along the big stallions neck and whispered, "Steady there boy. She's teasing you, but I think she likes you."

Dusty snorted again and took another step closer. The mare whinnied, shook her mane, then turned and disappeared into the trees. Dusty moved forward several steps, but Elliott tugged on the reins. Obediently the big horse stood firm. They rode around the pond to where an ancient lightning-struck pine stood and Elliott tied up the horse near some sweet grass. Elliott, as he always did, leaned back against the trunk of a fallen tree and a half buried granite boulder in the cool shadows and watched the rays of the setting sun dance across the water. A cool breeze came down the mountains and dragon flies darted and dashed across the still water of the pond. As Elliott closed his eyes he murmured, "Such a beautiful land."


After Elliott returned Dusty to the barn he walked slowly back to the ranch house. As old as the big horse was he still had heart. He could run for miles and had worn Elliott out. He was more tired than he could remember being in a long time. He switched on the Hi-Def big screen in the den. He clicked through some of the news channels and they were all covering the same thing; the simultaneous massive escape of prisoners. CNN was calling it 'The Great Escape II' and many commentators were speculating as to who was behind it and what the purpose might be of such a concerted effort. FOX News was sure it was a terrorist plot. One PBS station reported forty former prisoners had been recaptured and the spike in crime which had been anticipated had so far failed to materialize.

Elliott sipped his scotch and rubbed his eyes. Reaching over he picked up the phone and called his attorney.

"Robert, it's time to start phase two."

"Yes sir. The writers have been itching to start."

"Good, I'll talk to you in the morning."

Elliott rose, padded to the bedroom, changed into his bed clothes, brushed his teeth, took six Advil and went to bed.

# Chapter Thirteen

THE PROPER AUTHORITIES were approached by Robert Dale, Elliott's lead attorney. An agreement in principal was reached and a news conference was hastily called. A team of writers, well paid by one of Elliott's closely held corporations, submitted articles to TIME Magazine, People Magazine, Newsweek and a host of other weekly standards. Bloggers took to the Internet and other writers submitted editorial pieces to major newspapers across the nation and the Associated Press. They all carried the same message. The escapees were being offered amnesty. If they turned themselves in they would be given food and shelter, but more importantly they would be offered vocational training in a field of their choosing and their sentences would be commuted.

Standing before the sea of news cameras and microphones, Attorney Dale spoke slowly and purposefully.

"I am speaking to the prison escapees. I hold in my hand a check for 1.2 million dollars. Upon orders from my client I will sign a purchase agreement for the former and now empty prison complex outside Beaumont, Texas. It will be converted into a virtual university. Libraries, gymnasiums, pool and spa as well as specialized vocational wings will dot the campus. Job training and special vocational classes will be available. Meals will be provided at no cost. All convictions will be reviewed and sentences will be commuted upon completion of your chosen course curriculum. All you need do is approach the nearest police station and surrender to the authorities. You will be transported to the Beaumont facility as quickly as possible. You are being given a new lease on life. You will be housed, fed and given a general education as well as vocational training in the field you wish to pursue. This is not a trick, ruse or underhanded attempt to place you back in jail. This is an attempt at total rehabilitation. It is being offered to you with the belief that you have not been given a fair shake in life. You will be given a second opportunity to prove you are good people and good citizens. Thank you very much."

The news wires sprang alive carrying the speech to every corner of the nation. Again speculation ran rampant as to who the mysterious benefactor might be and what he, or she, might have in mind long term. FOX News was certain it had to be a plan hatched by Oprah.

Later that same afternoon the heads of all the major banks held a news conference. Blankenship was the spokesperson, flanked by the rest of his cronies. He read from a prepared text.

"Due to the nature of the economic situation in the United States, what some call the 'jobless recovery' or 'The Great Recession', we at all the major banks as of this moment are reducing the interest rates on all outstanding credit card balances to 7%. It is our way of saying, 'we understand, America'. We're all hurting and we'll do our part. It is our intention to hold these rates this low for at least three years, and possibly more if we can."

Not one of the faces behind him, nor Blankenship himself, showed any great joy in the announcement. Each anticipated their vast holdings of company stock would plummet. Some had even sold off immense numbers of shares. Their fears proved to be well founded. Investors howled. By late that afternoon even the blue-chip stalwart Bank of America had seen its shares fall from $51 to a low of $38 before rebounding to $42.

Something little watched in the aftermath of these two huge announcements was a statement by the head of Sallie Mae that he was reducing the rates on all the outstanding student loans to 7% as well. Kenny Borel looked equally as uncomfortable as the bankers had.

Eddie Kelley and James Lally, still ensconced at the Comfort Inn, didn't miss the speech. They jumped, whooped, hollered and gave each other high fives.

# Chapter Fourteen

ELLIOTT EASTMAN GROANED as his cell phone on the night stand rang. It was five in the morning. He pressed the button and said, "Hello, Elliott speaking."

"Can you hold for a moment sir? The President would like to speak with you."

Leaning back on his pillows Elliott explored his right side with his hand, pressing in here and there to determine the extent of the area where pain registered. As his hand slipped below his ribs he gasped in pain.

The President came on the line at that moment and heard the gasp.

"Is everything okay Elliott?"

"Yes, it's fine. Good morning, Mr. President."

"I wanted to pass along the good news. I've spoken at length with my cabinet and advisors. We're going forward with the Transaction Fee Bill on one condition. I'd like to meet with the chairman of the Securities and Exchange Commission and you at the White House at your earliest convenience. I would also like to hear from your experts from Harvard, Stanford and MIT. I want to hear it straight from Sam Goldman that he backs the idea. I'll have the head of the Treasury Department and probably the chairman of the Congressional Budget Office here as well."

Elliott was silent for a moment and then said softly, "I'll be there Paul, but I was hoping to keep my name out of this so the fewer folks you invite the better. They can still vet the plan in great detail after we have concluded our meeting."

The President was silent for a moment and then said, "I understand your wish to remain anonymous, but perhaps you can be an impartial observer and merely say a few words. I promise your name will not be bandied about to the media."

"Thank you, I think it's important I keep a low profile. Paul, I have a question. Was it the ten million dollar donation to your re-election that swayed you?"

The President paused again.

"I'd be lying if I said no, but it's more than that. Did you see Blankenship's speech last night? They're stepping up. If the banks are stepping up then now might be the time to cut the oil company and farm subsidies. It might be time to go for the whole economic package. I could be remembered as the president who finally brought it all together, the president who brought us back from the brink. I'll be honest with you Elliott, I've seen the numbers. We are on the brink. This is the time and the place to get America back to what it should have been all along, and this is the way to do it, with big, bold ideas. The Transaction Fee will be the centerpiece. I'll be honest, I've had some of my people explore the numbers and it looks very promising. It looks as though what you have suggested is easily within our grasp and doesn't impact the average Joe."

"Okay, you don't need to be speechifying to me. You already had my vote, but don't forget the spending cuts. It's the other side of the bill and is equally important."

President Paul White laughed more freely than he had in a long time. It was good to hear, Elliott thought.

"Okay, okay. I'll contact Sam Goldman at the SEC and see when he can make it and get back to you."

A short while later Elliott was in the shower, having taken another six Advil, and in spite of the pain actually found himself whistling softly. The president was on board!

# Chapter Fifteen

THE RESPONSE WAS overwhelming. Within twenty four hours, thirteen thousand former prisoners had reported to the nearest police station. An equal number of parolees inquired as to whether they might be eligible for some of the training programs. Robert Dale, the lawyer who had initiated the news conference, duly completed the purchase of the former prison and handed off the responsibility for hiring the necessary contractors to modify the existing structures to an architectural firm. A team of hand-picked former educators made recommendations for the hiring of teachers, administrators, personal trainers and health technicians.

Again Elliott's army of writers began expounding in various forms of media regarding the amazing willingness of people to try to better themselves. On the other end of the spectrum, the right wing argued the case that it was the prospect of reduced sentences that was the single biggest motivator behind the surprising response of the escapees to turn themselves in. This angered Elliott to such a degree that he brought three dozen mobile classrooms onto the prison grounds and took in an additional five thousand parolees who sought free educational opportunities.

Most of the evening news programs carried it as the lead story.

# Chapter Sixteen

SAMUEL GOLDMAN, THE head of the Securities and Exchange Commission, and Elliott Eastman were ushered into a closed door session in the White House Situation Room. An enormous 38 foot long highly lacquered Red Oak table dominated the room. It could easily seat eighteen people to a side. The walls were adorned with no less than a dozen fifty inch Hi-Def television screens with a full video set up on the far wall. Pitchers of ice water and glasses dotted the table.

Elliott recognized most of the faces of the men already around the table. Introductions were made and he was offered a cup of coffee. It was a virtual who's who of the Washington financial world. The Secretary of the Treasury Anthony LaScala was there as well as the Chairman of the Federal Reserve Ken Kenake, the President and Vice President, several scholars familiar with constitutional law, and leading economists including Paul Crugmann. The room was abuzz in conversation in low tones until the President tapped the side of his coffee cup with his spoon.

"Gentlemen, you all know why I've called such a hasty meeting. Obviously I feel it is of the utmost importance to review this proposal in depth before proceeding. I believe it would be best for the esteemed Mr. Elliott Eastman to open the meeting by reiterating his proposal in great detail."

Elliott gave the President a look as if to say "what part of low profile did we not understand?"

Most of the men in the room knew the story of the Master Sergeant. He'd refused many an offer of advancement, many a suggestion by his command officers that a rank of colonel or at least lieutenant was more appropriate for him. He'd refused them all to remain in the field with his men. That is until he was badly injured, had the lower portion of his right leg removed, and was forced to leave the service. Since then he'd become vastly wealthy and earned a reputation in the Senate as a tenacious fighter for the rights of the common man.

The President took a seat while Elliott set aside the notepad he had in front of him, opened his brief case, pulled out a thick manila folder and set it on the table.

"Perhaps a little back ground is in order before commencing on the nuts and bolts of the plan. I've had my staff working on various issues for the past few months, and they are some of the brightest minds in the nation. A staff, I might add, consisting of some of the best and brightest from Harvard, Stanford and MIT. Together they've determined the single greatest threat to our national security is our massive, and I might add growing, national debt. Foreigners could stop buying our treasuries, and they are in discussion to do just that, leaning towards a currency basket including the British pound, the Chinese Yuan and others. If that were to happen our interest rates, in order to make our currency more attractive to foreign investors, would soar to 8% or perhaps 9%, or even higher. This would crush our economy. Lending would cease. No homes, cars, or appliances would be sold. Short term borrowing for company finance, new machinery and payroll needs would stop. Essentially our economy would grind to a halt. Within six months starvation, food riots and general anarchy would ensue. Now bear in mind, to pay off 18 trillion in debt simply cannot be done by raising taxes. The tax burden would be a crushing weight on the common man and this scenario leads to the same result, anarchy. This team of brilliant economists came up with a new source of tax revenue, a very modest transaction fee I might add, that when coupled with some sensible spending cuts would eliminate our debt within five to seven years. I'll repeat: it would eliminate our debt in seven years, possibly less."

Elliott stopped speaking for a moment and studied the faces turned towards him. He opened the folder in front of him and handed a single sheet of paper to each man in the room.

"You will find before you a basic statement addressing a flat fee transaction tax on all stock transactions on the two largest U.S. stock markets; the NASDAQ and the New York Stock Exchanges. Recent computations suggest there are 928 million daily transactions in the U.S. with a buyer and seller for each side. The fee structure is $10 for trades over $1000, $100 for trades over $100,000 and $1000 for trades over $1,000,000. These fees will also apply for the futures and derivatives markets which amount to $703 trillion worldwide each year and are growing. This will generate almost 1.4 trillion dollars a year in additional revenue which will be applied first to the national debt and then to Social Security."

Ken Kenake, the Federal Reserve Chairman and former CEO of JP Morgan interrupted saying, "you must realize that almost every president since Ron Reagan has considered such a tax and shelved it."

"I'm aware of that. The World Futures Industry indicates there were 3.961 billion daily futures contracts executed in 2016, the last year for which figures are available. Of that, 42% were originated in the U.S., or 1, 653 billion contracts, each worth many millions of dollars. A $1000 transaction fee on each of them, an amount they wouldn't even feel, would generate another one and a half trillion dollars annually. This is a vastly different world than the one Ron Reagan faced. There are five trillion dollars in dollar foreign exchange transactions daily. Commodities, another two trillion daily trades, derivatives, another fifteen trillion dollars in trades and mind you those are daily trades. Half the products we're discussing didn't even exist when Reagan was alive. JP Morgan alone holds 90 trillion in derivative contracts. Think about that gentlemen. That's six times the entire Gross National Product of the U.S. It is a changed world. We are awash in capital and a lot of it, probably close to 60%, isn't taxed at all."

There were murmurs around the table.

Ken Kenake spoke up. "You do realize that Sweden tried the very thing you're suggesting and they lost most of their derivative and bond trading to the London exchanges."

"I'm aware of that situation. That was in 1995, a few lifetimes ago when the total world and derivative volume was $17 trillion. Now it is $703 trillion. There must be great profit for that market to grow so huge in less than two decades. Sweden is a small country located quite close to London, one of the biggest financial centers in the world. If companies want to move out of the US because of a miniscule transaction fee so be it, but they will not be allowed access to our capitol markets. I think they'll see the light and pay the fee. Now most of the world is in favor of a transaction fee. In 2011, before Greece, Spain and Portugal defaulted on their debt; the whole Euro zone was pushing for a transaction fee to solve their financial issues. US Treasury Secretary Tim Guttner shot it down. They needed the US to participate and we punted. The Euro zone almost went ahead on their own and imposed a transaction fee, but in the end couldn't put it together. We all know how Europe suffered after that."

"Still, Sweden was a failed experiment," Kenake insisted.

"Ken, I understand there are going to be reservations, but most of those have been generated by the financial community. In 2010 350 economists, including Nobel Laureate Joseph Stiglitz and Jeffery Sachs, from 35 countries signed a letter urging the G-20 to adopt a financial transaction fee. Angela Merkel of Germany, god rest her soul, Gordon Brown of England and Nicholas Sarkozy of France all came out in favor of the fee approach. Frankly, it's only the US and their enormously influential financial sector that stands in the way of successfully implementing this plan."

Elliott concluded with a sharp glance at the Treasury Secretary.

"Duly noted," Kenake said.

"Now, included in this proposal would be a sunset provision, probably about seven year's duration or until the deficit is eliminated. Although, I will add, I have spoken with the President," he nodded in Paul Whites direction, "and he and I are personally in favor of extending it for the purpose of making Social Security solvent again. This would serve two goals; addressing the current crisis with Social Security and garnering the popular vote in this country."

"Gentlemen, and please correct me if I am wrong Mr. President, but I believe the President stands ready to make this the centerpiece of his re-election campaign, but there is another part of the plan. I've spoken with Bob Gates, the former Secretary of Defense, and he stands ready to cross the country giving stump speeches in support of what we intend to call the 'War on the Deficit.'"

Elliott paused for a moment and took a sip of water.

"This is the other side of the ledger," Elliott said pulling a second sheaf of papers from his brief case.

"That is cuts to the spending side of the ledger. Do you know we have 1,118 military bases around the world? Again, I've spoken with Bob Gates and Secretary of Defense Bruce Holland and they are in agreement that almost half of these are redundant and superfluous. Hell, just one of our super carriers has more firepower and personnel than many of these bases. The savings from eliminating just four hundred of these bases is close to three hundred billion a year and we must not stop there. We must dust off some of the cuts that have been proposed time and time again over the years. Why do we send three billion a year to Pakistan, a country that reviles us, 1.3 billion to Egypt, six hundred million a year to Colombia, as well as many others? Those should go immediately. Personally I'm in favor of eliminating farm subsidies that would save 25 billion a year. Oil companies don't need subsidies and tax credits from the American people. I've spoken with Dick Henghold, Director of the Office of Management and Budget. He and the President's staff are putting together some numbers, but I imagine it could come close to two trillion a year in savings if properly enacted. I'm leaving the scope of the cuts up to the President and his staff, but I think cuts are a mandatory part of the whole package.

"In summary, our proposal to the American people is decisive. It's a massive source of revenue enhancement, but not on the backs of the average American family. In fact, it's on those they perceive as fat cats, the money guys shuffling trillions each day, so it's painless to the American people and it's temporary. Seven years is the blink of an eye in the history of a nation. This is an idea whose time has come. Thank you very much."

Elliott sat down, exhaustion creeping into every muscle in his body. Again a sharp pain like a punch in the gut hit his right side. He bent forward slightly in his seat. Bob Gates leaned towards him with a look of concern on his face. Elliott straightened quickly and held up a hand holding Gates at bay. Not another man seated at the table noted anything different about the former Master Sergeant.

The head of the United States Treasury, Anthony Lascala, rose to speak. "Elliott, gentlemen, I applaud the former senator's eloquence and leadership, however I must caution all of us from becoming overly optimistic. Congress has shot down, time and again, proposals that are far less reaching than this. I believe much of this proposal is what we desperately need to do, but I doubt you'll find a single congressperson to sponsor such a sweeping bill and few to support it in its entirety. You'll have the banking industry, the Futures Industry of America and all the military contractors against you. You're talking an army of lobbyists going against you."

"I've considered this and I intend to push back. If a congressman resists, we'll expose him and the lobbyists backing him to the American people. We need to do this and we need to do this now," Elliott replied.

"And just how would you expose him?"

"Leave that up to me. I've had my people conduct a poll recently. It was a phone call survey to five thousand families across the nation. The margin of error is 3 to 6%. 73.3% are in favor of the basics of this plan, with 18% undecided and 8% against it. When we included the Social Security funding portion of it the numbers changed dramatically. 92.7% approved of it with 3% against it and 3% undecided. I feel safe in saying that assuming the President runs on this platform you are almost assuredly looking at a president who will win a second term quite handily. Lastly my economic team is exploring the possibility of a National Referendum. This is the age of the Internet, Facebook, Twitter and others. A National Referendum could be completed more easily than at anytime in history. We don't have the answers yet, but it's looking like a simple yes or no text response may be sufficient, rather like voting for 'Dancing with the Stars'. A National Referendum, or even the threat of one, should motivate Congress mightily because it hits them where it hurts. It hits them in the smug assumption of their power. It hits them by bypassing them completely and taking the questions directly to the people. The American people deserve better than they have received in the last thirty years as Congress has kowtowed to the power of the corporations. It is time for change, and the time is now."

"A National referendum, or a direct vote by the people, was addressed eloquently by both James Madison and Thomas Jefferson during the constitutional debates," spoke up one of the scholars, Martin Wheeler. "They both spoke of the tyranny of the majority. If the majority is uninformed and out of control they might pass laws that dramatically upset the very nature of government."

Elliott spoke softly, for he was feeling a little light headed and queasy. "True, and yet Herodotus wrote of a mere six Roman families owning most of North Africa, so we know when the people have no voice it can go the other way and lead to a great concentration of wealth and power much like we're seeing take place today. An informed electorate can and should be trusted to keep the economy and the government on an even keel."

"Still, it will be difficult to get Congress to pass such a bill," the scholar responded.

The Treasury Secretary chimed in. "I should think a referendum won't be necessary. I think someone along the lines of Paul Rand would be willing to endorse such a bill and put it before Congress."

A low murmur of laughter rippled through the assembly.

"I suppose, but simply the push to initiate a referendum should give them impetus to consider the bill we are proposing. You may be selling our electorate short my friend," Elliott responded. "D'Toqueville in his diaries wrote that even in the 1820's, when traveling to the smallest town in the remotest regions of the Ozarks, the common man could speak eloquently regarding the current affairs of the nation. I think you'll find when the electorate truly believes they have a voice, a true stake in the outcome of an election, they will surprise you with how well informed they are."

The President spoke up. "I like it. We'll send the bill to the House once the wording has been finalized, but at the same time start the wheels rolling. I'll have my staff prepare a reasonable and wide reaching array of defense budget cuts, including a serious cut in the overseas bases and our funding for Egypt, Pakistan and the lot of them. I trust I can have the backing of those present?"

A stinging silence greeted his request and Elliott felt his ire getting the better of him.

"You think the status quo is going to get us anything but the same trash we've put out for the last twenty years?" he asked. "We need to take bold steps. Our country and particularly our government is slowly becoming the laughing stock of the world. All we are is empty rhetoric and lawgivers controlled by corporate money. We supported Mubarek in Egypt with 1.8 billion dollars a year and then applauded the Arab spring when he was over thrown. We have high school students who can barely read, an apathetic electorate and a military bent on supporting our corporate interests overseas. The list of our immoral atrocities worldwide goes back further than I care to remember. Anyone wish to hear the tale about Torres and United Fruit in Panama? C'mon people. As I said a moment ago, the time is now. Should we idly sit by and watch the government print money until we're in the poor house, paying interest to other countries and supporting their quality of life? Let's get our house in order. Let's get …" A rush of dizziness overwhelmed the senator. He felt himself falling. For a moment he gripped the armrest of his chair, but then he was falling again. He heard the crash of the chair on the floor and felt a dull thump. A cacophony of voices erupted in the tight confines of the Situation Room and then slowly, darkness descended and all was quiet.

# Chapter Seventeen

SLOWLY ELLIOTT BECAME vaguely aware of his surroundings. A faint whirring sound came from not far away and a rhythmic beeping seemed to be closer yet. He opened his eyes to find white curtains hung around his bed and he could hear voices speaking in low tones. He rolled over and a sharp stab of pain coursed through his right side. He groaned and instantly the screens were pulled aside. His personal physician, Dr. Paul Yates stood framed in the harsh fluorescent lighting.

"How do you feel, Elliott?" he asked, the genuine concern clear in his tone of voice.

"Okay, I guess. Rather tired. What time is it?"

"It's two a.m. on October third."

"October third? Are you telling me I've been out for two days? I've got things to do," Elliott said and made as if to get out of bed.

"Hold on there Tiger," Dr. Yates insisted while gently placing a hand on Elliott's chest and pushing him back against the pillows.

"I've got your phone and have been speaking to various parties. The list of visitors is quite impressive and growing. I've taken extensive notes and will review them with you shortly, but first I must review what the recent tests reveal."

"Keep it short and sweet," Elliott growled.

"A few questions first. Have you fainted or experienced light headedness before?"

Elliott shook his head.

"Shortness of breath or fatigue?"

"No shortness of breath, but I've been mighty tired recently," Elliott replied.

"I think it's an adverse response to the medication we've prescribed. I'll review the dosage with the pharmacists. You'll need to monitor it carefully. If you find yourself growing faint take a seat, and if you are driving pull over immediately," the Doctor carefully explained.

"Got it."

"Now for the update on your condition, which I'm afraid is not good. The cancer has spread to the lymph nodes under your arms. Unusually aggressive cancers often use the lymph systems to travel throughout the body. The operation is simple; we remove the nodes. It takes about an hour and a half for the operation and another hour of stiff coffee for the anesthesia to wear off. We'll put you on some heavy pain medication and you'll be out of here in the morning."

"Tell the doctors to start sharpening their scalpels. I'm out of here by nine a.m."

"Always the ever gracious patient," Dr. Yates replied. "Are you sure you have the time to die Elliott?"

The Master Sergeant stared for a moment at his long time friend.

"I'm sorry," he said. "Go ahead Paul."

"How do you feel?"

"Fine most of the time. I get a sharp pain in my side occasionally and a dizzy spell from time to time."

"Appetite?"

"It's normal. Come to think of it I am kind of hungry."

"That's good. I'll see what the hospital staff can rustle up in the way of food in a moment."

"How is this going to come down, Paul?" Elliott asked in a soft voice as if comprehending for the first time that his life was currently being counted in months, but that soon it would be weeks, days and then hours.

Dr. Yates looked at his friend of thirty years and struggled mightily to keep his voice from cracking as he spoke. "You'll get weak. Jaundice will set in. The pain in your side will become constant. You may have more dizzy spells, trouble standing and the pain will become quite acute. You'll probably begin to experience incontinence. We will give you medication to reduce the pain. Eventually you will not be able to stand or sit. Your organs will begin to shut down and that's when we normally begin the morphine treatments. When that starts, you're only a few hours or days away from saying goodbye."

With that final sentence the doctors lips began to tremble and he whispered, "I'm so sorry, Elliott."

Doctor Yates turned away and Elliott could see his shoulders shaking.

"How much time?" Elliott asked.

"I don't know. The movement to your nodes is not a good sign, but hopefully we caught it in time and the removal of them will slow the spread. And chemo would help."

"Well, there's a lot yet to do, so let's contact the doctors and get these nodes removed," Elliott said.

"First let me read my notes to you," Paul responded, quickly collecting himself.

"Eddie Kelley and James Lally are on their way into town. They said they were your body guards."

Elliott laughed at the comment. "How did they know I was here?"

"It's been all over the news. Don't forget you're a very well-known person."

"I didn't think I was national news."

"Well obviously you are. Kelley and Lally? I think I remember them from Iraq," Paul said.

"They are pretty unforgettable," Elliott replied.

"General Gates said the President is putting the finishing touches to his State of the Union speech and including everything you discussed. He said, and this is a quote, 'you better put on your boxing gloves, because the gauntlet is going to hit the table and Congress is going to howl.'

"The President's secretary has called twice asking about your condition. Representative Bruce Bennet called to say he's talked to the President at length and he's signing on to sponsor the 'War on the Deficit' bill."

"Hot damn," Elliott almost exclaimed, rubbing his hands together, "now were talking. Bruce is a little green yet, but a tiger for detail and he's a salt of the earth human being if there ever was one. We'll get this bill to the floor yet."

"Okay, that's about it. You get some rest and I'll talk to the doctors. Let's shoot for about six a.m. for the operation."

"Sounds good."

# Chapter Eighteen

ELLIOTT CAME OUT from under the anesthesia slowly. A nurse came in and checked his pulse. Dr. Yates came in and said, "Well everything went off without a hitch. You are no longer the owner of four lymph nodes."

"Great," Elliott moaned. "How soon does the anesthesia wear off? I feel sick."

"Are you going to throw up?"

"No, I don't think so."

"Good. General Bob Gates came by to see you. We wound up having a long conversation. Apparently the President wants the two of you to be on stage when he delivers his State of the Union speech two weeks from now. You've been a busy fellow, haven't you? The 'War on the Deficit' sounds like a bad B-movie, but he did have some words of wisdom. He said, 'do what you need to do to regain your health'. He'll keep you informed up until the State of the Union. I would suggest you listen to him. We could get three chemo treatments in and still give you four days of recuperation before your stage appearance."

"You're not getting me on some damn death treatment. I feel like all I do these days is lie around in bed."

"Rest is very good for you. It might add a month to your life; a month that sounds like it might be a very important one."

Elliott sighed. "What are we talking about?"

Dr. Yates explained and Elliott reluctantly agreed. It was a grueling two weeks with Elliott getting double the normal dose of radiation. He was usually down for a day and a half after that, but then began eating and swimming to rebuild his strength as quickly as possible. The attending doctors were awed and marveled at his stamina. He began drinking Starbucks Double shots and taking a brisk walk twice a day. By the time of the State of the Union he was feeling as fit as he did ten years ago.

He slipped into a newly purchased tuxedo, took the President's limo from the hospital to the Halls of Congress and was quickly whisked backstage. There he met General Robert Gates, Richard Henghold of the Office of Management and Budget, Secretary of Defense Bruce Holland, and Samuel Goldman, the Chairman of the Securities and Exchange Commission. Lastly there was Bruce Bennett of the House of Representatives, a young freshman Democrat from Colorado, who enthusiastically wished to introduce the bill to the House. Of course the President agreed to throw his support behind one of Bennett's pet projects; eliminating lobbyist access to government leaders and eliminating earmarks. Elliott remembered Bennett. The young man had contacted Elliott for advice two years before when he was contemplating a run for the House. He'd asked if they could have lunch together and Elliott had agreed. Elliott was impressed with him. He was convinced his heart was in the right place when it came to correcting the ills that beset America.

This was a most extraordinary gathering, and the President's plans for them were even more outlandish. The standard format for decades had been to have the Speaker of the House and Senate to be seated, along with the Vice President, behind the President at the podium. Instead, President Paul White had the seats removed, requested that the speakers stand down, and made room for these august collaborators of his to stand shoulder to shoulder behind him.

He touched on everything they had discussed; the transaction fee, the cut backs on military bases and spending, farm and oil subsidies, foreign aid to Pakistan, Colombia and other countries, reforming the prison system and even the basis for a National Referendum. The applause was thunderous at times, but towards the end of his speech became rather muted. He closed by saying, "This 'War on the Deficit' is going to succeed. The enemy of our nation, with its bloody blade hanging over us these many years will be vanquished. We will be beholden to no other nation to fund our existence. We will free ourselves to return to the country we should be. The greatness of America lies ahead of her and we will witness it together, or my name is not Paul White, the President of these United States!"

Bob Gates leaned over to Elliott and whispered, "He always could give a damn good speech."

"I'd say the game is on. We'd better ready ourselves for the worst they can throw at us," Elliott replied.

As Elliott left the stage he strode to a quiet location in the shadows and spoke into his cell phone. "Eddie, the game is afoot. Call all the teams in and get rooms at the Four Seasons until you can find an adequate safe house. I want you ready at a moments notice. Oh, and buy a half dozen of the smallest video cameras you can find."

"Consider it done, Sarge."

These days it was a rare occasion, but Elliott felt energized and began to hum an old rock tune, 'Takin' Care of Business', as he stepped into the cool Washington night.

# Chapter Nineteen

REPRESENTATIVE BRUCE BENNETT and six of his staffers worked closely with the Chairman of the Securities and Exchange Commission Samuel Goldman and his team of lawyers, along with Elliott's attorneys carefully crafting the wording of the bill. A week later Bruce Bennett handed the eighty page document, 'The War on the Deficit', to the Clerk of the House who placed it in a wooden box to the side of his desk called the hopper. Representative Bennett didn't really care for the name of the measure, but the President wanted it to be recognized as something different; something far reaching and vast in scope. The clerk entered the name of the measure in The House Journal and listed Bruce Bennett as the primary sponsor. Later that day, 'The War on the Deficit' became known as HR 2239. The Speaker of the House Nick Cobbings assigned it to The House Appropriations Committee because of the bill's obvious impact on defense spending and foreign operations, and to the House Financial Services Committee because of the stock transaction fee aspect of the bill. Immediately the lobbyists went on the offensive. Representatives of dozens of Washington's most powerful lobbying firms began contacting members of the Appropriations Committee and the Financial Services Committee, but Elliott's men, including Eddie Kelley and James Lally, were there armed with video cameras capturing every meeting in great detail. In several cases, posing as lobbyists themselves, Elliott's' men were able to get the business cards of some of the most aggressive of the money men.

In the meantime, Elliott placed a call to another long time friend Archie 'Backspace' Conner. Mr. Conner had been the troops' radio man in Iraq and literally spent years in the war zone at Elliott's side. The two men had become as close as brothers over that time frame. Archie, with a natural gift for anything having to do with air waves and electronics, had become an accomplished political satirist, nationally recognized photographer, frequent editorial contributor and general cynic. When Mr. Conner heard what Elliott had in mind he laughed harder than he had in a long time.

"I love it," he said. "Sure I'll be glad to do it. When is the vote going to be held?"

"The bill has been sent to two committees. Ninety percent of the bills sent to committee die in the committee, meaning they are shelved and never sent to the floor of the House for a full vote. Assuming the committees release them without any major amendments, the vote should take place about a week from now."

"Perfect. That's plenty of time," Conner agreed. "All you need to do is e-mail the photos to me."

"Thanks, Archie," Elliott replied. "You know where to send the bill."

Elliott contacted his men in the field and the photos they'd taken of the Committee members were forwarded to Archie within fifteen minutes.

Forty eight hours later, several YouTube videos appeared on the Internet. Videos and articles were sent to Taxpayers for Common Sense, Common Cause and dozens of other liberal groups. Photos and attached editorials were also sent to the Wall Street Journal, The New York Times, the Washington Post and the USA TODAY.

The first was a full page spread in the New York Times. A photo showed two men locked in deep conversation in the hallway outside the congressional chambers. One of the men was House of Representatives Republican from Florida Barney Martin meeting with Dana Pogue of Atherton and Associates. The caption below the almost full page color photo read: "Now why would Rep. Barney Martin, the leading member on the House Appropriations Committee where money is doled out to defense contractors, want to talk to Dana Pogue of the lobbying group Atherton and Associates, one of the most powerful groups representing GE, Lockheed Martin, Boeing and many other defense related companies?

"One guess might be the bill to reduce the number of military bases around the world. They can't be happy with that idea. They want to keep wasting your tax dollars so they can line their pockets. Don't you, the American taxpayer deserve better? If you think you deserve better and you think lobbyists should be barred from Capitol Hill, text 151. If you think everything is fine and wish to preserve the status quo, text 152. Note: Rep. Barney Martin and his entire family took a trip to Italy and France a few months back. The whole $38,000 bill was paid for by Maliburton. How do you think he'll vote?"

The YouTube version went viral in a matter of hours with over 9 million hits.

Another full page exposé in the New York Times showed Rep. Wilson Jenkins walking down the steps of Capitol Hill laughing with Aaron Barr of Podesta Group, a lobbying firm with ties to Pakistan, Saudi Arabia, Egypt and the Arab Emirates. The video was shot from a hundred feet away and the two men obviously believed they were alone and could not be recorded, but Elliott's men had some of the most sophisticated listening devices available. Rep. Jenkins is on the House Financial Services Committee.

Jenkins could be heard saying, "Some damn fee to cut into derivatives and futures earnings. Who do they think they are dealing with? We'll just add an amendment to cut Medicare funding. We'll see if the Democrats are willing to throw grandma out of her rocking chair or cut into banking profits."

A voice over as the men continued down the steps said, "The American Government is a disaster. Corporations and special interest groups run the country through the influence of lobbyists in Congress. Congress does not check the power of lobbyists because of greed. The only way to end government corruption is to eliminate the power and access of the lobbyists. As an American citizen, if you think you deserve better text 151, if you are happy with the status quo, text 152."

When Elliott saw it he couldn't suppress a smile.

"Oh that's beautiful work, Archie," Elliott said to himself.

The last op-ed piece, again paid for by Elliott Eastman, was displayed in all the major newspapers across the country. It showed an elderly man with a stocking cap and grizzled gray beard sitting in a large cardboard box, his hands wrapped in socks with the ends cut out, a grimace on his face as he scooped a wedge of cat food out of a can with one filthy finger. The picture, which took up half a page, was a startling one that universally caused a revulsion reflex in most people.

The editorial read; "You've worked hard all your life. You played by the rules and paid your dues."

The photo on the lower half of the page showed an elegantly dressed gray haired man climbing into a Rolls Royce with the door being held by his chauffer beneath the Wall Street sign.

The caption read: "Don't you think it's time someone else paid their fair share. Text 151 if you think a nominal fee on stock transactions (for five years) is fair, or if you're happy with the status quo, text 152."

Elliott's cell phone rang for the hundredth time that day, but he recognized the President's private number.

"Hello Paul," he answered.

"Elliott. You've outdone yourself. That half page ad with the old man in the box was a thing of beauty," the President stated enthusiastically.

"Thanks, although I can't take credit for it. I just happen to know an Internet whiz that is linked to hundreds of other very creative people."

"Still, it's got to be sending a powerful message to the House of Representatives and will probably cost Wilson Jenkins and Aaron Barr their jobs."

"I wouldn't want to be in their shoes. What's really going to rattle their cages is the results of the text messaging," added Elliott.

"Any numbers in yet?"

"I was about to check with my man Archie."

"Good, let me know what he has for us."

"Will do, but let's not get carried away. This was the first salvo. The opposition will gather their forces and fight back. Winning over a majority of the House to our way of thinking is going to be a much tougher battle," Elliott reminded the President.

"I'm realistic, but look what we've accomplished in just a few short weeks. The banks have reduced consumer lending rates and Sallie Mae has done the same. Consumer spending is up and rising dramatically. The GDP numbers for the fourth quarter are going to show a two percent jump, at least that's what the projections are on a preliminary basis. And from what I hear from my people in Congress, we almost have enough votes to pass HR 2239. I will be the president who tamed the deficit."

"The big banks will fight the transaction fee. They don't like the fact that the Securities and Exchange Commission is going to set up its own lock box for the fees."

"It's the only way I will set it up. We must keep our promise to the people and make this a dedicated account for the sole purpose of eliminating the deficit."

The pain in Elliott's side suddenly flared anew and he struggled to stifle a groan.

"Paul, let me touch base with my Internet people and I'll get back to you shortly."

"Are you okay? Your voice sounds funny."

"I'm fine, just a case of the hiccups."

The President laughed. "Okay, I'll let you go. I look forward to your next phone call."

Elliott clicked off his phone, then doubled over and gasped. He struggled over to his desk, grabbed the small bottle of pills Dr. Yates had given him and took three. He fell into his chair and wiped the beads of sweat from his forehead. He sat still for about five minutes until he started to feel a little better and then placed the call to Backspace.

"Archie, Elliott here. Is there any news on the text survey?"

"Yes, it's huge. I've never seen anything like it. All three of the surveys are off the charts. Reports from my number crunchers indicate over 92% of the responders are texting with 'yes' answers on all three questions and, get this, there have been over 30 million responses!"

"Good lord," Elliott exclaimed. "That's far beyond my expectations."

"And they're still coming in," Archie added. "You know what the pundits will say. They'll call it the youth vote, because mom and dad don't text."

"Can we run a demographic on who sends text messages? I'm sure Verizon and AT+T will have some numbers on that, but my thought is 'it's about time'. The young are the most disenfranchised of all Americans. To get a response like this is nothing short of extraordinary."

"I agree."

"Maybe we should play that angle up," Elliott said thoughtfully.

"Consider it done. I've got the perfect idea."

"I'm sure you do."

The two men hung up. After Elliott passed the good news on to the President he retreated to the restroom and vomited several times. There was blood in the mix. He then walked slowly back to the den, took four more pills and went straight to bed.

# Chapter Twenty

THE 'WAR ON the Deficit' bill became a hot potato. Any member of the House who was seen as voting against it would be a pariah in the eyes of an aware public, but any member voting for it would be ostracized by the corporate community. It was becoming a showdown of epic proportions, but a bill in committee is different. Committees are run by a chairman who may have a different agenda, a chairman who may have to answer to a lobbying firm which he is beholden too. Committee meetings are supposedly for investigating the relative merits of some aspect of a bill. Lobbyists lurk in the hallway outside the committee meetings just waiting for chance to bend the ear of those in the know once they emerge.

But the real meetings are off site where the power brokers exert enormous pressure on committee members. Little is shared regarding what happens in those sessions.

In this case, both the Finance Committee and the Appropriations Committee were selected by the Speaker of the House to review the bill. They had thirty days to send their recommendations to the floor of the House. If they did not respond at all, the bill would die. It was called 'being killed in committee', and many a bill had met its fate this way. Three weeks passed and nothing was heard from either committee. It looked as though the bill was going to fade away.

Elliott was seething. He was pacing the floor of his home office in his Colorado ranch when his cell phone rang. It was President White.

"Hello Paul," Elliott said.

"Hi Elliott. I've got that sinking feeling."

"I do too."

"How could they shelve a bill that is probably the finest piece of legislation on behalf of the American people since the Civil Rights Bill?" the President asked.

"If I recall correctly, the Civil Rights Bill didn't get passed without a fight," Elliott commented.

"Fight? I'd love a fight. I've had Jeff Archer, my head of the Government Accounting Office, look at the bill and crunch the numbers. He enthusiastically endorsed it. I've also spoken to George Madsen, the Director of the National Economic Council, and he thinks it's a stroke of genius. It provides a road map for solving all our ills in a few short years. I've asked both men to talk to the committee heads, the Republican Sam Whitback from Kansas for the Appropriations Committee and the Republican from Texas Ray Haley Hutchinson for the Finance Committee, but they couldn't get anywhere with them. I took it upon myself to speak with Hutchinson and he said he couldn't back it. He said it was too far reaching. The economy was too fragile for something that was such a game changer on so many levels."

"Oh hog wash," Elliott growled. "Isn't Hutchinson the one who was backing an earmark for almost a million bucks for 'Beef Improvement Research' at some plant in Texas owned by his cousin?"

"The same."

"How did we reach such a sick and twisted place in our history, Paul? The framers of the Constitution would jump off the roof of the Capitol if they could hear what goes on behind those doors."

"It's the damn lobbyists, but what can we do?"

"We have seven more days to wait and see if the committees do anything, but I think we both know what they are going to do. They aren't going to report it to the floor where the House members can vote on it, so it is dead. We could press for a Motion to Suspend the Rules and force the bill to the floor, but the Speaker of the House, Nick Cobbings, is a Republican from Oklahoma and close friends with Sam Whitback. The Speaker has the discretion for recognition of a Motion to Suspend and will request a ruling from the Committee that has jurisdiction over the bill. Sam Whitback will simply suggest the Motion to Suspend be denied."

"And even if H.R. 2239 made it to the floor, the Motion to Suspend allows for the addition of amendments. They'll amend the thing until it no longer looks anything like what was originally submitted," The President added.

The two men fell silent mulling over their limited options.

"This is November eighteenth?" Paul asked.

"Yes."

"The House will adjourn for the balance of the year in eleven days. We don't have any time."

"We could try for a Motion to Discharge which would pull the bill out of committee and bypass the Speaker. It sends the bill right to the floor for a vote by the entire House, and it cannot be amended, but let me think. When the Motion to Discharge is approved by a majority of the House it still has to sit in layover for another week, so the House members get a chance to review it. There are only eleven days until they adjourn for the year. Even if we tried for a Discharge Petition the layover period is another week, so we're three days short, we don't have time to pull off a discharge before they adjourn for the year. Damn."

"If I recall my congressional history correctly there have only been two successful Motions to Discharge in the last twenty five years," Paul White observed.

"Good, then we're due," Elliott replied. "If we could just find those extra three days."

"And it sometimes takes months to get the 218 majority votes needed in the House for an approval of the Motion to Discharge," the President interjected.

"I know," Elliott responded in a dejected tone, "but it doesn't have to take that long. In theory it could take fifteen minutes to get the 218 votes."

"You're dreaming," the president murmured.

"There has got to be a way. I'm tempted to try for a National Referendum."

"This isn't Romania. The United States does not allow for Mandatory Referendums, we have only 'Informational or Optional Referendums'," the President reminded the former senator.

"I know, I know, but if the percentages of approval are anywhere near what the text message survey revealed, it still might serve to put the House members on notice as to what their constituents would like them to do."

"So you think the members of the House are concerned with what the wishes of their constituents might be?" the President asked with an ugly chuckle.

"You seem to have become more cynical than when I knew you as a senator," Elliott observed.

"And you're not?"

"We have eleven days," Elliott murmured. "If we put on a major media blitz and file the Motion to Discharge on the 31st day, in other words the moment the thirty days is up in Committee which is this

Friday, then we can somehow force congress to delay the adjournment and then force a vote on the Motion to Discharge …"

The president chuckled. "You're going to keep congress in session over Christmas?"

"If I must."

"Fat chance. Don't torment yourself. We don't have time. It's the damn one week layover provision that's killing us," Paul replied.

Elliott swore under his breath. "Layover so the members of the House can read the bill. They rarely even bother reading the bill; they just go along with committee recommendations."

"I've only been part of one Motion to Discharge. Are you sure once it reaches the House floor it doesn't allow for the amending process?"

"I'm ninety nine percent sure, but I'll consult my rules manual and get back to you."

"Okay."

"Look Paul," Elliott pleaded, "we can do this. There must be something we can do. Can you have your staffers contact the committee members and see what they're up to? We have to try. I plan on going on the offensive first thing in the morning."

"Knock yourself out. I'll talk to the staffers, but don't get your hopes up."

Before they hung up Elliott said, "Paul, I still feel like there's something we've missed."

"What we're missing is time. Once the House adjourns sine die, for the remainder of the year the bill is dead."

'And so am I' though Elliott.

# Chapter Twenty-One

THE FOLLOWING MORNING Elliott woke early and went to work. Over coffee he flipped through the pages of the massive publication of Congressional Research Services rules and procedures and determined the Motion to Discharge didn't allow for any amendments to be added to the bill which worked in his favor, but he found little else to give him hope. The former senator was angry, and this was becoming a no-holds-barred fight. He contacted Backspace and suggested a new video. The Internet wizard ran with it. He called Eddie Kelley and James Lally with explicit instructions regarding Sam Whitback, Ray Hutchinson and Nick Cobbings.

He then pulled up an article he'd cobbled together in support of H.R. 2239 with bullet points aimed at certain demographics. The elderly he approached with the funding of the Social Security lock box; the groups against war and the deficit hawks with the cutting of the military bases; the young with a general comment about the stock, futures and derivatives fees eliminating their obligation to provide funding for previous generations retirements, and a closing comment about there being a much brighter future in just a few short years He sent it to his printing company for fine tuning along with instructions to buy three pages in USA TODAY. At the bottom of the article was an attachment of a tear out and mail in coupon requiring the voter's name, address, a statement warranting they were of voting age and a space to write a comment to their legislator. He included the mailing address and phone number for every member of the House of Representatives. He closed with a phrase meant to exhort the reader to make a change today and tell your friends to do so too.

By noon he was feeling weak and frustrated and needed to lie down for a while. As he closed his eyes he quietly wondered if he was going to wake up again.

Mr. Archie 'Backspace' Conner's next YouTube video went viral faster than the first. It showed a dark haired young woman in a tank top and cut-off blue jeans with a backpack. She stated in a very clear voice, "Hey you, yeah, I'm talking to you; the guy in the suit sitting in Congress. There were over 65 million text messages in response to three political questions. Over 90% of them were 'yes' responses. What does that tell you? I'll tell you. The American people have spoken. We're here. We're watching. We're aware and we will be heard!! If H.R. 2239 dies in committee we will be looking at you!"

It ended with a shot of thousands of people, probably at a rock concert, standing up and cheering. The mail campaign over the next few days resulted in millions of letters and calls to members of the House of Representatives, but still the bill sat stalled in committee.

A second YouTube video went out just as the 30th day dawned over H.R.2239. It was still not out of Committee. This video was brutally blunt. Eddie Kelley and James Lally had done their jobs well. They had managed to capture video of Sam Whitback conferring with a lobbyist outside the House Finance Committee meeting. They were even able to identify the lobbyist. They did the same for Ray Hutchinson and Nick Cobbings. Archie converted these to still photos and submitted them to major newspapers across the nations.

The caption at the top read roughly the same for each photo. "Your House of Representative member Sam Whitback working closely with Buford Birnbaum, a lobbyist from Rogers, Cahalan and Birnbaum, to defeat your future; H.R. 2239."

Below that followed another photo of Nick Cobbings and a lobbyist, while the third photo showed Ray Haley Hutchinson eating lunch at a posh restaurant with a lobbyist identified as Burt Donaldson. When the photos hit the New York Times on the morning of November 26th every member of the House on Capitol Hill saw them. Those that were not depicted in the photos breathed a sigh of relief because they knew it could just as easily have been them. The three gentlemen that were shown were in an absolute fit and demanding to find out how this had come to pass.

Letter writing and phone calls to various representatives spiked at 22,000 an hour. The House Finance Committee reported the bill to the floor unchanged, which was a remarkable event, but both the President and Elliott knew it was meaningless until the House Appropriations Committee reported it to the floor as well.

Elliott spoke with the President.

"It's half the battle won," Elliott said. "Now all we need to do is get the Appropriations Committee to do the same."

"It's a small step, but a move in the right direction," the President agreed. "What it really means is your newspaper and YouTube approach scared the heck out of Hutchinson."

"And Hutchinson knows if he reports the bill first it makes him look good. The bill could still die in the Appropriations Committee, so it takes the heat off of him," Elliott theorized.

"And the Appropriations Committee is where defense firms and military suppliers and all their ancillary suppliers get their bread buttered, so it will be harder to bring it out of that committee. And Sam Whitback, the chair of the Appropriations Committee can be one mean son of a bitch. I've seen him in action."

"All we can do is wait and see what Appropriations does," Elliott concluded.

Four days later the two men had their answer. The 30th day in the Appropriations Committee came and went with no release of H.R. 2239. It had died in committee.

Elliot was tempted to call the President suggesting there was something they could do, but he knew it was hopeless. They could file the Motion to Discharge, but the bill had to sit in layover for a week before they could vote on it. And with Sine Die Adjournment, the final day of the year for this session of Congress, less than six days away they were simply out of time. They had lost. Over the course of the evening while watching the news, he poured himself several stiff drinks. It didn't seem right that America went blissfully on heading towards financial Armageddon and the evening news didn't even mention it. There should have been some sort of comment regarding H.R. 2239 and the fact that it had disappeared without so much as a whimper. He fell into a fitful sleep on the couch with the T.V. droning on into the night.

He awoke with a start at about four in the morning. He knew there was something that had been bothering him, nagging in the back of his mind and now he knew what it was. 'Sine Die Adjournment' is what the President had said. The final day of this term of Congress was but six days away and that could make all the difference. He rushed into his library and searched the shelves. Again he perused the pages of the Congressional Research Service's Rules and Procedures and found what he was looking for.

"If after 30 days the committee has not sent the bill in question to the floor the member who sponsored the bill can file a Discharge Petition to release it from committee for full consideration of the House. If 218 members, a true majority of Congress, sign the Discharge Petition then the bill can be considered by the full House after waiting seven days. The bill can only be heard on 'Special

Procedure Days', the second and fourth Mondays of the month when the Discharge Petition would be considered as 'Privileged Business', meaning it would be the first order of business for the day. The 7 day waiting period, or the layover period is waived during the last 6 days before 'Sine Die Adjournment' and then can be heard immediately."

Elliott almost leaped for joy. With trembling hands he dialed Representative Bruce Bennett's cell phone number.

"Hello," a sleepy voice answered.

"Bruce, Bruce? Elliott Eastman here."

"Good lord Elliott, do you know what time it is?"

Elliott glanced at his watch and noted it was four fifteen in the morning.

"Yes, sorry, it's four in the morning, but this can't wait. Listen, I'm going to read you something."

Elliott read the caption from the Rules of Floor Procedure and then asked, "Do you know what this means?"

"Not really."

"How many days are left in session?"

"I don't know what, five or six."

"So tomorrow we're within the six day window of Sine Die Adjournment."

Elliott could hear the bed covers rustle as Bennett sat up in bed.

"So this means …"

"Tomorrow is the fourth Monday of the month and the day for hearing the Discharge Calendar. Motions to Discharge are Privileged Business and as such are the first business of the day. Here's what we have to do. This is going to be tough. Once the Speaker, Nick Cobbings, figures out what you're doing he'll not recognize you again. Have you got others in the House you can trust?"

Bruce thought for a moment, not really sure where the conversation was going.

"Yes, there's always the Minority Leader Jay Stephens, the Democrat from Oregon, and the Minority Whip Earl Bishop, a Democrat from Wisconsin."

"Cobbings is a savvy vet and if he's under as much pressure from the lobbyists as I think he is, he'll be wary of calling on those two. He'll know they will likely push for an approval of HR 2239. Who else can you count on?"

"There's Representative Kathy Morris Rodgers, a moderate Democrat from Washington who has been around a long time and knows the ropes. And Rosa Sparks, a Democrat from Connecticut we can rely on. They have both read the bill in its entirety and enthusiastically endorse it."

"Good, very good. Can you contact them and make sure they will support you? If they agree to support you then ask them to contact every Democrat they can and inform them that we need their help on a very important vote tomorrow. Tell them they must be there."

"Consider it done," Bruce, now fully awake, replied swiftly. "I'll get back to you as soon as I've spoken with them."

# Chapter Twenty-Two

THE FOLLOWING MORNING Elliott was feeling weak and couldn't keep any food down. He wasn't sure if it was the medicine, the cancer, or just a case of nerves like a ball player before the big game. He turned on C-SPAN and sat down on the edge of the couch clutching his cell phone in one hand and a glass of ice water in the other. He could see Bruce Bennett moving about the House floor.

From what Elliott could see it looked as though Bruce was the first member of the House of Representatives to arrive in those hallowed halls. He met with the Clerk of the House and dutifully filled out the Motion to Discharge. It just so happened that Mary Evans, the Clerk of the House, was a close friend of Bruce Bennett's and decided to go the extra mile for him. She made copies of the Discharge Petition and as members of the House filed in she had congressional pages, young governmental interns, approach them with the document. Many were signed and she dutifully entered them into the Congressional Journal. Once over half of the House members had filed in, the Speaker Nick Cobbings cried, "Call to Order!" He banged the mace down firmly on the podium several times and then carefully placed it in the upper position meaning the

House was in session. He then stood and said, "We will now bow our heads in prayer."

Reverend David James Ford and the 200 some odd Representatives began the day as they always did, with a prayer. Once the prayer was completed the Speaker moved to the next order of business, which was the approval of the journal. The United States constitution requires the House keep a journal of the previous day's business and the Speaker is required to state for the record that it has been approved or disapproved.

Nick Cobbings stood and stated, "The Chair has examined the journal of the last day's proceedings and announces to the House his approval thereof. Without objection, the approval is acknowledged."

Although any of the members of the House could object and give cause for a reading of the journal, they seldom did so and this was the case today.

The next piece of business was the Pledge of Allegiance. Bruce Bennett watched as Representative Jay Stephens, Democrat from Delaware, stood and placed his hand over his heart and solemnly stated the Pledge. With the Pledge completed and the members seated, the Speaker said, "There is no unfinished business so we will now move to one minute speeches."

Rosa Sparks, a Democrat from Connecticut, stood to be recognized.

"The Speaker recognizes the gentlewoman from Connecticut," Nick Cobbings said.

"Was there not unfinished business regarding the naming of the Federal Court building in St. Louis?" Rosa asked.

"That has been handed over to the Oversight Committee," Cobbings responded.

"Thank you Mr. Speaker."

As soon as Rosa Sparks was through speaking Elliott said softly into his cell phone, "Stand now to be recognized and ask for a vote on the Motion to Discharge."

"We don't have enough votes yet," Bruce insisted. "The Petition has only been moving around the floor for fifteen minutes."

"I know, I know. Trust me."

Pressing the tiny earpiece so that it would not fall out of his ear, Bruce did as he was instructed. With a fleeting frown Nick Cobbings, the Speaker of the House, said, "The gentleman from Colorado is hereby recognized."

"Thank you Mr. Chairman," Bruce replied. "I would like to request the Motion to Discharge regarding H.R. 2239 be called up for vote."

Cobbings' frown deepened further and Representative Sam Whitback instantly stood to be recognized.

"The Chair recognizes our esteemed colleague, Representative Whitback from Kansas."

"Thank you Mr. Chairman. I object to the call for the Motion to Discharge being called up for a vote. The requisite number of members, a true majority, has not signed the Petition."

Pages could be seen moving amongst the members' desks bearing documents.

"Stall," Elliott whispered into Bruce's earpiece.

"Mr. Chairman, if you would be so kind I'd like to respond to my esteemed colleague from Kansas."

Cobbings hesitated for a moment but did not wish to appear adversarial towards the young Democrat, at least not until he knew where this was going, so he reluctantly said, "You may proceed."

"Representative Whitback, I believe this to be one of the most important pieces of legislation to come before this august body in many a generation. The provisions contained in H.R.2239 are going to change the nature of this country. It will redirect the resources of

America in a way that will benefit every man, woman, and child in this great nation of ours. It will spark economic growth. It will reduce needless spending. It will create a vast new revenue stream and only burden the elite of this country in a minor way, and 75% of the populace will not bear the brunt of the tax burden as they have for so many decades past."

Mr. Whitback stood again. A sharp intake of breath by those assembled greeted Mr. Whitback's action because he was interrupting a member in good standing while the gentleman was still speaking and the chair had not yet recognized Whitback. "Isn't there a five minute rule in place at the moment, Mr. Speaker, or are we to be lured into debate of the bill before the Motion to Discharge has even been put to a vote?"

Cobbings' face reddened. "Representative Whitback, you will refrain from speaking out of turn and in the future wait until the chair has recognized you; however your point is well taken. Representative Bennett, the rules of the House do not permit debate of a bill that has not been sent to the floor by committee and we have no vote on the Motion to Discharge."

Bruce Bennett heard a shuffling of feet as more members of the House, sensing something momentous was afoot, began appearing in the chamber.

The young Representative from Colorado responded to the reprimand by the Speaker. "Mr. Speaker and my assembled colleagues, I beg the House's forgiveness if I appeared to be doing anything that is proscribed by the House Rules."

Whitback stood again. Cobbings recognized him and Whitback spoke in a stern manner. "Isn't the Five Minute Rule in effect? Have we not been listening to our colleague from Colorado far longer than five minutes?"

Bruce sat down and then stood right back up again.

"Good, keep up the pressure," Elliott said into his phone.

Rosa Sparks stood again.

At that point Cobbings would have done anything to get Bennett off the floor and Rosa's previous question had been regarding the naming of a little known Federal building, so she seemed safe to call upon.

"The Chair recognizes Representative Rosa Sparks, Democrat from Connecticut."

"Thank you Mr. Chairman, I rise in support of H.R. 2239 as it may provide additional funding for Health and Human Services, which as you know ..."

With a look of exasperation Cobbings interrupted her and said in a scathing tone. "Representative Sparks, I have just said we are not debating the relative merits of this bill at this time. It has not been released from committee."

"Oh, I'm sorry. I yield the balance of my time back to Representative Bennett."

Cobbings rolled his eyes.

The brief respite had given Bruce a chance to see how the forms were moving through the assemblage. He was pleased with the progress.

Elliott smiled as he saw the look of dismay on Cobbings' face as Representative Bruce Bennett stood to be recognized again.

At the same time Representative Kathy Morris Rodgers stood to be heard.

Elliott whispered in Bruce's earpiece. "Nice work, we're almost there, but I don't think Cobbings will be recognizing you again."

"What do we do?" Bruce asked with a hint of alarm in his voice.

"Sit tight and let them stumble into it."

With an almost audible sigh Cobbings said, "The Chair recognizes the Honorable Representative Kathy Morris Rodgers, Democrat from Washington."

"Thank you, Mr. Chairman. I move to recess for fifteen minutes."

"Motion to Recess is seconded?"

"I second the motion," Whitback instantly agreed.

"Sustained. Ladies and Gentlemen, please return to these chambers in fifteen minutes at exactly 10:35 a.m."

With a sharp blow of the gavel, Cobbings stood and exited the room in unseemly haste.

"That's perfect. It's playing right into our hands by giving us more time to gather signatures," Elliott said. "You should go thank Rosa. She did a nice job of running interference for you. She's as sharp as a tack and I suspect she knows exactly what's going on."

"That makes one of us, but I'll go thank her."

As Bruce made his way towards where Rosa was seated, Mary Evans the clerk passed close by him and discreetly whispered, "We have well over 218 yeas."

Bruce exhibited no outward sign he'd heard a thing, but was deeply overjoyed at the news.

# Chapter Twenty-Three

IN SPEAKER COBBINGS' office he, Whitback, Ray Haley Hutchinson and Majority Whip John Bainer were fuming. "I was just informed the Motion to Discharge is making the rounds of the floor. We must have over three hundred members here. That's a quorum. Someone is counseling the Democrats. Someone who knows what they're doing and is very, very good," spat Whitback.

"The question is what can we do?" Hutchinson asked.

Bainer was leafing through the Congressional Rules of Procedure. "Aha, here it is. The answer to our prayers and I quote. 'Until the vote on the Discharge Petition has been concluded and approved, and the underlying bill has not been debated or voted upon, the Committee can still report the bill to the House floor rendering the Motion to Discharge moot.'"

"I don't want it sent to the House floor. I want it dead," Cobbings snarled. "The big banks and military suppliers will have my ass."

"We don't have a choice," Bainer replied, "If the petition gathers enough signatures then the committee is out of the picture and the legislation is out of our hands. It doesn't even allow for the amendment process."

They could hear the clerk ringing the bell calling the members back to session. As they walked back into the vast congressional hall, Speaker Cobbings leaned over to Whitback and whispered, "Has the Committee even drafted a response to H.R. 2239?"

Whitback paled noticeably and said, "No, we just tabled it. We haven't even looked at it."

"Have you seen the Appropriations Committee manager John Cole?"

"I think I saw him earlier."

"Find him and get that bill in the hands of clerk ASAP. I'll try to stall."

Once the fifteen minutes expired and the assembly returned from recess Representative Bruce Bennett stood to be recognized again, but in this instance Chairman Cobbings pointedly looked away refusing such recognition. Representative Kathy Morris Rodgers, Democrat from Washington stood and the Chair immediately recognized her.

"Representative Rodgers is hereby recognized," Cobbings said.

"Thank you Mr. Chairman. Pursuant to Section 3 of House Rule XXVII I call up the Petition to Discharge the Committee on Appropriations from further consideration of the bill H.R. 2239."

Kathy Rodgers was a seasoned veteran and knew her stuff. After Bruce recommended her she had been heavily counseled as to procedure by the President and heavily supported by Elliott to stand at this occasion.

"Has the Gentlewoman signed the petition?"

"I have Mr. Speaker."

Representative Sam Whitback almost jumped out of his chair.

"The chair recognizes Representative Whitback."

"Thank you, Mr. Chairman. I would like to raise a Point of Order."

Elliott spoke softly to Bruce through his ear piece again. "A Point of Order? He's making a claim that the proceedings are in breach of the Standing Rules of the House."

"Please proceed," Cobbings said.

"The Standing Rules of the House mandate that a Motion to Discharge may not be called to the floor until it has been in layover for seven days. The motion to call up the petition is in violation."

Cobbings sat for a moment and then said, "The Speaker respectfully supports the Point of Order that the Motion to Discharge has not been in layover for the requisite seven days and therefore cannot be called up at this time."

Kathy Rodgers stood again.

"The gentlewoman from Washington is recognized."

"Thank you Mr. Speaker; if I may be permitted I would like to read a short statement from the 'Congressional Research Service brief regarding Calendar of Motions to Discharge from Committee in the United States House of Representatives.'"

"You may proceed," Cobbings wearily replied, as he watched Whitback leave his seat and physically remove John Cole from the room.

"The Motion to Discharge is placed on the Calendar of Motions to Discharge Committee and becomes eligible for consideration on the second and fourth Mondays of the month after a seven day layover, except during the last six days of any session when the layover requirement is waived. The discharge motion is debatable for twenty minutes, one half the time for the proponents and one half for the opponents. If the discharge motion is adopted it is then in order for the House to immediately consider the bill itself."

Cobbings paled. He had no choice but to allow the vote to proceed.

"Voting is now open on the Motion to Discharge the Appropriations Committee for consideration of HR. 2239," he said.

Whitback looked back in horror from where he was near the door with John Cole.

Ten minutes later the voting was complete.

The Tally clerk stood and said, "Voting is closed on the Motion to Discharge the House Appropriations Committee from consideration of HR 2239."

Bruce was about to stand and cheer when Elliott's voice cautioned him. "Wait."

John Bainer, the Majority Leader of the House, an old Republican warhorse from Tennessee, and a staunch conservative stood and the Speaker of the House instantly recognized him, "I move to lay the motion on the Table."

Elliott spoke into Bruce's ear piece. "Damn, that Bainer is a crafty old bastard, Bruce stand to be recognized and say you object to this motion. If no one objects to the Lay on the Table motion the measure will be disposed of adversely and that's the end of our efforts. And conclude by saying you want a simple voice vote of the yeas and nays."

Bruce Bennett stood to be recognized. Reluctantly the Speaker recognized him.

"I object to the motion to table the proposition," Bruce stated firmly. "And request a voice vote regarding said motion."

"Sustained," the Speaker acknowledged. "I will require a voice vote. A yea vote means you are voting in favor of tabling the motion and a nay vote means the proceedings will revert to where they were before the Motion to Table was made."

The voice vote was administered by the Clerk of the House and took another twenty minutes. The Nays carried, but Bainer stood to be recognized again.

"The Speaker recognizes the gentleman from Tennessee."

"The Motion to Table did not pass which means we are now voting on the H.R. 2239. I object to the vote on the H.R.2239 on the grounds that a quorum is not present and make a point of order that a quorum is not present."

Elliott smiled and spoke to Bruce. "It's a smart move. If any member of the House suggests there's not a quorum, not enough members present to provide a majority vote on the bill, it forces the Presiding Officer to have bells rung through the Halls of Congress calling members back to the floor and it forces a recorded vote by the Speaker of the House. It's a delaying tactic."

Elliott put down his phone and called Archie 'Backspace' Conner on his landline keeping the cell phone open to Bennett.

When Archie answered Elliott asked, "Do you still think you can do it?"

"Give me three minutes."

"They are yours, good luck."

Minority Whip Earl Bishop, a hard-nosed Democrat from Wisconsin was noted for his impatience and willingness to stay until midnight if need be to see that the House business was completed stood to be recognized.

"The Speaker recognizes the good gentleman from Wisconsin."

"Thank you Mr. Speaker. I object to a quorum call at this time as it is obviously dilatory in nature and an abuse of this assembly's time. The Clerk of the House has already stated the voting is closed on the Discharge Petition meaning a majority of the 435 House members are present and have signed the Discharge Petition. No one has left so a majority is still present."

Speaker Cobbings stared for a moment at the gray haired gentleman with the bushy white eyebrows and the defiant stance. 'Where the hell was Whitback with John Cole?' he thought. 'They needed to get the paperwork from the committee together before sending H.R. 2239 to the floor where it could then be amended.'

"I'm going to instruct the Clerk to conduct a recorded vote," Cobbings said. "I'll allow fifteen minutes for the aforementioned vote."

During the fifteen minutes Republican Majority leader of the House John Bainer tried to play the jobs card in hopes of convincing any of those members who might be on the fence to vote against the bill, saying the closing of so many bases would flood the nation with unemployed. Bruce Bennett downplayed the issue suggesting, "Millions of soldiers came home after World War II and we assimilated them. And if anyone is watching the remarkable events in Texas where over thirteen thousand convicts quietly turned themselves in with hopes of getting an education and a second chance at life, we could certainly employ many soldiers as teachers and mentors for many of these prisoners. A whole new industry may be starting right before our eyes and frankly reflects the type of people we are, the type of nation we should be."

Once the recorded vote was complete the Speaker declared, "The quorum call is complete. There is a majority present. The Discharge Petition is approved and has been signed by a majority. H.R. 2239 is now on the floor for consideration."

Whitback, with John Cole in hot pursuit, rushed at the clerk waving a stack of papers just as a voice boomed over the House of Representatives video system saying, "Aaand here's Nicky."

Archie had hacked the system just as he promised he could. On the enormous jumbo screen above the floor of the House appeared the now infamous YouTube video of Representative Jenkins saying, "Cutting funding for our friends overseas? We'll just add an amendment to cut Medicare Funding. We'll see if the Democrats are willing to throw grandma out of her rocking chair or cut Foreign Aid."

But in this version Archie had cut and pasted Nick Cobbings' face in place of Jenkins' and changed the wording a bit. The entire room went as still as an Egyptian tomb until Cobbings stood and screamed while extending an arm and pointing a finger at the offending screen, "THAT'S NOT ME. I NEVER SAID THAT."

He turned to whoever might listen, "I swear it's true. I never said that."

The video started to play again.

"Turn it off," he shouted. "Turn that damn thing off."

Pages rushed to try to stop the video. It played three more times before they finally pulled the plug on the entire system. Many members of the House were visibly shaken by this strange turn of events.

Whitback and Cole hurriedly resumed talking to Mary Evans, the Clerk of the House of Representatives.

"I am the Chair of the House Appropriations Committee and we are sending a recommendation to the floor regarding H.R. 2239 with a negative declaration."

"I'm sorry gentlemen, but as you can see the Discharge Petition has already won approval and they are now voting on H.R.2239. The vote cannot be stopped now, as you well know."

It was considered one of the fastest votes in modern history and there wasn't the slightest mention of touching Medicare as the bill passed 401-22 with 12 abstaining, one of the largest margins in history.

Cobbings looked like he was going to tear his hair out as he rushed from the room. Elliott could see John Bainer visibly fuming as he marched over to where Bruce Bennett stood, smiling and shaking hands with his fellow members.

Bainer leaned in and whispered. "That was a fancy piece of work, but you have made yourself some very powerful enemies with long memories. We're gonna kill this thing in the Senate and you're going to be a one term Representative."

The young freshman representative glanced at his heavy-set squint-eyed associate. "Do your damnedest, Bainer. Bring it on," he snarled right back.

Elliott watched the vote on C-SPAN and immediately called Eddie Kelley and said, "Start phase three."

His next call was to Archie 'Backspace' Conner. "Beautiful work. It passed the House."

"I know. I saw it."

"Be ready. We're starting phase three."

Hanging up the phone Elliott felt the pain in his side growing and a wave of exhaustion wash over him. Slowly he stood up, swayed for a moment and then shuffled back to the bedroom where he collapsed on the bed.

# Chapter Twenty-Four

IF NICK COBBINGS was furious when he walked off the House floor, he was purple faced livid when his exchange with the House video system made the evening news and all the rounds of the morning news shows as well.

"That was not me. I want to know who is behind this. I want the bastard's name and the names of all his relatives!" he shouted as he tossed a chair across his office.

"Let's get on the phones right now to every senator we know," Cobbings said. "This damn bill is dead meat!"

Bainer and Whitback were reluctant to do so. The senators were off on break at the moment, but Cobbings' rage was such that they felt compelled to make the calls.

He, Bainer and Whitback worked the phones far into the night calling in favors from senators they'd worked with over the years. It was Washington politics at its darkest. They cajoled, offered their votes on a senator's pet project, threatened to withdraw a vote and even suggested an earmark or two, like a library in the senator's district named after the good senator. They played every card they could and each ended their pleadings with the comment that all they were asking for was a no vote on a bill that was very questionable in the first place. They made each senator feel as though his or her influence in the Senate, their vote, would be so important as to be considered the final deciding factor on whether H.R. 2239 lived or died. The three men met with considerable success. Before the night was out they'd made arrangements to meet with several influential senators and contacted ALEC, the American Legislative Exchange Council, and arranged for a sit down the following day to brainstorm amendments to the bill that would effectively shelve it forever. Bainer's statement to Bruce Bennett had been no empty threat. The freshman representative had indeed made some powerful enemies.

The meeting was held in Nick Cobbings' private office and consisted of Senator Tom Coryn, Republican from Texas who sat on the Senate Armed Services Committee, Senator Wade Biggs, Republican from Nebraska who chaired the Senate Finance Committee, and Senators Jim Johnson and Brian Nelson who sat on the Appropriations Committee. Bainer, Cobbings and Whitback were there, as well as two senior consultants from ALEC, William Allison and Carl Hayden.

"So how badly do we want to damage this bill's chance of survival?" Allison asked, setting the tone of the meeting as he sipped his coffee.

"I want it sent to the Banking, Armed Services and Appropriations committees," Cobbings said with a sly smile. "I have friends there."

The four senators laughed as one.

"I want to amend it in a myriad of ways. I want it so twisted by the time it leaves committee it will be unrecognizable," Cobbings growled. He was no longer concerned with the merits of the bill. He was concerned with one thing and one thing only: vengeance. He wanted the bill utterly crushed and those backing it humbled for the entire world to see, just as he had been.

"Done," Allison said as he jotted notes on a yellow legal pad.

"I want to hit them with every conceivable committee response and let them figure it out. I want it to be years before that bill sees the light of day," Cobbings continued.

"Just who is 'them'?" Allison wondered aloud.

"Good question," Bainer chimed in. "I was wondering that myself. Some smart bugger is running the show behind the scenes. Bennett is too young and inexperienced to have pulled that off by himself."

"Which reminds me," Whitback broke in, leaning down and opening his brief case. He pulled several photos from it and laid them on the table.

"I have had several reports from some of our colleagues in the hallways that these two men are posing as lobbyists representing The Anvil Group, but they seemed more intent on gathering information from those who were waiting to speak to the various representatives on those committees. I have never heard of The Anvil Group, nor are they registered as a lobbying firm."

The photos depicted Eddie Kelley and James Lally gathering business cards and information from the lobbyists waiting in the hallway outside the House Appropriations Committee hearings. Several were close up.

"And your point is?" Cobbings asked.

"We've got a situation where we were hornswaggled in the House and we have new faces gathering information for a company which doesn't exist. I think there may be a connection," Whitback explained.

Cobbings attention was instantly galvanized into action. "I want the names, addresses and life history of each of these jokers."

"That will cost something," Allison said.

"I'll handle that," Bainer interrupted. "I happen to know that Senator Graham, the Chairman of the Senate Banking Committee, has worked on occasion with a certain Doc Hastings. Doc has a certain individual who does a lot of night work, which is what we're going to need here."

"Doc Hastings of Breaux Lott Leadership Group?" Allison quickly asked.

"One and the same. You know him?"

"I know of him? How do you know him?"

"Senator Graham and I did some work together recently pushing through some earmarks for a pharmaceutical company, research funds and the like, which was authored and backed by the Hastings team. It was a last minute affair and the kickbacks didn't go through the usual channels," Bainer explained. "There's a money drop tonight."

"There's actually to be two separate money drops tonight for Graham. The kickback is one, but there is a second drop from some banking groups to ensure Graham votes no on SB 1190. In fact, I happen to know from a very reliable source that the kickback payment is in the 50k range," Wade Biggs interjected.

Cobbings released a low whistle. "Fifty thousand, well at least we've secured one no vote. We can be certain that Graham will vote against the bill," Cobbings said with a laugh.

The other men in the room enjoyed a hearty chuckle.

"If you'll trust me with the photos I'll see they get to Doc Hastings," Bainer said.

"They're all yours. I have copies," Whitback said, pushing the photos across the table.

"So, I think I have a reasonable understanding of the sentiment in the room towards this bill. Let me put some people to work on it and we'll come up with wording for some amendments which should please you," Allison suggested.

"We'll meet a few days from now," Bainer agreed.

They all shook hands and filed out of Cobbings' office. Wade Biggs was the last to leave. As he was retrieving his heavy over coat from the guest closet Cobbings pulled him aside.

"$50,000 for one senator?" Cobbings asked in a low voice. "That's a far larger sum than I've ever heard being delivered before. Are you sure of your facts?"

Wade Biggs smiled. "I am sure. I happen to know a number of the bank lobbyists personally. I believe there is a larger sum coming my way within the week."

"You're kidding."

"Look Cobbings. I don't think you understand what you're dealing with here. They are worried. The over-the-counter derivatives market is 600 trillion dollars annually. It's virtually unregulated and they can claim there are 1,100 commercial banks involved, but 80%, hell 90% of the business is controlled by five big banks. You know their names. They know that once the ball gets rolling and the feds start taxing the trades it's likely to snowball. The feds need money desperately and the transaction fee is likely to grow in size. This will take a considerable chunk out of their earnings. They want this bill killed more than you do."

Cobbings stared at Biggs in quiet disbelief. It was true he had little idea of the immensity of the market.

"I'll tell you something else, just between friends; this derivative stuff scares the hell out of me. These banks are leveraged to the hilt. If we get another 'credit event' it will make Lehman Brothers look like a walk in the park. I, for one, don't put my money anywhere near those banks. Good night."

# Chapter Twenty-Five

THE FOLLOWING MORNING Elliott woke early after a fitful night's sleep. He stared at the dozen pills in the palm of his hand. At one point he'd known what each of them was for, but he'd long since forgotten. Gulping them down with a cup of black coffee he clicked on the television remote and tuned it to CNN. Settling into his chair he switched on his computer as well. CNN repeatedly showed Nick Cobbings marching ashen-faced from the House floor while the scroll underneath indicated the Speaker had suddenly taken ill and would not be working today.

With a second cup of coffee he read the New York Times and the Wall Street Journal online. The account of the passage of H.R.2239 was second page news, but each paper covered it thoroughly. Each speculated that the effect of the YouTube videos, the text message onslaught, and the online infomercials and regular print attack ads had raised the awareness of the public as to the issues at stake and played a pivotal roll in pressuring the House to act quickly and responsibly.

"If you only knew the whole story," Elliott murmured as his phone rang.

"Elliott here," he said.

"Elliott, Paul White."

"Good morning, Mr. President."

"Not really. My people on the hill are telling me that Bainer and Cobbings have been calling all the power seats in the Senate demanding they be placed on any joint conference committee dealing with the 'War on the Deficit' bill. And Bainer is suggesting none too subtly that the Senate's Finance Committee, where he has close friends, should be the first to review it as well as Armed Services and the Appropriations Committees. He's out for blood."

"We can deal with him," Elliott said softly.

"I would caution you not to be over confident. Bainer has been around. He's an old junkyard dog and I suspect Cobbings, who is no slouch either, is behind all these maneuvers as well. I can't recall a time when so much attention was being paid to a bill behind the scenes to ensure which committee investigates. Once the wheels start moving in the Senate they can crush almost any bill, no matter how deserving it is of passage."

"We're going to pull out all the stops, Paul," Elliott stated calmly.

"We'll have to," the President said. "They're lining up a veritable who's who of bill killers up there."

"We've still got a few tricks up our sleeves. And Paul, I view this as the most important piece of legislation in our lifetime. I'll not play their games this time around. If need be, heads will roll."

When the 'War on the Deficit' bill reached the senate it was given new life as Senate Bill 1190.

# Chapter Twenty-Six

EDDIE KELLEY'S SIXTH sense was telling him they needed more help. The test run was a success, but still they would need to bring some additional hands on board. He sent e-mails to former members of the Master Sergeant's team from Iraq. There were a few dozen he knew he could trust completely. He outlined the multi-faceted plan in great detail to each of them and received unanimous agreement, with only Mike Murphy registering the slightest reluctance.

"Mike, we can't hack phones or computers. Remember Rupert Murdoch and News Corp a few years back? That's how they were busted. They could identify the hackers. We're operating under old school rules with old fashioned listening devices."

"Isn't that kinda underhanded?"

"And you think these guys in the Senate are playing the game by the rules? You and I know they were bought off by big money years ago," Eddie stated firmly.

Murphy laughed. "Okay, okay I get your point."

"We've executed a successful test run. We need to know how to bring extraordinary pressure on key senators, enough to counteract the influence of the corporations, lobbyists and the Super Pacs. As I said, we've already made a test run. James Lally, posing as a United Parcel deliveryman, has already dropped in on several senators' offices and some big time lobbyists, I might add, and slipped listening devices under the desks so the wheels are in motion. Can we count on you, Mike?"

"You bet."

Twenty-four hours later Mike Murphy was seated at a posh Washington watering hole. It was happy hour and he was monitoring several interesting conversations using a pencil sized recording/video device. Senator Wade Biggs, head of the Senate Finance Committee, was seated in a booth with one of his secretaries, a married and very attractive red head. Mike's miniature camera and recorder could work wonders picking up single conversations in a crowded and very loud room.

"Take my word for it. The bill will die a slow death," Wade was saying as he caressed the woman's leg. The video camera resting in Mike's lap was recording every detail.

Meanwhile, Eddie Kelley followed Ricky Funk from his office at the lobbying firm Breaux Lott Leadership Group to the swanky Four Seasons Hotel in Upper Manhattan. Ricky liked to think of himself as an up and comer. He dressed in stylish suits, drove a big black Mercedes and liked to be seen with pretty women. He'd started work as a congressional page and then found himself on Senator Graham's staff, often running 'special' errands. It wasn't long before he'd come to the attention of Doc Hastings. They called him 'Doc' because he had a knack for fixing problems. Soon Ricky found himself in the personal employ of Doc and enjoying a six-figure income.

Once at the Four Seasons, Ricky took the express elevator to the penthouse. Eddie waited in the bar. Two hours passed before Ricky returned. He stepped out of the elevator, looked furtively both ways, and then made a beeline for the front doors. Eddie followed at a discreet distance. When Ricky opened the door to his Mercedes Eddie appeared beside him. Shoving a gun in the courier's side Eddie said, "No quick moves. Get in and move over to the passenger side."

"Who are you?" Ricky began to protest.

Eddie shoved the gun viciously into the smaller man's side again and spat one word at him, "Move!"

Ricky complied. As Eddie climbed in after him he hit the record button on the tape recorder inside his jacket.

"You are Richard Funk from Breaux Lott Leadership and you just met with representatives of Senator Curt Graham. You delivered $50,000 in small bills in exchange for a vote against SB 1190. The money was provided by a consortium of big banking houses."

"Who are you? How do you know all this?"

"It doesn't matter who I am, but there is something you need to know. I am part of a grassroots effort to clean up our government. We're targeting companies like yours. Now we're going to turn in the facts regarding your little escapade tonight to the Justice Department. I can leave your name out of it. You're just the bag boy, the little guy who usually gets 25 years to life while the bigwigs get a slap on the wrist. I want the name of your superiors who set this up."

"You wouldn't dare."

"Give me the name and I step out of your car and you never see me again. You don't give me the name and we drive to a secluded location where a couple of my friends are waiting. They are not nice people and you give me the name anyway."

For a moment Ricky hesitated and he cast a quick glance at the door handle. Eddie pressed the button on his side locking all the doors. Ricky sighed.

Ashen faced he whispered. "It was Doc Hastings."

"Doc?"

"Arnold, Arnold 'Doc' Hastings arranged the drop, but I don't know what companies gave him the dough."

"Thank you. Have a nice evening," Eddie said and disappeared into the night.

When he was a block away Eddie ducked into a bar and called Elliott.

"It worked like a charm. Got the name and recorded his admission of what went down at the Four Seasons," Eddie said.

"Good. Nice work. So merely sticking a listening device under a desk we can snag their plans and throw a wrench in them."


"I'll say. It was like clockwork. And remember that was just an old garden-variety bug. I've got the DARPA stuff coming and I've been told those bugs will pick up the voice on the other end of the line as well. We'll get both sides of the conversation," Eddie added.

"What's the world coming too?" Elliott asked.

"You said you wanted to go after them. The DARPA stuff is not even available on the commercial markets. It's the stuff of legends."

"I know, I know. I'll send you an e-mail with the letter we're going to deliver to our bag boy's boss. Can you make copies of the tape?"

"No problem."

"Can you contact James and tell him we need his skills as a United Parcel Delivery man again?"

"Sure thing, I'll have him meet me tomorrow morning at the safe house in Alexandria," Eddie replied and then added, "Say, are you feeling okay? Your voice sounds a little different."

"I'm just tired. Thanks for asking."

"Okay. Talk with you soon."

# Chapter Twenty-Seven

THE FOLLOWING MORNING Eddie downloaded and printed Elliott's letter.

Dear Senator Graham,

Please listen to the conversation on the enclosed disk. Once you have listened to it, please be aware that we have an identical copy. We know it was Arnold 'Doc' Hastings who set up the meeting at the behest of a number of banks. Please understand it is not our intention to do anything with the disk. We will be expecting you to vote with an affirmative on Senate Bill 1190. If you do not vote accordingly our copy will be hand-delivered to the Justice Department. Thank you.

A similar letter was attached in a second e-mail, but with the names Doc Hastings and Senator Graham reversed.

Elliott sent a third e-mail asking Eddie to make copies of the letters and the tapes; one set to be delivered to Graham and the other to Hastings as soon as possible. Eddie smiled. "You're one smart chap, Mr. Eastman."

Elliott wasn't going to send the information to the Justice Department and have Graham removed from office just so another money grubber could take his place. No, he was going to leave Graham in place, but require his vote. Elliott was also going to put Hastings on notice thereby drying up a major source of funding for the good senator. It was blackmail pure and simple and yet could it truly be considered a crime if it prevented a crime, prevented a vote from being bought by the big buck banking companies? Eddie knew the way he felt about it. Right is right. The courts might rule differently, but that didn't faze Eddie. He was seeing this through to the end. He was going to see a change in the way of life for the better for every American. He looked up to see James Lally standing in front of him dressed to the nines in his light brown United Parcel outfit.

"Special delivery today?"

"Very special," James replied with a smile.

James arrived at Senator Graham's office and dropped the package with the secretary. Half an hour later he appeared at the offices of Beaux Lott Group and asked for Doc Hastings.

"He's busy at the moment," his secretary explained.

"I'm sorry, but I must have my receipt book signed by him."

"I'll sign for him."

"I'm sorry. This form indicates personal delivery, only he can sign for it."

"Hummpf. That's odd. I've signed for him before."

"I'm sorry."

"Let me see if I can interrupt him."

The secretary left for a moment and then returned saying, "You may go in. It's the fourth door down the hall on your right."

"Thank you."

James knocked softly and then entered. Doc Hastings was a heavy-set man with a ruddy complexion and almost pure white hair and an expression that reflected the fact that he did not like being interrupted.

"I'm sorry sir, but I must have you sign for this package."

"Sure, sure bring it here."

As Doc scrawled his name across the ledger James looked around at the mahogany walls, the glass and mirror bar in the corner and the plush décor.

"Nice digs you got here," James stated.

"Yeah, yeah," Hastings responded in a dismissive tone as he handed the pen and ledger back to the United Parcel delivery boy.

James dutifully handed him the receipt adding, "I suggest you open it and listen to what's on the disk right away."

Hastings looked up, a puzzled expression on his face. "Huh, you know what's in here?"

"No," James said innocently, "but I don't get many packages that require a face to face meeting with someone like you. Have a nice day."

James strolled at a leisurely pace back towards the front door, briefly made small talk with the secretary again and as his hand touched the front door knob he heard Hastings' voice as he screamed, "Ricky!"

# Chapter Twenty-Eight

AT FIRST ELLIOTT was reluctant to draw more people into the inner circle, but Eddie felt it was necessary and with what was at stake the smart move to make.

"You never go to war knowing you're outnumbered," he insisted.

Finally Elliott agreed. However, he was feeling weak and traveling back to Washington once more didn't sound appealing at all. He suggested the meeting be held at the Colorado ranch. He brought in a chef, slaughtered a corn fed beef cow, ordered several cases of wine, kegs of beer, the finest scotch and Cuban cigars. Dinner was an amiable affair with the men making small talk and enjoying the fine repast. Afterwards, with cigars, scotch and Cognac, they retired from the dining hall to the great room and Eddie opened the meeting. All of the original members of Operation Anvil were there as well as a half dozen new faces. They were all former soldiers, some Navy Seals and some Special Operations personnel. All had worked with Elliott in some capacity over the years.

Eddie stood on the hearth dressed in army fatigues, his hair close cropped, broad shouldered and ready to take on whatever was sent his way. He exuded an air of confidence, but a confidence tempered by wisdom in the ways of war and a wariness of the strange twists of fate that war could introduce.

"We all know why we are here and have proven ourselves to be of one mind. It is time to take our government back. It is time to take matters into our own hands. Throw out the rules and make our representatives do the right thing. If I am mistaken in this assessment then please correct me now or forever hold your peace. If you are not in agreement with the foregoing statement then I would ask you to leave at this time."

No one spoke and no one left the great hall.

"Good. You all know the Master Sergeant and the sacrifices he is making in this cause. He will address you now."

Elliott rose from his chair, strode to where Eddie stood, shook hands and thanked him and then turned to the forty or so faces in the room.

"As you know we have opened what may be considered a war on the status quo, but is being termed the 'War on the Deficit.' I believe this is a desperate measure, but long overdue. We have a once in a lifetime opportunity where the President, the Secretary of Defense, the Army Chief of Staff, the Chairman of the SEC, the Chairman of the Federal Reserve, the Treasury Secretary and many others all stand united in this effort. However, I doubt even these esteemed men know the array of forces against us. What we are up against has been going on for some time. In short it is the financial, military and congressional cartel with a stranglehold on the economy, siphoning off massive profits for themselves at the expense of our nation. Their agenda is not in the national interest, but if they can hold on for another twenty years they will have made their fortunes and the country be damned. We don't have twenty years. We may not have five with our debt soaring so uncontrollably."

Elliott paused and looked around the room.

"I hold in my hand an article from the New York Times, April 25th, 1896 and this is a quote, 'Senator Barney Martin of New York has been the subject of congratulations this evening for the part he took in summarily ridding the Senate floor of a lobbyist at this afternoon's session. He literally chased him out of the room.'

"I won't read the whole article, but the point is that the date was 1896. Over one hundred years ago, lobbyists were stalking the floor of the Senate and a senator threw the bum out. I don't think that would happen today.

"You can bet a bill requiring change of the magnitude that is currently being discussed will bring out the lobbyists in full force. Lobbyists will literally throw millions of dollars at the Senate in an effort to defeat SB 1190. They will attempt to filibuster the bill, tie it up forever in committee. This means that our efforts thus far, although quite successful, must be redoubled. Eddie has approached me with a number of ideas. The single most effective idea in my eyes is information. We need to know the most intimate facts of everyday life for every senator; we need to know their every weakness. We need to apply pressure on them as it has never been placed before. We are up against a system of graft the likes of which the world has never seen before. It reminds me of a quote from the French economist Frederic Bastiat, 'When plunder becomes a way of life for a group of men living together in a society, they create for themselves in the course of time a legal system that authorizes it and a moral code that glorifies it.'

"This, my friends, is what we are up against. I will turn the meeting back over to Eddie and he will explain how we intend to proceed from here."

Eddie took his turn at the hearth.

"Gentlemen, I think what the Master Sergeant is trying to say is it's time to kick some greedy ass!"

This comment drew cheers, whistles and 'huzzahs' from the men. After a moment Eddie held up his hands. The room slowly quieted down.

"We intend to fight fire with fire. I know that's a dreadful cliché, but we intend to do just that. We've completed a test run, thanks to the efforts of James Lally."

James was standing off to one side of the room and doffed his green beret in deference to those assembled and the mention of his name.

"James and I happened upon information regarding a cash drop by Doc Hastings of the Beaux Lott group, a lobbying firm, to Senator Graham Brown. We intercepted the courier and recorded the conversation where he admitted to the pay off and named names. We then delivered a copy of the tape to Senator Graham's office. James was able to gain access to the senator because he posed as a United Parcel delivery person; an innocuous bystander if there ever was one, but it proved it could be done."

Eddie paused and took a sip of Cognac.

"Does anyone here know what DARPA stands for?"

A dark haired young man in the back with a deep tan and a build like Arnie Schwarzenegger in his heyday raised his hand. "The Defense Advanced Research Projects Agency. I worked with them briefly at Notre Dame."

"Correct. They have developed nanotechnology to a degree that many in the public sphere would find hard to believe. Sure, they've trotted out a few things like a mechanical hummingbird that sits in your hand, a dragonfly and moths with micro-transmitters attached to their bodies and computers controlled by GPS satellite. The claim is they will be used to monitor battlefield conditions. What was not disclosed was they have developed full Hybrid Insect Micro-Electric Mechanical Systems. We have been provided an opportunity to purchase sow bugs. These little guys are equipped with a full complement of micro-listening devices and transmitters. To give you a little perspective, a nanometer is one billionth of a meter. A human hair is about 75,000 nanometers wide. These little sow bugs are mechanical, nearly invisible, and can be dropped anywhere in the senator's office and will listen in on every conversation he has until the magneto-batteries run out about two months down the road. We intend to arm you with a wonderfully comfortable United Parcel outfit and a letter to deliver to every senator cordially inviting them to a big bash meeting at the Four Seasons Hotel with a representative from their favorite lobbying group. At that time a listening device will be placed in his office."

Eddie paused.

"And it is true. We are sponsoring a big bash at the Four Seasons. We will have a number of special assistants at the party who will photograph each senator enjoying the party and well, from there we'll take it the rest of the way …"

Eddie gazed at the men scattered about the room. Some sitting on couches, Lazy-Boys, foot stools or standing. A heavy-set man in the front with a thick black beard stood up and began clapping. The applause slowly spread until it reached a thunderous crescendo a moment later.

Once the applause died down Eddie asked, "Any questions?"

The man with the beard stepped forward saying, "Where do I go to get fitted with my UPS delivery boy outfit?"

"George, first things first, we're going to have to use a machete to cut the underbrush off your face," Elliott replied. "UPS drivers are clean cut young men."

The room exploded in laughter.

After the meeting adjourned most of the men went to the bunk house for a little card playing and reminiscing while Elliott strolled out to the porch. It was long after midnight, but a full moon was up and the soft white light glistened off the small trout pond not far away. Elliott sat down and sighed. He was going to miss this place. The pain in his side was constant now in spite of the barrage of pills he was taking, and the jaundice was sapping his strength. How much time did he have before he met his maker? This was a question he could not answer. Elliott was determined to leave this planet a better place than when he found it. There simply had to be enough time. Elliott took a sip of his drink and tried to dispel these dark thoughts. He sat staring at the moon floating on the water for a long time and finally stood and went to bed.

# Chapter Twenty-Nine

SENATE BILL 1190 was spread across the various committees of the Senate just as Cobbings, Bainer and Whitback had requested.

Elliott's cell phone rang and he answered it on the first ring.

"Elliott, Paul here."

"Yes, Mr. President," Elliott said sensing the seething anger on the other end of the line.

"It looks like they are setting up to do battle with us."

"How so?"

"My people in the Senate confirmed they have sent SB 1190 to the Senate Committee on Appropriations, the sub-committee for Financial Services and General Government, as well as the Senate Armed Services Committee. They will send it to their sub-committee for Emerging Threats and Capabilities and lastly the Senate Committee on Banking, Housing and Urban Affairs with the intention of sending it to their sub-committee on Economic Policy."

"So they are going to amend the hell out of it and then send it back to the House for revision," Elliott said softly with a sinking feeling that he had no chance of seeing this through.

"We can't be sure what they're going to do. We knew they weren't going to simply forward it to me for signature, but I didn't think they would send it to three committees and three sub-committees."

"Triple whammy times two," Elliott commented.

"I think Cobbings is behind this. My sources say they have never seen him so angry. He was throwing things around his office and fired one of his favorite interns."

"Rightfully so. I might do the same if my mug had been photo shopped into a conversation where they are planning to attack Medicare in an effort to kill a bill and it was plastered over every newswire, newspaper and website in the nation."

"There's not much we can do for the time being. The next move is theirs," the President concluded in a dejected tone.

"Actually, we've already put the wheels in motion for the next move, but let me think on this a bit," Elliott said. "I think we need to approach this very carefully. We'll need the names of every person sitting on all those committees, what pet projects they have in their districts, and when they are up for re-election."

"Okay, I'll have my secretary forward the info to you via e-mail shortly. I'll talk with you later."

# Chapter Thirty

THE ANCIENT CLERK of the Senate Armed Services committee looked about the expansive room, noted everyone was here and leaned forward speaking into the microphone.

"The Senate Armed Services committee pursuant to the Senate calendar is hereby in order on this the 3rd day of January, 2018 at 2:30 p.m. to consider SB 1190, 'The War on the Deficit'. The Honorable Senator Carl Nevin presiding."

One of the oldest standing committees on the hill, the members thirty six strong sit in a semi-circle with the chairman sitting in the center facing the eighty some odd seats open to the public.

Senator Carl Nevin entered the oak-paneled room through a side door and took his seat.

"Hello ladies and gentlemen. The meeting is now in order. The Bill will be considered read by a simple vote of the yeas and nays. The yeas will be heard first. Those in favor of considering the bill read will say aye."

A rumble of ayes rumbled from the seated senators.

"And the nays?"

There was no sound. None of the senators were interested in spending four hours reading the entire eighty page bill before commencing the meeting.

"An opening statement will be read by the Honorable Joseph Blieberman, a senator from Connecticut."

"Thank you Mr. Chairman. I rise in opposition to this bill. It is too far reaching. The closing of so many bases at this dangerous point in the history of our great country is unwise. I have spoken to members of the sub-committee on Emerging Threats and Capabilities and there is grave concern that new cyber attacks could cripple our capabilities. Our ground troops are the front line of defense against aggressors who would harm the American people. They are the face of our great nation across the world. They are the reassurance to our friends across the world that America stands ready to side with them in defense of their lands, their families, their very lives. It is easy, especially during times when our budgets are under the microscope, to say these good people of our armed services aren't earning their keep, but I personally find this disingenuous, dishonorable and unpatriotic. I yield to the chair."

The chairman noted Roger Portman, Senator from Ohio was standing.

"For what purpose does the good Senator from Ohio stand?"

"I rise in favor of the bill. This bill is far reaching, but the portion we are gathered to deal with is an age old question and one that I feel is high time we dealt with effectively and sensibly. Ladies and gentlemen, we have one million four hundred eighty thousand troops deployed around the world. We have 762 bases, or it might be 862, or it might be 1088, or it might be 1077. The Department of Defense isn't even positive how many bases we have, although in fairness to them it depends on how one defines 'bases'. They don't count anything under ten acres in size. The point is we have so many bases we can't be sure what the total count is. I ask you, and please remember I mentioned the word sensibly, do we need 54,000 troops in Germany on thirteen different bases? Are we afraid if we left that Russia would attack Germany? Do we need 39,230 troops on 29 different bases in Japan? Do we need 8,300 troops in England? Do we need 9,170 in Italy? We spend 20% of our annual government income on defense. The good Senator and colleague from Connecticut mentioned cyber crimes. I agree with him cyber crime is the wave of the future. If we were to close just 400 bases, some which have been around for sixty years after World War II, we would have that much more in the way of funds to combat the wave of cyber crimes coming our way. I yield to the Chair."

"Thank you Mr. Portman."

Tom Coryn stood to be heard.

"For what purpose does the good Senator from Texas rise?"

"I rise in rebuttal to my colleague from Ohio."

"Proceed."

"Closing 400 bases at once is outlandish. It will flood the country with unemployed ex-service people. It is irresponsible and unconscionable to even consider such a move. We will abandon our friends around the world. Our word to defend and protect our friends overseas will mean nothing. Are we to turn our backs on our patriotic obligations? I cannot in good conscience consider such a thing. I yield to the Chair."

"Thank you."

Senator Portman stood to be recognized again.

"For what purpose does the good Senator rise?"

"I rise in rebuttal to my colleague from Texas."

"Proceed."

Portman turned to face Coryn, which was out of the ordinary. In most cases the senator would face the chair.

"Since 2001, defense spending has gone up 416%. We have the most extensive network of bases the world has ever seen. The Byzantine, Ottoman, Roman and British empires had nowhere near our numbers. We have bases in 150 countries. 360,000 pounds of mail are delivered to Iraq and Afghanistan every day. The military operates 172 golf courses. You want patriotic Mr. Coryn? You want protection for every country around the world? You want honorable … ?"

"I do not like the way you are addressing me, sir, and suggest you stop this instant!"

"You want patriotic Mr. Coryn," said Portman almost shouting. "Let's start the ball rolling in the right direction. Let's get this great country out of debt. Let's… !"

Chairman Nevin was smashing the gavel on his table, shouting, "To order! To order!"

Senator Portman finally fell silent.

"Another outburst by either one of you gentlemen and I will move to have you censored. Do you understand?"

Each of them nodded and sat down.

"For the record, make note they both have agreed," Nevin instructed the keeper of the journal.

Senator Portman stood again.

"For what purpose does the Senator from Ohio rise?"

"I have a question for Senator Coryn."

"Proceed."

"How much have you been offered to kill this beautiful bill? What are they promising you?"

Coryn stood again, shouting, "This is outlandish. You will impugn my character in front of my colleagues?"

Coryn lunged at Portman as the gavel came down again.

"Order! Sergeant at Arms! Sergeant at Arms!" Nevin cried.

The portly Sergeant at Arms rushed down the aisle, but Coryn held up a hand. "I move to recess."

"Move to recess denied," Nevin nearly shouted, then reconsidered. Soothing his coat and wiping his brow with a hankie he intoned, "A vote of the yeas and nays is ordered with regard to recess for fifteen minutes."

Thirty-six yeas responded almost instantly.

# Chapter Thirty-One

THE MEETING IN the Senate Finance Committee chambers was a much more subdued affair. The Chairman, Senator Graham and his staff along with the ranking members had been very careful in selecting who was to bear testimony in regards to the Financial Transaction Tax aspect of the 'War on the Deficit' bill. The room only sat 150 people and Graham made sure it was packed with representatives from the American Bankers Association, the ABA Securities Association, the Managed Fund Association, the Futures Industry Association, the Institute of International Bankers, the Financial Services Roundtable, the International Swaps and Derivatives Association, the Investment Company Institute and the Securities Industry and Financial Markets Association. Not a single soul represented any of the myriad groups who stood in support of SB 1190.

"The meeting will now come to order," Graham said. "The first guest to speak will be David A. Stanwick from the Managed Fund Association."

A rail thin man with wavy grey hair and horn-rimmed glasses approached the podium, cleared his throat and said, "Thank you Mr. Chairman and members of the committee for inviting me to speak today. The MFA appreciates the opportunity to express its views regarding the proposed Financial Transaction Tax, or more specifically the Securities Transaction Tax. As a result of market structure changes, many aspects of our equity market-spreads, fees, execution speed, efficiency and pricing have drastically improved over the last several years to the benefit of investors. Although the MFA supports the committees efforts to review our rapidly developing market structure and to collect data to assist in the evaluation of a Securities Transaction Tax, our overall judgment is that such a tax is ill-timed and will result in a rollback of many of the efficiencies we have achieved. With hundreds of thousands of trades per hour, the MFA believes the STT is going to slow down each trade while a certain percentage, however miniscule, is removed. Even if it takes a tenth of a second to identify the dollar amount and remove it, this will add hours to each trading day. I thank the committee for its time."

Elliott was watching on the Banking Committee's streaming video feed online and commented, "You already trade after hours. And if a trade takes a split second the fee can be reconciled later," he growled.

If he already didn't like the tone of the committee hearings he liked them even less when Graham didn't allow for a question and answer period, which was standard procedure in an investigative hearing, and moved right along to the next speaker.

"The next speaker is Chris Edwards, President of Futures Industry Association," Graham announced.

"Damn," Elliott shouted as he slammed his fist on the coffee table. "Isn't a single senator going to question this blatant breach of procedure?"

Edwards dove right into his testimony. "Thank you Mr. Chairman and esteemed committee members. The Futures Industry believes that any legislative proposal that seeks to expand regulatory control in this area and to establish a new tax compliance framework will, in the end, be counterproductive. The ultimate effect of enacting such legislation will be to drive the industry overseas. At the very least it will make the U.S. Futures exchanges much less competitive vis-à-vis foreign exchanges. Examples of similar failed attempts at a similar fee abound around the world. Japan imposed a transaction tax in 1987. At first it generated significant revenues, but in four years revenues dwindled over 80% because market volume shifted overseas. Sweden experienced similar results when they tried a transaction tax. In 1993 Taiwan imposed a transaction tax on the value of commodities futures contracts and lost trading volume to the Singapore Exchange. The Futures Industry has a long and successful and innovative history in clearing futures contracts including previously 'unclearable' over-the-counter derivatives such as energy and credit default swaps.

"The tax structure you are considering would, I fear, result in the same experiences as the aforementioned countries. I thank you again for your time."

"Hey Chris, you forgot to mention that both Japan and Taiwan imposed fees that are thirty times higher than we are recommending," Elliott spoke to the computer screen, his anger growing by the minute. "And maybe someone could mention that France, Germany, and England already impose such taxes and England gets $40 billion a year with a tiny fee. Hell, many cities have a transaction tax on the sale of a home."

There was a soft knock on the door and Greer stuck his head in the door. "Can I get you something sir? Perhaps a sedative is in order?"

Elliott laughed and then grabbed his side. "Sorry Greer, I'll keep it down. They are just tearing the guts out of SB 1190."

"I understand sir," Greer acknowledged and eased the door closed behind him.

Senator Graham moved right along to the next speaker, calling up Michael Ettlinger from the American Bankers Association.

"Thank you Mr. Chairman and Committee members, I thank you for asking me to speak here today. The ABA is deeply concerned that in a climate of extreme joblessness the leaders of this great nation would impose a potentially crippling financial fee which could exacerbate the situation and cost thousands of jobs on Wall Street. There are often unintended consequences as my esteemed colleague Mr. Edwards pointed out. One such consequence that may pose a great peril to us all is that such a fee structure would be a constant net drain on the money supply and would be highly deflationary. It is the ABA's position with no equivocation whatsoever that such a fee structure would establish an unnecessary impediment to investment activities and job creation in the United States. And again, I thank you for your time."

Elliott almost slammed his fist down again but hesitated because it still ached a little from the earlier blow. "Deflationary? And what do you think, my good banker friend, is the impact of paying $400 billion a year in interest on our debt to the Chinese and Japanese? And the proposed fee will only exist for a few years. Damn them they are so self-serving!"

His cell phone rang. It was the President.

"Did you see that charade?" he asked, his voice filled with pent up anger.

"Yes, and not one person on that committee questioned an obvious disregard for the committee rules."

"If this is how it's going to be then I will call an emergency joint session of Congress and bring in my Economic Council and give opposing views to every damn one of the points they just made."

"I like the idea, but let's hold off until we see what the Appropriations Committee does."

"Hold off … when do the gloves come off Elliott? This is a beautiful bill as written. Are we simply going to watch it die? We can't let it die."

"It won't die, Paul. And the gloves will come off, but we must pick the place and time."

In disgust Elliott turned off the computer and went out onto the deck to read the Wall Street Journal. He read it religiously every morning, but this morning his mind wandered.

Elliott set the paper down on the wooden deck and stared into the distance for a moment. The President's phone call had disturbed him more than he let on. He recalled the stark numbers; only two Discharge Petitions in the last fifty years had led to a bill being signed by the president. A Discharge Petition with SB 1190 sitting in three separate committees was never going to work. They'd been lucky in the House with the Discharge, but could not count on such luck in the Senate.

Pondering the situation he realized he needed to reach out to the public, to the good people of the land and somehow let them know what was taking place in the Halls of Congress. Much of what their congressional leaders did was hidden from the view of the public. There may be no legal way to introduce a National Referendum, but the next best thing would be to have a show of force in support of SB 1190. The text messaging had been a success. It had made people aware of what the bill contained and how it would change their lives, but the American public had a notoriously short attention span. He needed someone with connections, someone who could awaken the land, someone with the tenacity of a tiger. Suddenly a beautiful face appeared in his mind. Laughing blue eyes framed in a halo of auburn hair. He stood up and went back inside and pressed the on button of his computer.

"No National Referendum," he said aloud. "Maybe we'll go for the next best thing. This calls for someone with a special means of getting things done."

He opened his online rolodex. He stared at the number for a full minute before dialing. He'd not spoken to her in several years and now suddenly he wished to hear her voice.

Stephanie Wells had been a House Representative for the state of Wisconsin, while he was in the Senate representing the state of Colorado. They had sat on several special committees and sent several Joint Resolutions to the floor together. When her husband suddenly passed away ten years ago she had turned to him for solace. For each of them it had been an epiphany of sorts. Neither of them believed they would ever love again and yet their feelings for each other grew. They went to dinner, plays and carriage rides around D.C. together. The tabloids had a field day, but the two of them didn't care. The National Enquirer ran a front page piece asking, "Is the most eligible bachelor in Washington off the market?"

They began holding hands together and even kissed several times when they knew the cameras were watching. One time Stephanie laughingly suggested she felt like a high school girl again. The truth of the matter was they had both fallen very quickly in love, but the business of governing was beginning to wear on her. She'd grown tired of the congressional backbiting and squabbling. After a second term she retired from the House and took a position with the Board of Regents for Harvard University. Elliott had beseeched her to stay in D.C. and even suggested he'd retire and they could move to his Colorado ranch together. Stephanie told him she would have nothing to do with ending the career of one of the most beloved and successful politicians to walk the Halls of Congress. Elliott grew angry at her stubbornness and said he would never speak to her again if she left him. She left, and true to his word he stopped returning her calls and eventually she stopped calling. But Elliott had followed her career as closely as he could from afar. She was still the activist she had always been and she chaired several political committees on campus, educating and nurturing future politicians. She was still in the seat of power and in a position to pull off exactly what Elliott had in mind.

She answered her cell phone and sounded a little irritated. "Hello, this is Stephanie Wells."

"Hi Stephanie, this is Elliott," he said trying to sound light hearted.

A sharp intake of breath whispered through the line.

"Elliott, my dear Elliott, it's wonderful to hear from you. How are you?"

"Fair to middling. And you?"

"I'm fine. I was just about to hop in the shower."

"I can call back if you wish?"

"No, no it's okay. Just let me set the phone down for a moment and put my robe on."

A moment later she was back on the line.

"There, that's better. Now where were we?"

"You just said you were fine and I was remembering all that auburn hair surrounding those deep blue eyes and those little dimples of yours thinking fine isn't the word for it. Something more like breathtaking would apply a little better," Elliott replied with a smile.

Stephanie laughed gaily. "Ever the charmer. Obviously you haven't seen me in a few years. So how are things on the hill? I know you've retired, but I can't imagine you're not in touch."

"Sadly, if anything they are worse than ever and that's part of the reason for my call. Are you still in touch with all the taxpayer groups? You know, Common Cause, Taxpayers for Common Sense and Citizens against Government Waste?"

"Yes, and several others."

"Here's what I was thinking. I'm afraid SB 1190 is going to go down in flames."

"Are you behind that? I've been watching it. What a wonderful bill. I'd sign it in a heartbeat."

"No, I'm not behind it, but I'd like to see it passed. Maybe you could send an email or something to all those watchdog groups with a proposal. I'd like to suggest those who have RV's to execute an assault on the Capitol. I'll pay for banners reading 'Pass 1190 or else,' or something along those lines. I'm not really sure how to execute it, but you get the idea. I'd like something in the way of a major show of force by the people of our good land."

"You don't need to send any money for banners. We have a lot of Betsy Ross types out there who can make banners. I can send an email announcing the event to all those groups and they can start a letter writing and email campaign to their legislators, but I'll do you one better, how about AARP? If I'm right, the bill provides for funding of Social Security once the national debt has been extinguished. They are the ones we should be contacting. They'll hop in their RV's and head to Washington in a heartbeat."

"That's brilliant. Yes, the Baby Boomers, this is right up their alley. They can re-live the protests of the sixties."

"And they are retired so they have the time to make the journey," Stephanie added.

"I knew I was calling the right person."

"Is that the only reason you called?"

"Yes, I knew you were still very involved politically. And you've always been an activist where government waste was concerned."

"Okay Elliott, I'll buy that, but if you want to you can come visit me."

"I'd like that. I'd like it very much, but I've got a lot of work to do."

"A lot of work to do, he says. Elliott, I know you're behind this. It's funny, when I read the first few news flashes about the bill your face suddenly popped into my mind."

"I think of you every day," Elliott admitted as his voice softened, "but there is another group I'd like to involve in support of SB 1190 and that is the young. They are the future, and whether they know it or not they are in deep trouble."

"Hmm. Okay, he's changing the topic she said to herself."

Elliott laughed. "No I'm not. I would love to see you, but I've got a lot on my plate right now."

"Alright, the young, I'll bite. The first thing that comes to mind is what the banks and Sallie Mae have done. You know, reducing their interest rates. As I understand it this is just a temporary effort to help jumpstart the economy. Today's kids are the most indebted generation in history, at least for that age group. But they are the flip side of the social security play. It's a 'get out of debt free' card for future generations so they don't have to pay the retirement bill for the elderly. You need to play that up."

"That's exactly what I told Paul," Elliott exclaimed.

"Paul who? Paul White? You've been talking to the President. I knew you were behind this!"

"No, it wasn't Paul White. It was Paul, Paul ..."

Stephanie giggled. "You are the worst liar."

"Okay, it was Paul White, but I don't want that to leak out. Please don't repeat that to anyone!"

"If you don't agree to visit me I can guarantee the media will get hold of that information somehow."

"Blackmail, will you stoop so low?"

"I will."

"The truth is I would love to see you."

"That's better. I won't press for an exact date for our rendezvous at the moment, but I want you to give it some thought.

It's something we should do. We aren't getting any younger, but back to the matters at hand. I saw a YouTube video rather like the old Uncle Sam poster, 'I WANT YOU!', but with a young woman as the speaker. It seemed to be effective. I suggest you contact a photographer and film a video announcing the event. You know, dates and times to be in Washington for the vote. By the way, when is the vote?"

"It's just been submitted to several committees, but as soon as I have a firm set of dates I'll let you know," Elliott promised.

"I'll contact the various taxpayer groups and AARP and start the letter writing campaign and wait to hear from you."

"Okay, thanks for everything. I'll be in touch."

"Elliott? I meant what I said. I would love to see you again. Are you in Washington or Colorado?"

"Colorado."

"I want you to promise me you'll call me when you are planning to come to D.C."

Elliott glanced at the calendar on his desk and noted he had another dose of chemo to deal with in ten days.

"I promise you, Steph. I would love to see you. I still love you. I'll always love you."

"Oh, Elliott," Stephanie cried and hung up before he could hear the tears in her voice.


Elliott sat staring at the phone. 'He probably shouldn't have said that,' he thought. It was not fair to Stephanie if he were to reignite their passion for each other right before he … before he … left. The thought was not a pleasing one.

Suddenly Elliott felt very tired. He yawned and glanced at his watch. It was only noon, but a siesta seemed like it was in order. He went to the bathroom and brushed his teeth. As he brushed he studied his eyes, the yellow orbs staring back at him spoke of the stress his liver was under. They were slowly changing color to match the solid gold handles on the sink in front of him. The eyes, underlined with dark circles, sat in a face growing more hollow cheeked by the day. He also noticed that his hair was starting to thin due to the Chemo treatments. He'd grown so accustomed to the dull pain in his side that he barely noticed it anymore, but a new pain in his right leg just above his ankle was beginning to worry him. He pulled the brush from his mouth and noticed a faint pink to the bristles. After he rinsed his mouth he studied his gums and pulled at a tooth or two. One seemed loose and he noted blood seeping around the gums. For a moment he leaned heavily on the countertop and then in anger he spat a crimson glob into the sink.

He couldn't let Stephanie see him this way. As much as he longed to see her, yearned to hold her once again, the person he was slowly becoming was not the one he wanted her to remember him as. They had always laughed and poked fun and simply enjoyed each other's company. After a moment together she'd know instantly something was desperately wrong. It could not happen. In fury he threw the toothbrush at the mirror and retreated to the dark solace of his bedroom where he pulled a picture of her from his nightstand and sat holding it for a long time.

# Chapter Thirty-Two

THE FOLLOWING MORNING a fleet of chocolate brown mail cars left an old warehouse yard and sped towards Capitol Hill, the Beltway and the Senate offices. James Lally had briefed the men about how he'd approached the job and felt they would perform admirably. They were given three addresses each to visit. The senators in question had been chosen because they were seated on a committee or subcommittee that was going to be deeply affected by the proposed legislation and therefore were likely to be in a position to vote or amend SB 1190. According to the thick dossier compiled on each of them they had certain weaknesses that might be exploited, but this was to be the initial salvo; a simple invitation.

Each man carried a parcel which contained a glossy invitation to a brainstorming session at the Four Seasons hosted by American Defense International, Rodesta Group and Potomac Advisors. The lobbying companies had been chosen because they represented Lockheed, Raytheon and a number of other major players in the defense industry as well as the powerful big banks. The invitation spoke of a general evening of fine food and strategy sessions dealing with current affairs of special interest to senators. The first went to

Jim Johnson, Democrat from South Dakota who sits on the Appropriations Committee, and specifically on the sub-committee for Military Construction, Veterans Affairs and Related Agencies. Another invite went to Robert Durbin, Democrat from Illinois who sits on the Financial Services and General Government Committee, and another to Brian Nelson, Democrat from Florida who sits on the Armed Services and chairs the Emerging Threats and Capabilities Sub-Committee. Brent Conrad, Democrat from North Dakota who chairs the Budget Committee, and James Bingham, Democrat from New Mexico who sits on the Fiscal Responsibility and Economic Growth Committee were invitees as well. All told fifty eight senators, all sitting members on key committees such as the Appropriations, Finance, Foreign Relations, Armed Services and the Banking, Housing and Urban Affairs received the gaudy invites for the meeting at the Four Seasons two nights from now. At the same time they were signing the United Parcel receipt book a microscopic bug was dropped on each of their desks near the phone. The feeds from the bugs were set up to transmit to 'Backspace' Conner's set of servers down in Atlanta. Within an hour of the invitations being delivered, Senator Jim Johnson called Senator Brian Nelson and his secretary immediately patched him through. 'Backspace' was listening in.

"I saw your name on the invite guest list. Did you open yours yet?"

"Yeah, just did," replied Brian. "What do you think?"

"I'm not going to miss it. I'm sure the food will be terrific, and those guys are some heavy hitters. It could pay some big time dividends down the road."

"It seems a little strange to me. What does 'dealing with the current affairs' mean? Normally these invites are a little vague as to the topic, but this is down right mysterious."

Jim laughed. "Now what do you think they could be hinting at with that wording? Maybe it's the only topic on every ones mind in Washington. What is the one thing on the tip of everyone's tongue?"

"SB 1190?" Brian suggested.

"Bingo, my good man."

"And then to mention a 'Strategy Session'? That seems odd."

"Pretty bold, but I think these guys are shaking in their boots. Make no mistake about it. This is a meeting to map a plan of attack on SB 1190. The base closures will cost some big companies a fortune. The transaction fee on stocks and currency trades; I've already heard from some companies concerning the impact to some of the big players that trade millions of shares a day. And this whole prison thing down in Texas. I've heard they have so many escapees showing up and now parolees showing up they're referring to it as the new prison model. Complete rehabilitation. The 'for profit' prison is going to be a thing of the past."

"Was that in SB 1190?" Brian asked.

"It was added as a rider at the last second when the House passed it and will ultimately save the Federal government billions and save the states millions as well, and put the 'for profit' prisons and all their suppliers out of business."

"Somehow I missed that part of it," Brian Nelson admitted.

"Don't worry about it. If you blinked you could have missed it."

"Well, I'm going for sure," Brian stated.

"My wife loves these dinners. She'll be upset if she can't go. There's an R.S.V.P. phone number here. Maybe I'll give them a call."

"Go for it," Jim suggested. "If there are any earth shattering revelations, let me know?"

Brian hung up and called the number on the invite.

Backspace had anticipated the possibility and knew he would need someone to help with the phones. He paid his ex-wife a queenly sum to handle the phones for a few days. Archie and Goldie had first met when he was on a photo shoot for a Dallas Cowboys Calendar. He'd noticed her right off. Not simply because she was astonishingly beautiful, but because of a quirky smile she had with deep dimples and a willingness to laugh out loud at his silly jokes. They'd hit it off from the moment they met, with Goldie pulling his moustache and saying he looked vaguely like Sam Elliott. Two years later they were married. But with her traveling schedule and his shooting assignments they saw little of each other. Two years later they were divorced, not because they were no longer in love but because it was so difficult on both of them. It was with sadness they slowly gave up trying to make time for each other. Archie always thought when they were at a different point in their lives they might re-approach the idea of marriage and felt Goldie still loved him. She had opened a pastry shop in Dallas with a couple of her cheerleader friends, which was a great success, and soon had several dozen shops across the southwest. He was living in Atlanta pursuing his freelance photography, video and general high tech career. When he asked her to help with the phones, she had initially refused, but he sweet talked her into believing she needed a few days away. He also had to promise a couple of nights out on the town in Atlanta as well as a free flight.

"Good afternoon, Potomac Advisors. How may I help you?" Goldie said in a velvety voice.

"This is Senator Brian Nelson. I received an invitation for a gathering at the Four Seasons two nights from now. The wording seemed a little odd to me. If it is to be a strategy session are wives invited?"

"I'm not sure, sir. That's a good question. Can I place you on hold for a moment and find out for you?"

"Sure."

Brian held while Goldie lit a cigarette and blew Backspace a kiss and then scowled. Backspace was busy monitoring three other calls between senators and could only blow her a kiss back and then mouthed the word, not!

A moment later she was back on the line. "I'm sorry to keep you holding, Senator. I spoke with one of the organizers and apparently this meeting will be a little different than others we have hosted. There will be some sensitive material discussed, so wives are not encouraged to attend."

"Oh, alright."

Goldie sensed the disappointment in his voice and quickly said, "Senator Nelson?"

"Yes?"

"Perhaps it would help soothe any injured feelings if a gift card for dinner for two at the Four Seasons courtesy of Potomac were to arrive at your home address in the next few days?"

"Yes," Senator Nelson replied immediately. "That would be very nice."

She jotted down his address and wished him a good afternoon.

Turning to where Backspace was seated at a bank of computers along the far wall she smiled sweetly.

"Now who is going to pay for that?" he asked.

"Anyone who can afford this beautiful office should be able to afford a dinner for two at the Four Seasons," she quipped.

"We're seated in my basement," Backspace replied.

"Don't remind me," Goldie said stubbing out her cigarette.


Backspace placed a quick call to Elliott. "Better get your best party organizers ready because they are coming."

"I've already booked a conference room at the Four Seasons. Ask Goldie to call her girlfriends from the cheer leading squad and line up the photographers. It's a go."

After he hung up he had a pang of guilt. He knew what he was doing was certainly not ethical or moral.

A famous statement came to mind and he found himself saying it out loud. "Ask not what your country can do for you, but what you can do for your country."

Even though the plan he was contemplating was something that a few years ago he would never have dreamt of doing and today still proved very distasteful to him on many levels, there was the single focus and purpose to his actions that rose above all else, that justified everything. He repeated it for the hundredth time and wondered if it was becoming his mantra. "If we do this right we just might save our country."

# Chapter Thirty-Three

THE LINCOLN CONFERENCE room at the Four Seasons was lit up like Cape Canaveral at the moment of launch. The cavernous room was filled with linen covered tables and plush chairs. Orchids graced the center of each table and pitchers of lemon water stood alongside. Each corner of the room offered a bar with all manner of beverages including a tropical punch boasting a liberal dose of 151 Rum which was proving to be quite popular with the senators. Twelve breathtakingly beautiful women dressed in evening gowns with slits up to their hips and plunging necklines worked the crowd offering hors-d'oeuvres and cocktails. They garnered a great degree of attention from the assembled members of the Senate.

Senator Nelson leaned over to Senator Milton Whitehouse sitting beside him and whispered, "Wow, those babes could put the Baywatch cast to shame."

Whitehouse agreed saying, "I've got to get the name of this catering outfit and put them on speed dial."

Earlier in the day video cameras had been discreetly installed in the corners of the ceiling to record the event in vivid detail and two roving photographers made the rounds taking the occasional shot of the senators. Dinner consisted of an eighteen-ounce filet mignon served with a light béarnaise sauce and heads of romaine with choice of dressing. Red and white wines of the finest vintage were served in liberal quantities by the same gorgeous women throughout the meal. A fruit sorbet made with the same ingredients as the tropical punch was served as dessert. The speaker was an English stage actor who'd played rolls such as Julius Caesar, Abraham Lincoln and many other stately figures from the past. He had a commanding voice and a face that reminded some of the late great actor Richard Burton. As dinner drew to a close he stepped to a raised dais, the lights were lowered, and he introduced himself as Stewart Pourtnoy, CEO of Defense Analytics Incorporated.

"Gentlemen, I'd like to thank you for taking time out of your busy schedules to join us this evening. This discussion is not going to be a new one, but it is a discussion regarding something that threatens the very existence of our democracy and it is one that continues to grow. Even though it has reached crisis proportions it is still being discussed in terms that are not near realistic and will not be addressed until it is too late. Our national debt currently stands at over 18 trillion dollars."

A faint groan coursed through the vast hall.

"Now bear with me for a few minutes. Perhaps the girls should offer another round of drinks to make this discussion a little more palatable."

A round of applause greeted this suggestion and the women appeared a few moments later.

"The U.S. Comptroller stated recently that when a country's gross debt levels tops 90% of Gross Domestic Product economic growth suffers. We surpassed that amount years ago. By 2021 the cost of annual interest payments on the debt alone will top that of the defense budget and consume over half of the government tax receipts. That's because lawmakers have yet to seriously address how to rein in the country's long term debt. Of course it has been feverishly debated, but always to no avail."

The lovely ladies moved quietly through the assemblage serving drinks.

"Essentially the two ways that have been proposed to deal with this problem have always been to tweak the tax code and a reduction in spending across the board. The aspect of this problem that has hamstrung the discussions is the growing number of retirees and their demands on Social Security and Medicare. How do you cut our debt burden when those receiving government checks are growing exponentially? We should have, indeed we must have another source of revenue. Our problems cannot be addressed with a few cuts here and there. And this is exactly what SB 1190 does; it provides a huge new revenue source and a path to the future ..."

Mr. Pourtney went on for another forty-five minutes painting a picture so bleak that the senators' alcohol consumption not only kept apace but actually increased.

"I will conclude momentarily ..." He was instantly interrupted by a loud round of applause. "By asking you to open the slim envelope you have in front of you with your name on it. There is a single question on the enclosed sheet of paper. It requires a yes or no answer. If you would be so kind as to answer the question then we can finish the night with another twenty of these beautiful ladies' friends joining us for 'Dancing under the Stars!'"

Most of the senators answered swiftly. Another bevy of beautiful women entered the room bearing bottles of champagne while a number of workers moved the tables out of the way. An old time rock and roll hit from the Righteous Brothers, 'You've Lost that Lovin' Feelin' blared over the speakers. The women had been coached to aggressively approach the men seeking dance partners.

Two exceptionally beautiful blonds with very revealing gowns had been given explicit instructions and a photographer was dispatched to follow them around the room as they carefully executed the plan. They approached a senator and one would kiss him on one cheek and the other would kiss the other cheek. They were wearing heavy red lipstick which showed up well on the photos. They would generally smooch with the senator, kissing his lips and giggling like schoolgirls as the senators often kissed them in return while the photographer clicked away from a discreet distance.

The tropical punch was always near at hand served by waiters bearing full cups. The girls formed a dance chain, coaxing some of the men to join them as they snaked about the room. The party ended about three in the morning and Operation Anvil had several photo albums worth of very damning images.

# Chapter Thirty-Four

THE FOLLOWING MORNING Elliott awoke feeling as if he'd been the one drinking at the tropical punch bowl. Gazing in the mirror he noted more of his hair was starting to fall out, his eyes were still yellow from jaundice and he felt weak.

"You look terrible," he said to the haggard face in the mirror.

His cell phone rang and he answered it.

"Backspace here. I just sent you over the photos and videos from last night."

"Great. I'll check them and get back to you."

"Call me and we can look at them simultaneously. There are some real beauts."

"Okay."

After pouring himself a strong cup of coffee Elliott sat down at his computer and opened his e-mail. The messages from Backspace started pouring in. Elliott clicked the first one open immediately and couldn't suppress a grin. He called Archie.


As soon as Archie answered the phone Elliott asked, "Is that guy, I think it's Ron Emanual from Missouri, wearing rouge?"

"No, he's been kissed so many times it just looks that way".

"He sure seems happy, and the lady in the photo is a real looker" Elliott observed. "And look at those red eyes. He's had a few too many."

"He has."

"Wait a minute," Elliott said. "Emanual's in favor of the bill. Why was he there?"

"You wanted everyone we could get. And as you well know they can change their vote at any time," Archie replied.

"True," Elliott replied.

There were hundreds of photos of men and women in some form of embrace. Several showed the men being kissed feverishly by strikingly gorgeous women. Dozens of others showed senators returning the kisses in an equally feverish manner. Another photo showed Senator Graham with at least a half dozen bright red lipstick kisses covering his face, which also bore a foolish grin from ear to ear. One showed the back of a senator's head while his face was buried in a woman's cleavage. She was smiling. Another showed a close up of a man's hand complete with wedding ring clutching a woman's buttocks so hard her dress was crumpling beneath his grip.

There was still a degree of reluctance on Elliott's part to go this route. He sighed and said, "Well you've got the guest log with a photo of each senator as they signed in. Let's get the photos sent out with the letter I forwarded to you earlier indicating if they don't vote for SB 1190 the photos will be released nationwide in all forms of media and to their wives."

"You know Elliott, I can cut and paste every man in that room into a few of the best shots, but I was thinking. Why don't we go after the flip side of the coin? Why don't we go after the lobbyists?"

"They tried to get a bill passed banning lobbyists in 2006, but it didn't pass the Senate," Elliott responded, feeling that tiredness creeping over him again.

"No, I mean if you can get me the names of the most aggressive lobbyists you're up against I can copy and paste their mugs on these same photos."

"You have a very devious mind. I'll get a call into Eddie and James and see what they have on file for our lobbyist friends."

He refreshed his coffee and typed an email to Eddie requesting photos of lobbyists, but before he hit the send button he paused. Even if they were able to curtail the current lobbyists' activities, others would simply fill the void. There had to be a more effective way to address the situation and he thought he might just have the answer. He hit send anyway.

# Chapter Thirty-Five

THE PHONE RANG around midnight. Fumbling for a moment Elliott finally answered, "Hello."

It was Archie.

"It's Eddie and James. They're in a D.C. hospital."

"What happened?" Elliott asked fully awake now.

"They were beaten pretty badly."

A note was pinned to Eddie's chest and it read, "There is worse to come."

"What's the prognosis?"

"They'll live, but James may lose an eye. Eddie is awake but barely coherent. I could barely understand him. I think they might have drugged him."

"Damn," Elliott growled. "Where were they picked up?"

"Central Park, but the cops are pretty sure they were dumped there because no one heard a thing."

"It's the lobbyists."

"Or Cobbings," Archie added. "I think they were trying to get some dirt on Cobbings."

"Do we have Cobbings bugged?"

"No, we only did the senators' offices and not all of them."

"Damn."

Archie continued, "If they know Eddie and James' identities they can track them back to you."

"And possibly you too," Elliott countered. "You better pack your stuff and get out of there Archie."

"Only if you do too."

"They won't come after me."

"I wouldn't be too sure," Archie replied. "Do you have any idea what the legislation you're trying to force through Congress is going to do to the powers that be? This is not just upsetting the apple cart Elliott. This is taking the Titanic by the rudder and throwing it on shore. It's going to change the way the American people live. It's going to change bankers' incomes in a vast and irreversible way. People will kill over the amounts of money we are proposing."

"I get the picture," Elliott said. "Let me think a minute."

Archie continued. "Besides, if they come after me they'll be in real trouble. I've got more firepower tucked away here than we had in Iraq."

"I'm going to make some calls and get them moved over to Bethesda Hospital. Can you get a couple of the guys over there to provide security?"

"Yep, and I'm going to track where those guys were tonight and see if I can get a license plate number or some kind of identification on who did this to them."

"How can you do that?"

"We haven't forgotten all you taught us in Iraq. We watch each other's backs. I planted some homing devices on their vehicle which should give me a read on where they were. Then all I have to do is hack into the transportation department's camera network. We might get lucky and get a traffic light camera or a store camera that picked up what happened to them."

"I can't decide whether you are amazing or certifiable." Elliott quipped.

"Actually, these days you can track a person by cell phone, but that simply tells you where they are, not where they've been."

"I'll take your word for it. Can you get me their hospital info?"

"Sure, here's the phone number and room number. I'll have a couple of men over there in a half hour."

"Thanks for the call, Archie."

"Take care Sarge."

# Chapter Thirty-Six

THE MEETINGS IN the Senate Appropriations Committee and the Senate Banking Committee were extremely heated. The Washington Post got wind of the extremely elevated level of debate and ran a front page story entitled, "The Bill that Broke the Senate in Two."

Many people in Washington's power elite were slowly becoming aware that something very unusual was happening on the Hill. When he wasn't calling the doctors attending to his two injured men Elliott followed the progress of the bill, listening for any mention of it while watching C-SPAN six hours a day and answering reports from his men in the field.

Stephanie Wells called back two mornings later.

"Elliott? Hi, this is Stephanie, have I caught you at a bad time?"

"No, of course not, it's always good to hear your voice."

"I think I have some good news for you."

"Great, I could use some."

"I spoke to the head of the Association of Advancement for Retired People. He's very enthusiastic about the bill. And don't worry, I didn't use your name. He's sent out emails to every chapter of AARP instructing them to sign a petition endorsing the bill, but get this. The Florida chapter, which is a couple of hundred thousand strong, has a group called 'The Minute Men' which is about ten thousand strong and they have agreed to go to D.C. by RV, car, train and boat whenever the time for the vote on the bill is set. Of course loads of people will come from all over the country. He knows a lot of people in the music industry and is going to get the word out to them. It's going to be another Woodstock."

"That is good news. Nice work Steph."

"And he also brought up another idea which I thought was a good one."

"I'm all ears."

"It's a group called 'The National Federation of Independent Businesses', a group of small business owners. I say a group, but there are about six million of them employing two to twenty people on average. They have seen their sales numbers drop off dramatically since the financial meltdowns in 2008 and 2015. Sales haven't risen much since then, and they are one pissed off bunch of people. Please excuse my colorful colloquialism. They're angry that the big banks got all this bailout money and have used it to buy influence and they feel like big companies that donate freely to election campaigns get preferential treatment. Companies like General Electric with record profits paying no taxes. I was thinking if we could amend your bill so that when the deficit is paid off and the funding starts for Social Security we could move to end the payroll tax for Social Security. Employees get more take-home pay and the employers don't have their portion of the payroll tax and all the accounting costs for implementing the Social Security payroll tax. That's the equivalent of a 4.2% pay raise for the employee and a 6.2% pay raise for the employer. It's a lot of money Elliott. Employers will likely hire more people as it will cost less, and employees will have more money to spend and thereby jump-start the economy. The National Federation of Independent Businesses would go wild over that idea."

"Same old Steph, out in front of everybody and thinking outside the box. I think it's terrific."

"Careful there Mr. Eastman. I'm reaching that point where using my name and old in the same sentence can get you in real trouble."

"Sorry, but I think considering the fact that I'm twenty years your senior should get me off the hook."

Stephanie laughed. "I'll let it go this time, but you know it never felt that way."

"What never felt what way?"

"It never felt like you were that much older than I am."

"I know. We were a perfect fit," Elliott replied softly.

"Do you know when you might be out to D.C. next?"

"I'm not sure."

"I'd really like to see you Elliott."

"I know."

He didn't have the heart to tell her he'd flown in twice to check on Eddie and James.

They fell silent, each waiting for the other to speak. When the silence began to grow awkward Stephanie said, "Do you still have the same e-mail address? I'll send you the contact information for both of these men just in case you need it."

"It's still the same."

"Okay. I'll talk to you soon."

"Thanks."

As soon as he set the phone down it rang again.

"Elliott? Archie here. Eddie and James have been released. They were able to save James' eye, thank God. I suggested they head for your ranch to rest up, but they would have none of it. They're worried they might be followed and they want a piece of the guys that jumped them. I was able to do some creative hacking and I got a clear shot of the vehicle that cut them off. The video shows them being manhandled into the back of a black Escalade. I got a clean read of the license plate off a traffic light video cam. It's registered to one Reginald Soro who, get this, works as a private detective. We could talk with him and see who hired him."

Elliott was quiet, thinking for a moment. "Tell Eddie and James they are off duty for now. They will be followed. Get two new faces and see if they can track down Soro. I want to know who paid for the hit on Eddie and James. I want to know if there is a new player in the game."

"I'll get Jim Buckner and Gordon Harrison on it. They're good at the special ops stuff."

"Good."


Elliott stood on shaky legs and turned up the sound on C-SPAN so he could hear it in the bathroom. He went to shave and make himself presentable to the doctors administering the chemo today. As he entered the bathroom he glanced in the mirror and said, "Hello, craggy face."

He paused, shaving blade in shaky hand, and studied the dark circles under his eyes as the water in the sink heated up. His hair had thinned to the point where he could see areas of his scalp he'd never seen before.

'Damn chemo. I can't see Stephanie looking like a concentration camp escapee,' he thought. But he owed her some kind of explanation. He could hear the hurt in her voice today, and she'd done such a beautiful job, but he didn't want her to know his life was numbered in weeks, maybe days. It was true he did long to see her, more than she would ever know, but the last thing he wanted to do was resurrect their feelings for one another and then leave her grieving after he was gone. He supposed he was taking the easy way out, but nothing about it felt easy.

Setting the blade down he turned the water off and moved back out to the den where he put C-SPAN on mute and called Stephanie back.

"Hi Steph. Hey, I'm sorry. I'm just buried. I've got forty men in the field right now. I promise when I'm coming to D.C. I'll give you plenty of notice."

"I'd like to see the ranch again. It's been a long time," Stephanie said softly.

Elliott actually considered the idea for a moment. They'd enjoyed some marvelous times here. "It's just not a good idea right now, I'm sorry."

"I understand. Do what you have to do. I'll see you soon."

"Bye."

The call was supposed to make him feel better, but it didn't.

After showering and shaving he put on a Brooks Brother's suit and drove the forty miles to Colorado State University where Dr. Yates had arranged for him to get treatment.

Two days later after a double-dose of chemo, he was being helped to his car by an orderly when he heard his phone ringing from inside his briefcase.

"Please, it might be important, and I can make it the rest of the way to my car myself."

"Are you sure sir?" the orderly asked.

"Yes, thank you," Elliott said setting the brief case on the ground, opening it and quickly answering his cell phone.

"Elliott here."

"Elliott. It's Paul White. The Senate Banking Committee just sent SB 1190 back to the floor with no changes."

"They didn't even try to amend it?"

"No, the bastards didn't want a repeat of the Discharge Motion maneuver so they made sure they got it out of committee within the 30 days, but essentially they're saying it's fine the way it is."

"That makes no sense. I assumed the banking lobby would hammer us," Elliott commented.

"I know. I thought the same thing. I don't like it; I can't figure out what they're up to," the President added.

"I thought they'd attack the amount of the transaction fee, you know, cut it in half or something," Elliott added.

"I heard rumors the opposition was going to modify the bill to have the transaction fee apply to personal accounts."

"That would be dirty pool, but would effectively destroy the intent of the bill, if they could get it through," speculated the former senator.

"I think the Banking Committee moves are just a feint to lull us into complacency," President White speculated.

"They're up to something."

"And we'll see it out of Armed Services and Appropriations shortly. I can't imagine they'll leave it unchanged."

"We'll see. Who can you line up in the Senate that we can count on?" Elliott asked.

"We can count on …"

"Listen Paul, I'm just getting in my car. Can you e-mail me the contact information for the senators you can trust? I've got some driving to do."

"You know you just interrupted the President of the United States?"

"Yep, and I'm not even sorry about it."


As Elliott drove back to his ranch he had to stop twice because of the dry heaves. His stomach was as empty as a sun bleached gourd, but his body was telling him it had been through hell and something needed to be ejected from it. As weak as a kitten from his second roadside stop, he was climbing back into his car when his phone rang again.

"Elliott?"

"Yes."

"Archie, I've got a hell of an idea. Ouch, don't hit me."

Elliott could hear a woman's voice in the back ground, "Don't you go taking credit for my idea."

"Hit me again and I'll kiss you."

"Go on. You're keeping the Senator waiting."

"Elliott?"

"Yes, Archie, I take it you're with Goldie?"

"Yes, Goldie, my beautiful angel is right here."

Goldie put a finger down her throat and made a gagging sound.

"Goldie, or one of her girlfriends on the cheerleading squad, met Bono before he was married and developed a close friendship. They still talk once or twice a year," explained Archie, making sure to get the credits right.

"I've met Bono as well, quite an impressive fellow," Elliott mentioned.

"Agreed, well we had an idea. Bono knows a lot of people. If we were to make him aware of the sweeping impact of the 'War on the Deficit' bill, we're sure he would back it and he might bring in other famous friends and we could air a national TV ad. You know, kinda like the ones that Yul Bryner did about the dangers of cigarettes before he died of cancer? I'm excited about the idea."

"It's worth a shot. Run with it."

"I knew you'd like it. I'll let you know how it goes. Later."

Elliott was pulling onto the long gravel drive that led to his sprawling ranch house when his phone rang again. It was Robert Dale, his attorney.

"Hello Robert."

"Hi Elliott, here's the monthly report, as you requested. The manager of the prison inmate project is reporting they have had over fifty thousand hits on their web site requesting information on how to apply, and another ten thousand have simply shown up at the gates. This thing is going wild. And this is just in Texas. It's a whole new industry that's grown up over night."

"Of course, free food, a roof over their heads and a chance to get a leg up in life. It's simple human nature to want to improve their lot in life."

"We're running into a little trouble with getting accredited, but we're making progress. And our foundation has been approached by representatives from California, Georgia, New Jersey and Ohio inquiring how the costs are shaping up."

"And how are they shaping up?" Elliott asked as he climbed out of the car.

"They're coming in at about 66% of what it cost to run the former prison."

"That doesn't surprise me. I read somewhere the average cost to house, feed and clothe a prisoner for a year was around $71,000. 66% of that times fifty thousand ex-prisoners is one hell of a savings, while helping to make productive citizens out of serial prisoners. When word gets out, every state in the Union will be knocking on your door."

"And a lot of these teachers and other assistants were on unemployment. Some of the former prisoners were on welfare and soon they'll be gainfully employed, imbued with self-esteem and a sense of worth. We'll be seeing people dropping off the welfare rolls in very significant numbers very soon."

"We'll see quite a few prison guards on the unemployment lines," Elliott said softly.

"They negotiated themselves a CEO style severance package. They won't be hurting."

Roberts's voice grew husky and he faltered to a stop.

"Don't question it. Not for a second. It is a good thing you are doing, Elliott."

"You're the one who has made it happen, Robert."

"Me? I'm glad I was able to be part of it. I just had my paralegals move forward with the hiring process for unemployed teachers and managers and then let things run their natural course. You're the one footing the bill."

"Well, keep up the good work and please keep me posted," Elliott concluded.

"I'll be speaking with you soon," Robert replied.


Elliott's phone rang the moment he set it down. Glancing at the number he noted it was the President's private line and pressed the green answer button.

"Yes, Paul."

"Appropriations just sent the bill back. Their sub-committee on economic policy believes the transaction fees are too high and will reduce liquidity and possibly push up interest rates. They recommend a flat ten cent tax on all transactions over one million dollars. They also recommend that JP Morgan hold the transaction tax funds in a Wall Street lock box account."

"Ten cents on transactions over one million dollars is nonsense. That's nothing. It essentially guts the bill," Elliott observed.

"We were wondering why the banking committee wasn't the one to carve the bill up, and now we know. It was a smart approach. They don't want the bankers to be the ones who are against the bill, which might bring the wrath of the people down on the bankers who they despise already," the President said thinking out loud.

"So the banking committee sends it back to the floor unchanged knowing it would help mollify an angry public and at the same time instructing appropriations to decimate the bill," Elliott said.

"You got it," The President replied and laughed bitterly.

Elliott remained silent wondering if the growing nausea in his gut was from the news or the chemo.

"And the Armed Services Committee, undoubtedly pushed by Cobbings' close friend Larry Lanting, the senator who chairs the Emerging Threats subcommittee, has recommended closing eighty bases over the next seven years."

Elliott groaned and said, "I'll call you right back."

He hobbled as quickly as he could to the kitchen sink and threw up. After leaning against the sink for a few minutes to make sure he was done, he rinsed his mouth out, returned to the den and dialed the President back.

"Paul? Sorry about that. I think I have a case of food poisoning. The results don't surprise me. When you have one-sided guest speakers addressing the sub-committees there are few conclusions that can be drawn other than what we are seeing here."

"I'm so angry I can't see straight," Paul said, sounding utterly demoralized. "Now it will go to conference committee hearings and you know what that means."

"Yes, there will be select members of the House and Senate committees who originally heard the bill and they will attempt to reconcile the differences between the two bodies. This just means the bill will be back in the hands of Cobbings, Bainer, Graham and Coryn," Elliott concluded.

"This does not bode well for the bill," the President said in a dull monotone.

"There are still things we can do. Let me think on things. I'll call you in the morning."

# Chapter Thirty-Seven

THE NON-DESCRIPT LIGHT brown four door sedan eased up the street passing each address slowly.

"There it is," said Gordon. "235 Weaver Street."

After Jim Buckner pulled to the curb across the street and doused the headlights. The two men studied the small single story tract home for a few minutes. A waist high chain link fence ran around the perimeter of the front yard. Weeds grew along the fence and grew in the cracks of the concrete driveway and walkway.

"Hmmm," Jim said, "looks pretty run down, but there's the black Escalade Backspace picked up on the traffic cam. This is the place, and there's a light on in the front room so somebody is home."

Gordon pulled a file from between the car seats. "Soro lives with his mother. From the records we pulled Marilyn Soro is seventy eight and on oxygen. Maybe she likes late night TV?"

"I'm going to take a quick look in the front window, see who's home and if we have dogs to deal with," Jim said as he climbed out of the car and quietly shut the door.

Walking softly towards the front of the house, Jim moved up the driveway and almost tripped over a tangle of garden hose. It was just past midnight and most of the denizens of this unsavory neighborhood were already in bed. The chain link gate stood open. Jim crossed the dry front lawn and the grass crunched under his feet, but the TV inside the tiny house was so loud he was sure they heard nothing. He peered through the front window and spied a rotund man sitting on a worn couch in his skivvies drinking a beer. Jim retreated back to the vehicle.

"He's alone and there are no dogs."

"Let's do it," Gordon said, thinking of Eddie's badly bruised face.

"Okay, you stay with the car and keep a look out. Bring the car around when I'm ready. I'll handle the perp."

Jim climbed from the car again, opened the trunk and pulled a half full gas can from it. Quietly he moved across the street. In the shadows beside the Escalade he poured gas over one tire, laid a trail of the highly flammable liquid to the second front tire and dropped a match. With a whoosh the tires immediately burst into flames. Buckner moved back into the deep shadows beside the garage. A moment later Soro leapt through the front door. With an oath he ran over and began grappling with the hose trying to untangle it. Jim stepped from the darkness and said, "Hey."

When Soro looked up Jim pressed the point of his Zap Mini Stun baton against Soro's neck and pressed the trigger. A flash of electricity exploded from the end of the baton. With a grunt Soro fell to the ground and began shaking violently. Gordon pulled the car around while Jim lifted the nearly 260 pounds of unconscious man, dragged him to the car and tossed him in the back seat.

# Chapter Thirty-Eight

THE CONFERENCE COMMITTEE hearing was held at the Dirksen building of the Senate. The tension in the room grew with the appearance of each new face as they entered the pale marble walled room of the ancient chamber. News people crowded the perimeter of the room recording every nuanced motion of the assembly.

A standard Conference Committee combines the chairs of the original committees in both the House and Senate, sensibly assuming they were the most familiar with the bill, along with select members of both Houses as recommended by the Presiding Officer of the Senate and the House Speaker with input from the Majority Leaders and Minority Leaders. In this case other members of the Senate and the House, sensing this was an historical occasion, requested inclusion which generally was granted. Cobbings and Bainer were there as was Coryn, Larry Lanting, Senators Jim Johnson, Sam Whitback, Ray Haley Hutchinson, Wade Biggs, Brian Nelson and another dozen members of the House and Senate. Opposite, across the huge mahogany table, sat Representatives Bruce Bennett, Earl Bishop, Jay Stephens, Kathy Rogers Morris, Rosa Sparks and Senator Roger Portman.

Senator Roger Portman had been in the Senate long enough to sense that this conference meeting had all the earmarks of a real bloodletting. He spoke at length with Senator Carl Carimendi from California, and Senator Bill Spitzer from New York. These were two experienced and savvy veterans. He met with them several times. They were already in favor of SB 1190, but by the time he was done informing them of the forces arrayed against the bill and what had gone on already in committee, the two men were poised to request being appointed to the Conference Committee. They were here as well.

Cobbings, along with his cronies, made a point of finding seats opposite the instruments of their wrath. They sat glaring at Kathy Morris and Bruce Bennett, while Tom Coryn stared hard at Roger Portman. This was not to be a meeting of amiable counterparts working together towards a common goal. No, this was akin to the Godfather meeting with the heads of the five families. They would speak to each other cordially, but in the end each wanted to spill the blood of the other.

A stenographer recorded every word spoken and began typing as the Chair of the Committee, Carl Nevin, brought the gavel down hard on the circle of rosewood beside him and said, "Pursuant to the Congressional Calendar and concurrent notice, the Conference Committee hearing is now to commence in room D-538 of the Dirksen Senate Building."

Cobbings leaned across the table and whispered to Bennett, "This is never gonna happen. Do you know what you're up against? Funding is flowing in for our own attack ads."

Bennett shrugged. "Whatever."

Carl spoke loud enough to interrupt the threats being traded between the two warring factions at the end of the table.

"Ladies and Gentlemen, I would like to have your undivided attention. Beside you on the table you will find a summary of the SB

1190. The House and Senate versions of the bill are there for you to review. The House passed the bill as written, but the Senate modified it as specified in bold type."

Cobbings stood and said, "I rise in opposition to the SB 1190."

"You may proceed," Senator Nevin ordered.

"Mr. Chairman, I move that lines 22 through 44 of clause six are stricken from the bill."

"You wish to eliminate the transaction fee completely?" Nevin asked puzzled.

"Yes, and further I move to strike lines 139 through 217."

"You wish to eliminate the base reduction entirely?" Senator Nevin asked, inwardly realizing he was seeing the opening salvos of a battle the likes of which a Conference Committee had never seen before. He leaned back from the table and motioned to one of the congressional pages that hovered nearby to approach. The young man took three paces closer and bent at the waist so he could hear the Senator.

"Could you please inform the Sergeant-at-Arms his presence will be needed shortly?"

"Yes sir. Right away sir," the page replied and hurried away.

Representative Bruce Bennett and Senator Carimendi stood at the same instant and spoke as one voice. "Mr. Chairman, I rise in a Point of Order against the striking of these lines!"

Nevin looked over at the two men and shook his head, 'This is going to be a very long day,' he thought.

"Only one of you may speak."

"I yield my time to my esteemed colleague from California, Mr. Carimendi," Bruce said.

"Thank you, Representative Bennett. Mr. Chairman, pursuant to Rule XXVIII the striking of the entire subtext which Representative Cobbings has delineated is outside the 'Scope of Differences'. As we all know, implicit in the rules of both chambers is the requirement that conferees resolve differences by reaching agreements within the scope of the original bills sent to them. The House agreed to the original graduated flat fee arrangement while the Senate rewrote it with an across the board ten cent flat fee. Any proposed amendment must be within those extremes; therefore a complete elimination of the transaction fee is outside the scope. I might add the same statement applies to the base closures. The House accepted 400 and the Senate reduced the number to eighty. The Conference Committee must stay within those parameters."

The Sergeant-at -Arms quietly entered the room and stood by the door observing the proceedings.

Representative Bainer stood.

Carl recognized him.

"I request a voice vote of the yeas and nays on the Point of Order."

Bainer knew if the Point of Order could be overruled the amendments in question could be modified in almost any fashion they liked.

The vote was immediately initiated and Senator Nevin declared, "The yeas have it. The Point of Order is sustained."

Senator Graham stood and said, "Mr. Chairman, I rise in opposition to the previous question."

"Proceed," Senator Nevin said.

"I move that lines 22 thru 26 be modified. They currently read as follows, "The transaction fee shall apply to all specified transactions. The term specified transaction shall not include any transfer between accounts of a taxpayer and any deposit into a personal account of an individual.

"I move to insert the following wording; 'The transaction fee shall apply to all specified transactions. The term specified transaction shall include any transfer between accounts of a taxpayer and any deposit into a personal account of an individual.'"

Bennett's head shot up. Bishop glanced at Kathryn Morris and then his gaze settled on Bennett. The young representative's face was an ashen color.

'So this was it,' Bennett thought. 'They intended to rip out the heart of the bill. It was supposed to be a fee on the huge financial firms, the ones gambling with trillions of dollars every day. Now they wanted to impose the fee on every transaction the average American made including a simple transfer between accounts.'

Bennett could not control his rage. He abruptly stood up staring directly at Graham and then gazed at those others beside him, "You sirs, are the most despicable of human beings!"

With that he strode swiftly from the room.

To Graham the affront was more than worth it. Let Bennett think what he may. With a rapacious grin Graham stood to be recognized.

Nevin nodded.

"I move that we notify the respective chambers that we cannot agree and file the conference report in disagreement," Graham announced in a stern voice.

Cobbings instantly stood and seconded the motion. They knew that the chances of the entire bill dying when it was submitted unchanged back to the floors of the respective chambers was quite good.

Senator Nevin sighed. His ire was rising by the minute. "Gentlemen, we have been here for less than fifteen minutes. There are those in both houses of Congress, and I might add the American people, who believe some provisions in this bill have merit. I think they would like to see some minor effort at a reconciliation of the different versions. But considering the contentious nature of how this meeting has begun, I am going to move that we recess until a time agreed as ten a.m. on February third. That is two days hence and should give all of you time to reconsider your positions and make headway with your differences. I hope everyone returns with a more cooperative attitude. Meeting adjourned."

# Chapter Thirty-Nine

RICHARD SORO SLOWLY came around to find himself staring into a bright circular disk of light. His arms and legs were securely duct taped to a chair in the center of a shabby motel room. A heavy smell of gasoline permeated the air and his underwear seemed uncomfortably soggy.

"What's going on here?" he asked, struggling to make his jaw work after the torment his muscles had endured during the electric shock.

"Stay away from the light. Stay away from the light," intoned Gordon in a hollow inhuman voice.

"Huh?" Richard murmured.

"Just kidding, I couldn't help myself. I always wanted to say that," Gordon confessed.

Jim Buckner stepped up to a point just behind the light and said, "We have a couple of friends who were hospitalized by you and your boys. We're willing to overlook that if you can answer a couple of questions."

"I don't know what you're talking about," Soro responded.

Jim took a step closer and flicked the silver top off of his lighter and thumbed the flame to life. The flame wavered slow and lazy in the stillness of the room.

"Don't even go there. We have the entire attack on film. That gasoline you smell is your undies, you're soaking in it. If I drop this lighter you'll go up in flames, and I'll do it if you don't answer the questions to our satisfaction."

"You wouldn't."

"I don't think you want to test me. We have gloves on, so there will be no finger prints and we registered the room under false names. They'll never know who checked in and I don't think too many people are going to be saddened by your checking out. Now tell me, do you know a man called Doc Hastings?"

"Never heard of him."

Gordon stepped past the light and poured more fuel on Soro's crotch.

"Jesus Christ," Soro cried as he teetered back in the chair and almost tipped over.

"Okay, okay. I know Doc Hastings."

"That's better. You might just make it out of here alive. Do you know about his dealings with John Bainer or Nick Cobbings?"

"Who?"

The lighter flicked on again. The flame, like a viper's tongue drifted closer to Soro.

"God damn, don't drop that thing," Soro cried inching away.

"Talk!" Jim snarled.

"Alright. I never met either of them, but I've heard Doc say a few things. He doesn't think much of either one of them. I wanna say Cobbings has some sweet deal with his wife's Political Action Committee and a lease or something. Bainer I don't know nothing about, but I heard Hastings complaining about Bainer demanding some boxes of real fine scotch from him. That's all I got."

"Nothing else?"

"Naw, that's all I can remember."

"Have you ever heard the name Sam Whitback?"

"Nope, and I think I'd remember a name like that."

"Nothing more on Bainer or Cobbings?"

"Look, I'm sitting here with my nuts soaking in gas. Don't you think I'd talk if I knew anything more?"

"Fair enough, now talk to us about Doc Hastings."

Soro shifted uncomfortably and said, "I don't know much about him."

"You're really standing on the razor's edge pal. We know Hastings put you on our guys. Talk."

"Okay, I said I know Hastings, but all I do is run errands for him from time to time. It ain't like we hang out together."

"Give us some dirt on him and we're through here."

"I don't know nothin' about his personal life," Soro replied shifting uneasily again.

"C'mon, you've carried money for him. Who supplied it? Who'd you take it to?"

"Listen dude, do you think I deal with the higher ups? I meet a faceless nothing, drop some cash or pick some up and that's it. And them guys see the same thing; an empty nothing shuffling between orders. I'm telling it like it is and there just ain't no more."

For a moment Gordon was concerned the thug might start sobbing.

Jim stepped swiftly around the light, drove a sharp left jab into Soro's face and felt his nose snap. He then followed with a hard right upper cut that drove Soro's head back and the chair toppling backwards onto the floor.

"Leave him here?" Gordon asked.

"Yeah, the cleaning people will find him."

As the two men stepped from the seedy motel room and into the night, Gordon said, "Not much info."

"No, but I think a visit to Hastings' office might be in order."

"It's two a.m. You're not thinking right now are you?"

"Yep, no better time, and a stop by Cobbings' district office might be in order too."

With a sigh Gordon said, "Lead on."

# Chapter Forty

SENATOR GRAHAM TOOK up residence at the back of the cloak room where much wheeling and dealing took place beyond the prying eyes of the public and the press. He made it a point of bending the ear of any of his fellow congressmen who wandered into the room regarding what he perceived as the negative aspects of SB1190.

Senator Jess Willow was a heavy-set man in a pudgy sort of way and given to wearing inexpensive suits and colorful bow ties. He was soft spoken and considered a moderate in the Senate representing the state of Maine. He made frequent visits to the cloak room for a soda and to relax on one of the plush sofas that dotted the room. Senator Graham moved over beside him the moment Senator Willow took a seat.

"Hello Jess, how is it going out there in Maine?"

"Maine's a mighty fine place."

"What are your thoughts on this 'War on the Deficit' bill?"

"I think it has merit. It's high time we get serious about the deficit. The darn thing is like a coiled snake lying right at our feet. It's only a matter of time before it rears up and bites us in the behind."

"Come now Jess, you can't be serious. All kinds a fees on top of fees and more fees is not what the country needs right now. It will rock the recovery back on its heels. We need to stop this thing in its tracks right now."

"I know you're against it, but I'm not sure why?" An uneasy Willow replied, looking over at the craggy face of the Senator from Nebraska.

"Look Jess. You know I chair the Senate Banking Committee. I can tell you right now, we are very concerned that this is a deeply flawed bill with many unknown impacts on the economy. It's not going to pass, I guarantee it, so why waste your vote?"

"It seems like we must do something about the deficit," Jess said hesitantly.

"Look, we don't know what's going to happen in Conference Committee. It's a wild card situation. We need to be prepared," Graham insisted.

"I heard it was in trouble in committee. I heard it might not even come out of committee," Jess insisted.

"I know, I know, I heard the same thing, but you just never know. I tell you what I'll do. I know you've tried to get the Jess Willows library off the ground up there in Portland and are having a devil of a time."

"That's for damn sure," the portly Senator responded sitting up a bit and listening intently.

"What if I were to promise you I'll see you get the funding as a rider on an amendment or an earmark on some other bill?"

"I'd really appreciate it."

"Consider it done. If you vote no on SB 1190 I'll see to it your library gets built," Graham offered expansively.

"I told my grandkids about it … the library I mean, and they keep asking me when it's going to get started," Willows mused softly.

"Shake my hand, promise me you'll vote no, and we'll both get to work making your grandkids happy," Graham said, thrusting his hand at Willows.

Reluctantly Willows reached for the outstretched hand and Graham's clamped down on his. "You won't regret this Jess. You've made the right decision."

"Thanks Graham, I'm trusting you to get me that funding."

"I can hear the hammer and saws going already."

Willows made his way back out to the Senate floor.

And so it went for the next two days. Any Senator who ventured into the cloak room and some that Graham coaxed in as well were all subjected to similar arguments convincing them of the fruitlessness of voting for a bill when the banks and the military establishment were going to be so negatively impacted and would obviously fight fiercely to defeat it.

Bainer and Cobbings were doing much the same in the House of Representatives: holding meetings, dinners and outings with critical members of the Armed Services Committee, the Banking Committee and Appropriations exhorting them to vote against the bill and the futility of fighting the banks and the entrenched military establishment.

# Chapter Forty-One

"SO WHAT HAVE we got?" Elliott asked.

"We have good news and bad news. We have the still photos from the party at the Four Seasons," Archie replied. "Mike Murphy got some good video of Senator Graham and one of his female assistants, and Jim and Gordon took it upon themselves to visit with Richard Soro. He was quite cooperative."

"That's strange," Elliott said. "I don't know him, but I would think anyone Doc Hastings has as an off-the-books employee would be tough as nails. I would have expected him to clam up."

Archie chuckled. "Well, he was at first but then with a little gasoline …"

"That's okay. I don't need the details," Elliott interrupted him.

"Anyway, he mentioned something about a lease Cobbings was concerned about, so they went to Cobbings' office and um, borrowed some files. Get this, his wife's PAC leases office space from Cobbings and he's not declared it on his taxes," Archie explained. "We've already sent copies of the leases and his tax returns to the House Ethics Committee, but you know how slow they are to respond. In the meantime Eddie and James are posing as investigators and contacting every Representative Cobbings has talked to in the last year and they're following up with questionnaires and requests for meetings with them. I think Cobbings' credibility will be toast in week."

"So what is the bad news," Elliott asked.

"It's Bainer. We got nothing on him."

"Damn, he's chatting up every member on the Conference Committee, ringing up the no votes as fast as he can."

"Goldie has an idea, but you're not going to like it."

"Don't tell me," Elliott cautioned. "I'd hate to have to testify against you."

Archie laughed. "I know you better than that. You'd go down in flames before you'd rat any one of us out."

"True, but I still don't want to know. Is it legal?"

"Borderline, but definitely very, um, shall we say creative. So what do you think?"

Elliott was quiet for a moment. This was a point where all the cards were on the table. You either bet the house or meekly fold and walk away.

"Run with it, Archie. Do whatever you need to do and hit them as hard as you can."

"You got it."


Suddenly overwhelmed by exhaustion, Elliott retreated to his bedroom and lay down on his bed.

# Chapter Forty-Two

APPROXIMATELY ONE HUNDRED and eighty 8 x 10 glossies went out in forty four different envelopes the following morning to each of the partygoers from the Four Seasons along with a short, curt letter. "You will be expected to vote for SB 1190 or a copy of this photo will be sent to your wife, released to the news media and numerous websites. Please consider your options carefully. Democracy at the behest of corporations is not democracy."

Eddie and James refused to stand on the sidelines and despite their injuries they couldn't have looked more ominous, dressed in black suits and wearing dark sun glasses, when they caught up with Republican Representative George Madsen of Minnesota getting out of his taxi in front of his D.C. apartment.

"Mr. Madsen?"

"Yes."

"Jones and West, IRS," Eddie said opening his coat and letting the congressman catch a glimpse of his badge along with the butt of the gun in his shoulder holster. "We'd like to ask you a few questions regarding Nick Cobbings."

"Right here?"

"It won't take long, or perhaps we should step inside your apartment?"

Madsen looked terribly uncomfortable.

"Let's step up near the front door and I'll try to answer a couple of questions," the congressman suggested.

The three men walked up the flight of steps until they were near the front doors to the upscale condominium complex where Madsen rented a unit.

"Are you aware of Cobbings leasing part of his office space to his wife's Political Action Committee?"

"I most certainly am not."

"Strange, you were mentioned in our briefing as a close associate of his."

"I am no such thing. Sure, I've spoken to him a few times, but that's about the size of it."

"Are you aware of his concealing his wife's income from the IRS?"

"Absolutely not. What kind of questions are these? How would I know anything about his personal taxes?"

"These are merely routine questions we are required to ask," James said.

"Do you, or have you ever, been in a business partnership with Nick Cobbings?"

"No, never. Did he say that?"

"No, but the Bureau indicated you and he have met on many occasions away from the congressional buildings."

"Wrong, we may have met a handful of times, wait you said the Bureau?"

"Yes, as you know a member of Congress must declare their financial holdings. The IRS will investigate when we believe a case of tax evasion has occurred, but not declaring properly for the Congressional Journal is a crime and that draws in the FBI."

"I don't think I want to answer any more questions unless my attorney is present," Madsen said slowly.

"We understand," James responded. "Thank you for your cooperation."

"And please, don't leave town," Eddie added as they stepped away.

A shaken Madsen opened the front doors, took the elevator eight flights up to his unit and immediately got on the phone to one of his aides.

"Luanne, find Nick Cobbings and have him call me as soon as possible. Tell him it's an emergency."

Twenty minutes later the phone rang.

"Madsen here."

"George, what's the emergency?"

"I just had a personal visit from two IRS agents. They are investigating your lease arrangements and apparently the FBI is involved."

"Damn. And rumor has it the House Ethics Committee is beginning an investigation of me."

"Are the accusations true?"

"It was an innocent mistake."

"A mistake that you were funneling money to your wife's PAC while she was leasing space from you?"

"It's nothing. Hell, half the House has got similar arrangements," Cobbings growled.

"I think you are exaggerating just a bit. I know of no others, and if you're convicted you'll obviously lose your seat."

"I know."

Madsen sat for a moment in silence not sure what to say and finally merely stated, "I wish you luck."

Eddie and James had similar conversations with a dozen members of the House over the next two days. It was just enough to set the House abuzz with speculation as to Cobbings' fate.

Meanwhile Judy, all ninety pounds of her, read the lines Goldie had typed for her for the seventh time and said, in her high squeaky voice, "I think I have it down, Goldie."

"Remember, you're angry and sobbing."

"Yes, Goldie," Judy replied rolling her eyes.

"Okay, are you ready?" Goldie asked.

"Yes."

"This is me dialing," Goldie said with a smirk as she pressed the numbers on the phone.

A moment later, after a few rings, the voicemail kicked on.

"Hello, you have reached the offices of Congressman John Bainer. The offices are closed at this time. Please leave a message at the tone or visit our web site at www.johnbainer.com." The phone beeped and just as Judy began to speak Goldie gave her thigh a fierce pinch. Judy inched away and immediately began sobbing uncontrollably and cried.

"What you did to me was horrible. I'm only seventeen years old and you, you … you raped me. You are a monster! I'm going to tell the police what you did. I hate you. I hate you!"

Judy set the receiver down in its cradle.

"Perfect," Goldie breathed as she turned off the tape recorder.

"I was pretty good, wasn't I?" Judy said with a beaming smile as both women emerged from the phone booth.

"Now let's get this tape off to the police," Goldie said. "We'll go to the post office together."

The following morning Mabel Hessling, Bainer's aging secretary of twenty plus years, turned the key in the front door lock and let herself into the office at seven a.m. As soon as she set her overcoat on the back of her chair she noticed the light blinking on the phone at her desk.

Sitting down at her desk she responded to the series of commands that allowed her to access the voicemail message. She stared in horror at the phone as she listened to the hysterical woman on the other end of the line. After listening to it three more times, with her senses reeling, she quickly dialed Bainer's cell phone number.

"John, you must come to the office as quickly as possible."

"What is it?"

"There is something you must hear."

"It can't wait? I haven't even finished the Times yet."

"You must come now."

"Mabel, Give me some idea of what we're talking about."

"I … I can't, John."

"Okay, I'll be there as soon as I can," Bainer grumbled, "but this better be a true emergency."

"Believe me, it is."

Mabel waited patiently for the congressman to arrive and all the while her thoughts leapt about. Could he have done it? Either way he was going to be disgraced. Would he go to jail? Would she? She would undoubtedly be questioned. She would need to find another job.

After Mabel paced the floor of her little office for a number of minutes wringing her hands, she sat down again and began to quietly cry. Tears rolled down her cheeks as she thought about how bright eyed, naïve and optimistic she was when she first joined the Bainer operation. She, no they, were going to change the world. Slowly she'd learned how favors were doled out. Plumb positions for loyal constituents, and favorable legislation for big money donors was arranged. Her disillusionment grew and was eventually complete, but she stayed on the job because the market for someone with her limited skills was simply not there.

'And now this,' she thought.

Finally she decided her only course of action was to go to the police first. It would help absolve her of any complicity in some sort of cover-up and was the right thing to do. This poor young woman had been violated and needed to be protected.

Withdrawing a sheet of stationary from a nearby drawer she stifled a sob, pushed a strand of graying hair out of her eyes and quickly began typing her resignation letter.

# Chapter Forty-Three

CONGRESSIONAL PAGES SLIPPED between the men
and women seated at the enormous table laying thick sheaves of
paper beside the glasses and vases of water.

Bainer leaned back in his chair, cleared his throat and said, "I'm
comfortable with Senator Carl Nevin continuing to chair this
meeting."

Nevin looked up from the papers he was studying. "My last stab
at chairing a committee meeting was not a scintillating experience,"
he said gazing pointedly at both Portman and Coryn.

"Come on, Carl," Bainer said in his water well deep voice. "This
is Conference Committee. It doesn't get more informal than this.
We're just gonna kick around some ideas and be out of here in a few
hours."

Senator Nevin hesitated for a moment and acquiesced. "I'll
continue on, but I want some promises we're going to work hard to
make some real headway."

"I think we can do that," Bainer replied glancing around the
table.

Carl picked up his papers and moved to the vacant chair at the
head of the table fifteen feet away.

He immediately dropped his gavel and said, "The meeting for purposes of reconciling the differences between the House and Senate versions of the 'War on the Deficit' is now called to order on this, the eighteenth of February, 2018. Who would like to open the meeting?"

"I'd like to make a statement in hopes of setting the tone for this meeting," Senator Bruce Bennett said.

"You may proceed," Nevin said.

"I would like to say that I hope we can all come together and make some responsible choices, some responsible compromises that will change the very course of our country. This could be recognized in years to come as a turning point in the history of our nation, where we embarked upon a path of fiscal sensibility with a vast new revenue source and some long overdue spending cuts. A path where we begin a serious reduction in the enormous debt we and our children face."

"Humpf," Cobbings snorted.

Bennett's face reddened, but he bit his tongue and held silent.

After a moment of consideration Coryn took the lead and said, "I move that any wording regarding the Financial Transaction Fee be stricken and that the military base closure be reduced from eighty in the next seven years to sixty."

There it was, the gauntlet had hit the table once again.

Portman was the first to speak. "Are you saying you'll accept no transaction fee whatsoever?"

"Don't forget," Cobbings said with a sneer, "we never had a chance to amend the bill in the House due to a low down dirty trick."

"I believe it was voted on, was it not?" Representative Kathryn Morris Rodgers stated firmly.

Cobbings snorted again. "If you wish to call it that, you may do so."

"Well then perhaps we should consider changing the task completely and have no new revenue stream, which means we'll need to close 200 bases and cut military spending in other areas like pulling all our troops out of Afghanistan and Iraq and Libya within six months," Bennett said.

"That will never fly," Bainer said.

"It's worth a try," Bennett replied staring Bainer down. "I can summon my assistant and get the wording rolling in a matter of minutes."

Bainer glared at the young House member.

"Or I'll add it as a rider once we get something passed here," threatened Bennett.

"I've sat on the Armed Services Committee, and I can guarantee a 200 base cut is never going to fly," Whitback interrupted.

"Maybe we should lock in those low interest rates the bankers have agreed to and make them permanent. We can amend the wording and include a clause doing just that," representative Rosa Sparks suggested. "My constituents would love it."

"Point of Order," Bainer snarled, turning to the chair. "Carl, I object. The sole purpose of a Conference Committee is to reconcile the differences between the House and Senate versions of the bill. The bank rates were a voluntary gesture. As you know, there is no provision in the Conference Committee rules allowing for new amendments."

"You yourself said this is the most informal of meetings," Carl replied. "I'll listen to whatever you folks want to bring up."

"I move to adjourn," Cobbings said in a low threatening tone. "This is nonsense."

"We have barely begun," Senator Kathryn Morris Rodgers said, looking about the table in dismay.

"I second the motion."

"Meeting adjourned," Carl Nevin quickly said with obvious relief in his voice as he banged the gavel down, "until Thursday, February 21st at ten a.m."

The news of the shortest Conference Committee meeting in history quickly made the rounds of the Hill, but what was perhaps more important was the rumor that a summons requesting Nick Cobbings appear before the House Ethics Committee for a preliminary investigation at 10:00 a.m. the following morning had been served.

Meanwhile, later that evening two plain clothes policemen knocked on John Bainer's front door and gently insisted he come with them for questioning. He made his one phone call to his personal attorney and was humbly escorted to the waiting unmarked car.

Senator Wade Biggs opened his mail when he got home and discovered the video disk and note. Puzzled, he retreated to his home office, clicked on his desktop PC and inserted the disk. A moment later he could clearly see his face and that of his red headed assistant Maggie seated in a restaurant. The camera then panned down and showed his hand caressing the inside of her thigh and her hand moving his away while she said in hushed laughter, "Not here, Wade."

The Chair of the Senate Finance Committee looked furtively about, shut the computer down, broke the disk into many pieces, took it out to the garage and pushed it deep into the trash. In a quiet seething rage he marched back into the house and sat in his office, read the note several more times and then quietly began making calls to a number of his friends in the Senate attempting to explain why he was changing his position on SB 1190.

Lastly, several dozen members of the Senate received the photos from the Four Seasons party and the accompanying letter. There was much anguish, gnashing of teeth and sleepless nights, but more importantly there was a decisive change in the attitude towards SB 1190. Apparently the bill did have some merit after all. They all began to see the light and beat a hasty retreat from their previous stance regarding the bill.

Graham received his and promptly put a call in to Doc Hastings, explained what had happened and concluded by saying, "I want to know who is behind this. Spend whatever you must, but I want answers."

Doc put a call in to Soro saying, "Hire whoever you must. We need answers. The two jokers you roughed up will be your best lead. They must have been hired by someone. Find out and find out fast."

"I'd be glad to but the two jokers burned my Escalade. I won't have wheels for another day or two," Soro lamented.

"Rent a car and send me the bill. Get moving," was Hastings' terse reply.

# Chapter Forty-Four

ELLIOTT SIPPED HIS coffee on the covered deck while Greer forked hay to the horses. He'd taken his fistful of pills and some of the new pain pills Dr. Yates prescribed. 'The tiny pink pills really worked quite well,' Elliott concluded, for he felt better than he had in several weeks. He was reading The Washington Post and flipped to page two where a long article began by asking the question; 'What is going on behind closed doors on the Hill?'

The article speculated about the nature of the acrimonious debate which had led to one of the shortest committee meetings in congressional history. It went further saying; "This author would give his right arm to be a fly on the wall in that room. Cobbings, Bainer, Graham, Coryn, Biggs and Whitback wrangling with Carimendi, Bishop, Bennett, Portman, Spitzer, Kathryn Morris and Rosa Sparks is like Cardinal Richelieu's men against the King's Musketeers. There can only be one outcome; winner takes all. A gathering that is designed to promote a meeting of the minds and some measure of compromise is now filled with those that would rather bury each other in a pit and fill it with lime. Will one of the most significant bills since the Civil Rights Act wind up dead because a handful of people with utterly opposing views were locked in a room for a few days? It would be disgraceful if they can't give us something worthwhile to work with considering the impact on American life this bill would have. The shortness of the meeting bodes ill for the fate of the bill."

Elliott was just starting on a full a page article in Time Magazine with the heading of 'The Legislation of Visionaries' when his phone rang. He noted it was the President's cell and answered.

"Talk to me Paul."

"What the hell did you do?"

"What do you mean?"

"One moment Graham, Cobbings, Bainer and company are ringing up votes like a Wal-Mart cashier and the next thing I know they're being shunned like lepers at a pool party!" The excitement in his tone was hard to disguise.

"I can't say I did anything other than set a few wheels in motion."

"Well, those wheels are rolling all right. My people on the hill are telling me vast changes are afoot. Cobbings is contemplating recusing himself from the Conference Committee. Bainer and Cobbings are both possibly under investigation by the Ethics Committee. Thirty of the Conference Committee members are beginning to suggest the bill is perfect in present form. And word has it another forty not on the committee are actively urging their protégés to move forward with a vote in the affirmative when the bill comes out of committee," the President concluded with undeniable joy in his voice.

"That's terrific news," Elliott exclaimed.

"I know. My spies on the hill hear whispers we may have it out of the Conference Committee with the Senate and House members agreeing to the House version within three days."

"The House version was unchanged from the original version," Elliott said softly. "Could we be so lucky?"

"From what I'm hearing we just could, and then it goes on the legislative calendar for three days before it can be heard on the floor," Paul added, calculating the number of days.

Elliott let out a low whistle. "We're so close."

He could feel the excitement growing within him.

"I was thinking, considering a worst case scenario, if it doesn't get out of committee," Paul said in a decidedly different and more serious tone, "I've got an idea for calling an emergency session of the joint houses of Congress so a few guest speakers can voice their opinions regarding the bill. We've talked about that before. Anthony Lascala, the Treasury Secretary will address Congress regarding the Financial Transaction fee. Bob Gates, the former Commander-in-Chief of the Armed Forces will speak regarding base closures along with several others and, well, I'd like you to speak also."

"I don't know Paul. I've been away from Congress for what, eight years? Half those freshmen congressmen have no idea who I am. I doubt my presence would prove much good."

"My friend, you underestimate yourself. A lot of these young congress people remember you and me in their growing years. They remember how president after president granted Big Pharma years of locked in profits by eliminating Medicare's ability to negotiate for cheaper prescription drugs, and how you and I took them on and crushed them. We reduced the senior citizen's drug costs by a trillion a year."

"That was a fight," Elliott agreed, "and a good win."

"And they remember Libya and how we almost got caught up in a land war. We shot that down."

"I think you're being a little generous towards us. There are thirty bases scattered about Libya and we've got 80,000 troops still there."

"Yeah, between the two of us and some major arm twisting we got us out of a major land war there. Our bases were built by Exxon-Mobil and are concentrated in the area of the oil fields of Libya."

"Yeah, didn't see that one coming," Elliott said wryly.

"Sure, but you understand what I'm saying," Paul concluded. "Many in Congress still remember the ferocity of the Master Sergeant when his sense of fair play was offended. And that's why I have to insist on your speaking."

"Paul, please, I have no idea what I'd say."

"Elliott, I'm the President. I expect to see you in Washington in 48 hours. Air Force One will be in Colorado Springs evening after next."

"Wait Paul, I've got something to tell you … !" Elliott cried, but the line was dead.

For a moment he was tempted to call Paul back and inform him that he was dying of cancer, but instead he slowly set the phone down. Suddenly Elliott found himself with a beaming smile spreading across his face. They had not played by the rules, not by a long shot, but by God it looked like they were going to do it. They were on the brink of the most massive change in the fate of the nation since the end of World War II! It felt good.


But there was the next step which was critically important. He swiftly dialed Stephanie's number. She answered on the first ring.

"Steph, its Elliott. From what I'm hearing the bill may be out of committee in three days and then it has to sit on the legislative calendar for three more days before it can go to vote. So we're less than a week away … !"

"Wait, slow down. Are you saying it's going to come out of Conference Committee with no amendments?"

"That's what I'm hearing."

"Oh Elliott, you've done it! You are the most wonderful man on earth!"

"Stephanie, I didn't do this alone and there's still much that could go wrong."

"Don't you even go there, Mr. Eastman!"

"Alright, alright, don't get your Irish up. The purpose of this call is to alert you that your part of the task just kicked in."

"AARP has the Minute Men ready to go along with tens of thousands more members. The websites that are in support of SB 1190 are unbelievable. There are literally thousands of them. Common Cause, Alliance for Democracy, Policy Watch, True Majority Action, Taxpayers for Common Sense, Center on Budget and Policy Priorities, United for a Fair Economy, Washington Tax Fairness Coalition, People for the American Way and a hundred others. It's going to be amazing."

Elliott sounded a little choked up when he said, "Thank you so much for doing such a marvelous job."

"It was my pleasure. I've set it up as a group e-mail so I press one key, type my message and it goes out to hundreds of people and websites simultaneously."

"Terrific work, Steph."

"Thank you Mr. Senator. I assume you'll be traveling to Washington soon."

"I might."

"You promised to let me know."

"I will. I'll let you know as soon as I have a flight scheduled."

"Okay."

"Bye."


Elliott stood up and steadied himself, then quickly sat back down. It was one of those surreal moments when he wasn't sure if he was dreaming or not, but it was happening. SB 1190 was going to the floor. Standing up again he stepped out onto the deck.

"Greer!" he cried. "Greer!"

The butler looked up from where he was slopping the hogs.

"SB 1190 is going to the floor! It's a tequila morning!"

The two old friends hadn't had a tequila morning in years. There was one when Elliott returned home from Iraq, another when he had been elected to the Senate and then again when he'd retired from the Senate, but that seemed a lifetime ago.

Elliott could see his main man's smile from forty feet away as he said, "Not to worry boss, I got the limes cutting in my mind already."

While Greer gathered limes from the block house, Elliott stepped back inside to the bar where he reached to the top shelf and pulled down a twenty year old bottle of Asombroso Reserva Del Porto; arguably the finest and most expensive tequila in the world. The two men sat on the deck smiling like young boys with a brand new video game. Elliott filled Greer in on the latest developments. Several shots later Elliott stood and announced, "I feel like singing, but I don't know what song to sing."

"I know what I'd be singing," Greer said.

"Really, and what would that be?"

"I Feel Good."

"Hmmm, a little James Brown might be just the thing."

Elliott did his best impersonation of the bump and grind while he belted out the first refrain, and then tried the classic James Brown pirouette. He was three quarters around when a loud crack sounded and he fell to the deck clutching his right ankle. Greer was instantly on his feet by Elliott's side.

"I think I broke my damn ankle," Elliott said through gritted teeth.

"You stay right here. I'll call Dr. Yates."

Before he rushed off for the phone Greer took one last glance at Elliott. Their eyes met. Elliott said, "Be sure to tell him it's my good leg."

The two men gazed at each other for a moment longer, and then Greer said, "you only got one," and burst into laughter. Elliott followed suit.

# Chapter Forty-Five

THE THIRD DAY after his fall Elliott was resting comfortably in a private hospital room and waiting to be fitted with a walking cast. Dr. Yates spoke several times with the attending physician and insisted tests be run to determine if the bone cancer had spread and if the ankle was made particularly weak as a result of the cancer. The physician performed his job admirably and also made sure that Elliott's painkillers, which he no longer resisted taking, were very effective. The tests revealed the bone cancer had spread, but there was no conclusive evidence that the ankle break could be attributed to that unfortunate development.

At the same time, Elliott was watching C-Span and fielding calls from Phoebe, the President's personal secretary, who'd been instructed to keep him informed of the action in the Conference Committee. Apparently there had been an extremely begrudging acceptance of all the parameters of the bill. As required by the rules of Conference Committee, a Joint Explanatory Statement must accompany the report. The deep divisions within the committee revealed themselves in the Joint Explanation. The statements by Cobbings, Bainer, Whitback and Graham revealed the depth of their anger at being coerced by unseen forces into agreeing to the bill.

Whitback was predictably demurring in his criticism of the bill saying 'the true costs to the economy are unknown at this time.'

Bainer was more forceful in his critique saying it was a 'poorly designed bill with many flaws yet to reveal themselves,' while Cobbings barely concealed rage appeared as 'the true cost of the measure and the damage done to the economy will take generations to repair.'

Those in support of the bill sang a different tune. Bennett praised it saying, 'I am proud to advance this bill to those charged with the stewardship of America, for this single bill will return America to prosperity and its rightful place as the world's richest economy.' Portman went on to say, 'it is with tremendous confidence I endorse the first major economic initiative which will restore America's position of greatness and even more importantly restore the faith of everyday Americans in their elected officials.'

Rosa Sparks said in her normal blunt fashion, 'America's future had begun to dim but this bill paints a brighter picture of the future than many of us could have imagined.'

So the Conference Committee report and the Joint Explanatory report were placed on the legislative calendar and expected to be opened to floor debate in three legislative days which, taking into account the weekend, was a mere five days away.

The cast was placed on the injured limb and an hour later the doctor stepped back in the room and said, "Here are your release papers. Please sign where indicated by red arrows. If there is any discomfort please call me directly. Here is my card with my direct line."

"Thanks Doc," Elliott said. "You could do one more thing for me. Could you direct me to a phone? I want to arrange for a ride."

"I'm sorry. I thought one of the nurses told you. There's a taxi out front ready to take you to the airport where Air Force One is waiting for you."

For a moment Elliott was taken aback, but then he said, "Not Air Force One again. I told him I was tired of the same old ride. I guess I'm going to Washington."

Smiling, the doctor said, "It would seem so."

# Chapter Forty-Six

ELLIOTT SAT IN bed leaning against a pile of pillows dressed in pajamas and a silk robe, surrounded by crumpled pieces of paper.

"What a time to get writer's block," he grumbled as he crushed yet another piece of paper and tossed it on the floor. He'd spoken briefly with the President who had insisted he prepare a speech on the defense spending aspect of SB 1190, just in case.

"People respect you and will listen to you."

Elliott agreed to the request, but felt defense spending was a no-brainer. There were larger issues that demanded immediate attention that he wanted to address. The President was not sure when Elliott might be called upon, but instructed him to be ready.

Setting the legal pad down on the bed beside him he picked up the TV remote and began flipping through the news channels. He stopped on a channel and listened to Bono saying, "So here it is people; the time is now. You, each and every one of you, have an opportunity to change the world, a chance to change your future and the future of your children for generations to come. So get out there. Get out to the Capitol and make your voices heard. I am Bono and I paid for this message."

Elliott smiled and said to the television screen, "Nice work Bono. You're a good man."

He continued clicking through the channels and stopped at MSNBC where a news anchor said, "Now we'll go to our man at the Capitol Mall, Jim Fields. How's it going out there, Jim?"

"It's an unbelievable scene here, Bob. I hope you can hear me. There has got to be at least a half million people here. Pennsylvania and Independence Avenues are shut down. People are bathing in the reflecting pool. The music you hear is Bon Jovi live belting out, 'It's my life, it's now or never,' which seems to be the anthem of the day. Taylor Swift has already been on. Crosby, Stills and Nash are scheduled for later. Stevie Wonder and Bob Dylan are going to sing a duet of 'Blowin' in the Wind' tonight. Rumor has it Sir Paul McCartney has enlisted Mick Jagger, Keith Richards and others to join him in singing, 'You Can't Always get What You Want' and 'Gimme Shelter'. Clint Black, Tim McGraw and Faith Hill are scheduled to sing tomorrow. Jackson Browne is rumored to have written a song called, 'Don't Tread on 1190' and is going to debut it tomorrow. Bono has coaxed John Mayer to join him in a duet of 'Waitin' on the World to Change.'"

As Jim spoke into the camera, behind him a young man in stocking cap, with a stubble of beard on his chin and a broad smile, jiggled a sign from side to side that asked the question; 'I don't own a derivative. Do you?'

Elliott switched to CNN. The newsman was standing on a small ridge of grass overlooking the Potomac saying, "All manner of vessels are out there. From ninety foot yachts, Boston Whalers, canoes and rubber dinghies, they come in all shapes and sizes. Some are saying they have never seen so many ships crowding the Potomac since the inauguration of Teddy Roosevelt. They have filled the tidal pool behind the White House and the nearby Atascosa River. I would guess that one could walk from one shore to the other without getting ones feet wet! Back to you Marie."

"And by the looks of it one might agree with you. I can't see any water at all," the news anchor in the studio said with a laugh.

Elliott changed channels to a local affiliate.

"Traffic is snarled for fifty miles in every direction," the newswoman was saying, "and our eye in the sky says it's going to get worse as traffic levels are elevated for this time of day in every major artery leading into the city."

Elliott felt a smile cross his lips.

'Stephanie you are an angel,' he thought.

For a moment his hand was poised near his cell ready to call her, but then a sudden rush of nausea overwhelmed him and he hobbled from the bed to the bathroom where he threw up violently several times. Returning to the vanity, he washed his mouth out and stared at himself in the mirror. It was a haggard, worn countenance that stared back at him. His 'moon-faced' appearance had waned and his cheeks were now sunken and hollow. It was a death's head he was looking at. Wobbling between his prosthesis and cast he managed to stand on the scale for a few seconds. He weighed 157 pounds. Subtracting about ten pounds for his plaster cast and robes he was less than 150 pounds. 'I haven't weighed less than 150 since my freshman year in high school,' he thought. With a measure of dejection he returned to the bedroom and picked up the notepad again. He'd lost sixty pounds in the last two and a half months. 'How much time do I have left?' he wondered. Dr. Yates had guesstimated six months. That was three months ago, and he felt Yates was being overly optimistic. Could he last one more?

He began to write.

# Chapter Forty-Seven

THE HOUSE OF Representatives chambers were packed with reporters from every corner of the globe. Cameras flashed as the Speaker of the House, Nick Cobbings was introduced by the Presiding Officer and he approached the podium.

"House will come to order. Members please register."

He turned to the Clerk of the House, "Have all registered?"

The clerk nodded.

"A quorum is present. The Chair recognizes Representative Brian Hughes to introduce our pastor of the day."

Brian Hughes stood saying, "Thank you, Mr. Speaker. Members, it is my pleasure to introduce Pastor Don Garner to lead us in prayer this morning."

The pastor stepped up to the podium and read the prayer of the day. When the Pastor was done, the Pledge of Allegiance was recited by every member of Congress. The Speaker then stepped forward and said, "The House is now in session. Is there any unfinished business? None?"

Representative Rosa Sparks stood to be recognized.

"The Chair recognizes Representative Sparks."

"Thank you Mr. Speaker. Esteemed members of the House; The Conference Committee Report, supported by 850 pages of the joint explanatory statement, has concluded that the bill as written has been approved by the committee with the recommendation that the Senate recede from their amendments. I move we proceed to consideration of the report, and with a quorum being present, I further move we vote on the conference report. I return the floor to the Speaker."

Representative Bruce Bennett stood.

"The Chair recognizes Representative Bennett."

"Thank you Mr. Speaker. I second the motion."

"No objections?" Speaker Cobbings said slowly.

No one spoke.

It was difficult for Cobbings to send the conference report to vote. He was reliving the embarrassment he'd experienced just a few weeks before. He decided to delay as long as possible.

"I will remind the members that the conference report is open to debate under the one hour rule."

No one spoke.

The faint strains of Crosby, Stills, Nash and Young's famous anthem, 'Treat your Children Well' penetrated the thick walls of the building.

"We will now move to a reading of the Conference Committee Report," Cobbings said.

Representative Portman understood this was another delaying tactic. The report was 350 pages and the joint statement was another 850. It would take days to read. Portman stood up instantly.

"The Chair recognizes Representative Portman."

"Thank you, Mr. Speaker. I move for a vote by unanimous consent to waive the reading."

Representative Sparks stood.

"The Speaker recognizes Representative Sparks."

"Thank you Mr. Speaker. I second the motion."

Representative Bainer stood to be recognized.

"The Chair recognizes Representative Bainer."

"I move for a Motion to Recess."

"Recess? We just got here," Portman said.

Cobbings slammed the gavel down. "You are out of order, Representative Portman. You will wait for the Chair to recognize you before speaking."

Representative Bennett stood to be recognized. Cobbings was tired.

"The Chair recognizes Representative Bennett."

"Thank you, Mr. Speaker. I would like to remind the Chair that a Conference Committee report is considered privileged business. The vote should move forward as requested."

"Acknowledged, Representative Bennett, the House will proceed to a Unanimous Consent vote to waive the reading of the bill."

The ayes carried the vote easily.

"They ayes have it," Cobbings said. "The House will now move to an electronic vote on the Conference Committee report asking the Senate to recede from the addition of the three amendments."

It took less than a half hour for the vote to be completed. SB 1190 was approved by a vote of 418 for, 12 against and 5 abstaining, and it was forwarded to the Senate for final approval.

# Chapter Forty-Eight

AFTER THE VOTE Cobbings, Graham, Bainer and Coryn met in Cobbings' office. There was an air of resignation in the room.

"We cannot amend a conference report in the Senate," Graham said.

"You could try a filibuster," Coryn offered.

"Listen to the people out there," Bainer said. "There must be a million or so. Do you want to be identified as the Senator who attempts a filibuster?"

"Certainly not," Coryn responded. "Besides, they will just invoke cloture and close out the filibuster."

"These are not the days of 'Mr. Smith Goes to Washington,'" Bainer growled.

The four men fell into silence.

"We can send it back to conference committee by refusing to recede," Coryn suggested.

"There is a lot of support for the bill in the Senate. We don't have the votes to send it back," Graham said.

"The big banks are going to have our asses," Cobbings said. "I'll never get re-elected."

"Apparently the President has already sent a message to the Clerk of the Senate indicating he'll sign the bill if the Senate approves the House version," Graham announced in a dull monotone.

"You know, it's far more difficult to kill legislation when the whole world is watching. How did we get into this situation?" Cobbings lamented.

"Somebody out there has been coordinating this from behind the scenes. Somebody with a lot of money and willing to break the rules," growled Bainer with a quick squint-eyed look at Cobbings, "but as they say, it's never over till the fat lady sings."

"You say the President has already said he'll sign the bill?" Bainer asked Graham.

"That's what I heard."

Bainer rubbed the stubble on his chin between his thumb and forefinger. "Maybe we can set this up so the President can't do anything but veto it."

As much as Graham disliked the fat man with the gimlet eyes and bulbous red nose, his political acumen was undeniable.

"What have you got in mind?" Graham asked.

"A little of the old tried and true, but this time a massive dose of it," Bainer explained.

"Talk to us," Cobbings demanded.

A half hour later the men shook hands, each tasked with their own part of the plan and the meeting broke up.

# Chapter Forty-Nine

ELLIOTT FELL ASLEEP on his hotel room couch while watching the evening news. Several of the news feeds showed the reaction of the crowd when word reached it that the House had passed SB 1190 with instructions suggesting the Senate recede from their previous amendments. An enormous roar akin to the sound of six 747s landing blew through the crowd. The ground shook. People were hugging. Many men and women were in tears. One fellow on top of an RV painted in American flags, who had become a favorite of the media, was waving a banner which read: "Senate. Don't tread on SB 1190!"

The noise from the T.V. brought a groggy Elliott back to awareness. Soon he was bouncing between stations with his grin widening by the moment. Charlie Rose was interviewing former Treasury Secretary Thomas Guttner who said, "If the 'War on The Deficit' can get through the House and the Conference Committees, as it just did it might just have a chance to pass the Senate, although the Senate was where the last amending process threw a wrench in the works. If it does pass, we are looking at many structural changes to the way Americans live."

On 'The Last Word with Lawrence O'Donnell', Lawrence interviewed retired General Robert Gates who commented; "The bill is well thought out and grounded in common sense. It ought to pass, and I think it will. This Congress is showing that it may have more common sense than others we've seen in the past."

Jon Stewart opened his evening comedy show with a minute of silence showing the thousands of people on the Capitol Mall as news of the House passage surged amongst them.

Jon turned to his audience and said, "I know this is supposed to be a comedy show, but I'd like to take a moment to get serious and simply speak from the bottom of my heart. We might just be witnessing one of America's finest hours. If they can get this deal done, then I will truly believe a new day has dawned in America."

His audience roared their approval.

Elliott dozed off as one of the late evening pundits was asking a guest, "exactly how much has the roll of populist pressure played in getting the 'War on the Deficit' bill so close to becoming law?"


Elliott woke up around two a.m. with a bulging bladder. He found his cane and limped his way to the restroom. Slowly easing himself into a sitting position on the john he murmured, "Such tired, tired bones."

His mind wandered until he realized he wasn't going. He pushed as best he could, but still nothing happened. He tried urinating off and on for the next two hours with no success. Finally, with the pressure becoming unbearable, he called Dr. Yates.

"Hello," a sleepy voice said.

"Doc? Hi, it's Elliott Eastman. I have a problem which I don't think can be described in a graceful way. My bladder is killing me. I can't take a leak."

"How bad is it?" the doctor asked.

"Bad. I've been trying to go for hours and can't. I don't think I can take it much longer."

"Okay. I'm going to call Bethesda hospital and line up a doctor. You get yourself in a taxi and get over there right away."

"I'm on my way."

Forty-five minutes later Elliott was seated on the edge of a gurney having a slender tube inserted in his urethra. A moment later the urine began to flow.

After a few minutes Elliott released a large sigh and said, "Thank you so much, Doctor Glynn. That might be the best feeling in the entire world."

"I've heard patients say that before. Hopefully I will never have to experience it."

"Your personal physician Dr. Yates has asked me to take samples and hold you for observation."

"Hold me for how long?"

"I'll need to run some tests, but I think you'll grant me that time as I'm going to determine if this event is something which might occur again."

Elliott smiled. "Take all the time you need. I'd like to go out and buy a couple of newspapers to pass the time."

"Don't worry about it, Mr. Eastman. Dr. Yates explained you are having a little difficulty moving around. Being as you're a former Senator I'll just ask one of the nurses to pick them up on her way in. Why don't you jot down the names of the papers on the prescription pad?"

A half hour later Elliott was resting comfortably in a private room sipping a large black coffee and reading the New York Times. The front page showed the masses outside the Capitol Buildings. The headline read, "Woodstock II on Capitol Hill". The accompanying article went on to explain how the age of the Internet was connecting people and causes. A secondary article commented on the big names which had shown up to wow the crowd.

Elliott was just starting in on an article from the Financial Times which also showed the crowd, but delved into European reaction to the famed SB 1190 and the rising chorus calling for a financial transaction fee across the pond when his cell phone rang.

Archie was on the line. "So what do you think?" he asked.

"Nice work. We all came together when we needed too."

"Do you still need me? Goldie is starting to be a real pain. Ouch. You gotta start hitting me on my other shoulder. This one is simply one huge bruise."

Elliott chuckled. "I see you two are still getting along famously. If you don't mind, I'd like you and Goldie on standby for another few days until the final Senate vote."

"Roger that. Talk to you soon," Backspace replied and the line went dead.

Elliott was just returning to the article when his phone rang again. It was the President.

"How are things going? How do you feel?" Paul asked.

"Pretty darn good. I'm beginning to think we should start preparing a victory party."

"Not so fast. We still need to nurse it through the Senate."

"What's the word from your insiders in the Senate?"

"I can't say. It's hard to read, but I get the feeling something is going on that doesn't pass the smell test," Paul revealed.

"What makes you say that?"

"When you've been around Congress as long as I have you just get a sense of the undercurrents, but I'm having difficulty reading this one."

"I don't like the sound of that," Elliott admitted.

"We'll know soon enough. The Senate meets tomorrow morning. Keep your speech handy. We may not need it, but I'd like to know you're ready."

"I'm here, just keep me posted."

"I will. And by the way Elliott, since I let it be known that I'm ready and willing to sign SB 1190, my ratings are up to 79% of all voters."

Elliott released a low whistle. "That's up there with Kennedy at his high point."

"I know," the President crowed.

"There are good people in this land. Once they were made aware of the importance of this bill they stood up to be counted," Elliott said.

"My re-election is almost a sure thing."

"I won't argue with you there, but nothing is done until you sign the bill. Let's get this thing done and then we'll start tallying up your votes."

"Ever the voice of reason," the President said. "Talk to you soon."

Elliott hung up and his phone rang again.

"Hello, Elliott here."

"Elliott, it's Doctor Yates."

"Yes, Paul."

"There has been some damage to your bladder. You may have another episode like last night again. I can't say for sure. Your platelets and white blood cell counts are low."

"Meaning?"

"Your body is trying to fight back but losing the battle." Both men fell silent. "The unfortunate thing is if the urethra issues persist, the only answer is a colostomy bag."

"I'm not wearing some crap bag," Elliott argued, indignant at the thought.

"I knew you'd say that Elliott. We'll put that on the back burner for now, but listen, since you're at the hospital I've scheduled another series of radiation treatments."

Elliott groaned.

"I guess we may as well deliver all the bitter pills at once," Doctor Yates continued, "I've had your blood type for years and have asked a number of physician's groups to put out the word for a marrow donor. We may have someone who is willing to donate. We're doing blood tests to be sure he has no diseases such as hepatitis and the like."

"Okay, thanks Paul," Elliott said softly.

"I've also spoken with the staff at Bethesda and explained the importance of your position in the world and why the radiation treatment must be done in as precise and timely a manner as possible. They can have you prepped and in and out in two days, and that includes recovery time. It might help stave off further bladder issues, at least for a while."

Elliott imagined himself with a plastic bag slung around his waist and said, "Let's do it."

"Let me talk with Dr. Glynn and see how soon he can assemble his team and I'll get back to you."

"Thanks Doc."

# Chapter Fifty

ELLIOTT PLACED A call to the President at exactly 8:15 in the morning, when he knew the Commander-in-Chief would be winding up his morning oatmeal.

"Good morning Elliott. Your timing is perfect, as usual."

"Good morning Paul. A quick question; what do your people say is the pulse of the Senate regarding SB 1190?"

"My spies you mean?"

Elliott laughed. "Your word, not mine, but I was thinking about what you said last night about not being able to read the undercurrents in the Senate and, well, I was hoping you could expand on that."

"The word seems to be we might have a majority, but there are a large number of undecided, and the opposition is entrenched and unwavering. That's all I've got at the moment, but I'll let you know if I hear anything else. I think the raucous crowd is helping to sway opinion. How long can you keep them out there?"

"My people have arranged for various music legends to appear on different days. Morgan Freeman is going to give a speech at some point today, and I think Robert Redford is scheduled to say a few words right after, so we may be able to keep them at the Capital longer than we originally had hoped."

"Excellent, keep up the good work."

"Have a good day."


A thought had been lurking in the back of Elliott's mind, just an incomplete germ of an idea, but it had been growing. Elliott sat for a moment, went through the stored numbers on his phone and then placed a call to Senator Carl Carimendi. One of Carl's assistants answered. As soon as she found out it was Elliott on the line she put him right through.

"Elliott thanks for the call. It's been a long time."

"Yes, it has Carl. I wanted to personally call and say thanks for all that you and Roger Portman have been doing."

"Well thanks back at you, but we're just doing our job. We believe in this thing."

"Carl, the real reason for my call is to tell you how this vote is going to come down and ask you a question. You can bet the farm they are going to filibuster it, but here is the question. When we counter their filibuster with a Motion for Cloture, what usually happens?"

"Cloture essentially means 'closure', meaning the filibuster is over until we vote on the Cloture Motion, but still we must wait for two days for it to ripen on the calendar until it can be voted on."

"I understand, but what I'm asking is what happens to the filibuster? What does the opposition do?"

Carl thought for a moment. "Well, they know we have to wait forty-eight hours for the cloture vote, so there is no longer a need for a filibuster. Usually the Senator who has the floor, the one doing the filibuster, gives up the floor and the opposition leaves for their offices to take care of other business, or whatever," he answered slowly.

"Absolutely correct, now here's what we're going to do ..."


The conference report with the re-write striking the wording in the three amendments the Senate had proposed and reinserting the original wording passed by the House was entered on the Senate Calendar. After the normal Senate business was disposed of in the morning session, the consideration of SB 1190 began. Senator Thomas Coryn of Texas was still smarting from the tongue lashing he'd received from Senator Roger Portman at the Conference Committee meeting. Although only two days ago he had agreed with Cobbings and Bainer that a filibuster was a fruitless endeavor, he made the snap decision right then to move forward with one. He stood to be recognized. The Presiding Officer Pro Tem, Senator Will Campbell from Wyoming, said, "The chair recognizes the Honorable Senator Thomas Coryn from Texas."

"Thank you, Mr. Chairman. I have ambivalent thoughts regarding this bill. There might be a time and place for this legislation, but with the current weakness in the economy ..."

Elliott was watching on television from his hotel room, putting the finishing touches on his speech, when he heard Coryn begin speaking.

"Okay, here we go," he said to the screen. The filibuster was made possible by Senate Rules which allowed a Senator to speak as long as he or she wanted as long as they held the floor.

An hour later Coryn was still speaking and Elliott was starting to get agitated.

"How long are you going to wait before making the Cloture Motion?" he asked the screen.

When Senator Curt Graham stood to be recognized, and the Chair did so, he asked, "Would my colleague Senator Coryn yield for a question?"

Elliott shook his head. "Smart move, Graham."

Elliott knew if Graham had asked Coryn to yield the floor then the filibuster was over, but asking him to yield for a question allowed Coryn technically to continue to hold the floor, while Graham took his sweet time to ask his question. Essentially, Graham was giving his conspirator a little time for a breather. Coryn got a glass of water, two Starbucks double shots and some snack peanuts from one of the Senate Pages while Graham took a rather lengthy time to frame the background for his question. Six hours later, cots were brought into the Senate building in anticipation of a long filibuster as Coryn continued speaking into the night.

It was nearing midnight when Elliott saw a number of pages begin moving papers between various senators.

"Good work guys," Elliott said softly. He knew they were gathering the sixteen signatures required to invoke cloture. Cloture limited debate on a bill to only thirty hours after cloture was approved, thus ending a filibuster, but the Cloture Motion had to sit on the Senate Calendar ripening for two days before it could be voted on.

Senator Carl Carimendi of California stood to be recognized and spoke immediately. "The Senate submits sixteen signatures as required to make a Motion for Cloture."

Coryn slowly fell silent, but remained standing and Carimendi repeated his statement.

"The Cloture Motion has been presented in accordance with rule XXII. The chair directs the Clerk to read the motion," the Presiding Officer stated.

The legislative clerk stood and proceeded as ordered. "We, the undersigned Senators, in accordance with the provisions of rule XXII of the Standing Rules of the Senate, hereby move to bring to a close debate on Senate Bill 1190. Signatories are as follows: Senators, Carimendi, Portman, Batt, Morgan, Ampara, Roberts, Liu, Frontieri, Davis, Landry, Schlageter, Morales, West, Dumas, Hays, Lewis and Flynn."

Coryn sat down and glanced at his watch. It was well past midnight. He knew the Cloture Motion had to sit in layover for two days, so his work here was completed. Carl Carimendi stood to be recognized again.

"The Chair recognizes the good Senator from California."

"Thank you, Mr. Chairman. While we are all still here I would like to say a few words in regards to SB 1190 and the filibuster procedure in general. The urgency of reforming the Senate rules is evident from the increased usage of the filibuster in recent years. The filibuster again and again is being used as a de facto veto by the minority party. This is an abuse of power. And this bill, which I've studied in great detail, offers a blueprint for the future, the likes of which ..."

With those words Coryn, Graham and two dozen other Senators stood and made their way towards the exits.

Carimendi continued as he watched them leave. "This document offers not only a new revenue stream which doesn't hurt the common man, but ..."

A few minutes later Carimendi stopped and said softly, "Mr. Chairman, I would like to suggest the absence of a quorum."

"Good work," Elliott whispered as his hands began to sweat. He stood and began pacing as best he could without turning his back to the screen.

Puzzled, the Chairman Pro Tem Will Campbell shrugged and said, "The Clerk shall call the roll."

It took fifteen minutes but the clerk determined that a quorum, a majority of the senators, was present. Elliott knew most of the remaining senators in the room and all were, in varying degrees, in support of the bill.

"The Chair represents a quorum is present."

Senator Portman stood to be recognized.

"The Chair recognizes the good Senator."

"Thank you, Mr. Chairman. May I ask my good friend from California to yield two minutes of his time?"

"I yield the two minutes," Senator Carimendi agreed.

"Thank you, Senator. Mr. Chairman, I hereby lay the Motion for Cloture on the table."

"You're withdrawing the motion?" Chairman Campbell asked, surprise written across his face.

"Yes, Mr. Chairman."

Chairman Campbell waved the Senate Parliamentarian to come over. The two consulted briefly. The Senate Parliamentarian is the resident expert on Senate rules and procedure. They whispered back and forth for a short while longer and then turned to the Clerk and said, "It is so ordered. The Motion for Cloture on SB 1190 is hereby tabled."

"I yield the balance of my time back to Mr. Carimendi."

"C'mon guys, you can do this," Elliott whispered with his heart pounding.

Senator Carimendi spoke. "I move for the previous question before the body."

"What is before the body?" Chairman Campbell asked momentarily confused.

"SB 1190, that's what I was addressing before the honorable Senator Portman asked me to yield two minutes."

It was well past midnight. Chairman Campbell was growing tired, but his attention was suddenly sparked. 'They're executing a sort of modified nuclear option,' he thought, and sat straighter in his chair attempting to remember the next step required of him.

"C'mon Will, you've been around long enough," Elliott whispered. "You know what to do."

"I hereby make a parliamentary ruling citing the argument that the constitution requires that the will of the majority be effective on Senate rules and procedures. A quorum is present. A vote on the previous question is so ordered. The Clerk will conduct a roll call vote regarding SB 1190."

The Clerk, as duly ordered, began calling the roll where each senator was required to stand and state their yea or nay and their vote was then recorded by the Clerk. The vote seemed to take forever in Elliott's eyes. As each Senator stood and voted yea his anxiety grew. When the final vote was tallied by the Clerk a few minutes later, it was sixty-one yeas and seven nays.

"The yeas have it," the chairman said in a solemn tone.

"Mr. Chairman, I move to adjourn," Carimendi said.

Senator Portman stood and said, "I second the motion."

Campbell brought the gavel down. "Meeting adjourned."

Elliott stood stock still for a moment not sure he could believe his eyes. As he watched the senators shaking hands and congratulating each other the truth sunk in. It was a majority vote in the affirmative. The bill had been passed. As soon as the president signed it SB 1190 was law!

He wondered who he might call at one in the morning, but he didn't want to bother anyone this late.

"It's another tequila moment, Greer."

With that he called room service and ordered two tequilas on the rocks; one for Greer and one for himself.

# Chapter Fifty-One

THE PRESIDENT RECEIVED notice of the passage of SB
1190 at two in the morning. Around 5:00 a.m. Archie woke Goldie
with a nudge when he got a call from one of the operatives that it had
passed. Goldie gave a whoop and hopped out of bed, made coffee
and began texting her girlfriends.

Elliott's phone was in the charging station and he missed the
calls from the President and Archie. He was sitting up in bed in what
was in his opinion a far too revealing hospital gown waiting for the
last of the radiation team to arrive watching CNN and Headline
News. He'd requested copies of the Wall Street Journal, the New
York Times and the Washington Post be brought to him. They had
been delivered a short while ago. Each of the papers had the story
buried back in the last few pages of the front section, primarily
because most of the reporters had gone home by the time the vote
had gone down. Each newspaper hailed it as a major achievement.
CNN was discussing the impact of the million strong crowd on the
mall. Headline News was suggesting the people had carried the day
and was asking if a new third party had been created, calling it the
'We the People' party. And party it was. When news of the passage of

SB 1190 reached the masses on the Capitol Mall the music and love fest began in earnest.

Elliott was wheeled into the radiation room, but never the less he had a smile on his face.

"You seem awfully pleased for a fellow getting prepped for a rather strong dose of radiation," Doctor Glynn commented.

"It's a good day Doc. A very good day," was all Elliott said as they helped him into the radiation chamber.

# Chapter Fifty-Two

"THE BASTARDS! THE rotten stinking bastards. If I ever find out who these two are I'll have them strung up by their heels."

Even through the fog of recovering from the radiation treatment and feeling weak as a kitten Elliott understood something was very, very wrong and interrupted the President's rant asking, "What's happened?"

"While the approved bill was being typed at the Government Printing Office, someone in the Senate put a secret hold on it. It may never be released for my signature."

"Damn," Elliott whispered, feeling the nausea crawling up his throat.

"It's the same thing they did with the Whistle Blowers Act. The public and congressional proponents thought the bill had passed, but the secret hold killed it. How can they call this a democracy if one or two people can hold up or kill important legislation?"

"Don't lose hope. We can find out."

"Find out what?" Paul asked.

"We can guess who they are. Who were the most vociferous voices against the bill?"

"Obviously Coryn and Graham."

"Agreed, but we must be absolutely certain they were the ones who put the secret hold on the bill. What we need to do is ask the public to contact their senators and ask each of them if they were the Senator who put the hold on the bill. In fact, I'd like to see each senator sign a pledge swearing they are not the ones placing the hold. We need to be absolutely certain who put the hold on the bill before we can act. This is a process of elimination. We must have people call each of their individual senators and ask them point blank if they're the ones who have put the hold on. Once we know who it is, we'll plaster their names across the heavens. The public wants this bill passed, and if we can prove we know who is holding it up without a shadow of a doubt we can put an incredible amount of pressure on them to remove the hold. I'll contact some people I know and start the wheels in motion."

"I like it."

"I'll get the word out."

"How?"

"Paul, please trust me. I'll get it done, but I have to go now."

The President was about to say something but Elliott tossed the phone on the bed, threw the covers off of his legs and painfully made his way to the bathroom where he threw up. He threw up until his stomach was empty and then experienced dry heaves for another ten minutes. When he was done, his eyes were watering to the point he could barely see and the stomach acid had burned his throat raw. He crawled on all fours back to his bed and pulled himself up to a point where he could collapse face down on the mattress. As he fell asleep again, with a pounding headache the likes of which he'd never experienced before, he kept thinking he had a bone marrow transplant scheduled twelve hours from now.

# Chapter Fifty-Three

SORO MET WITH Senator Graham at about eight in the evening in the latter's home office. He'd parked down the street and walked up a side path to the Tudor mansion so no one would see him enter. He knocked softly on the side door and Graham let him in.

"Do you want a drink, Rick?" Graham asked.

"Sure, a gin and tonic sounds nice."

As Graham poured the drink he eyed Soros. The big man had a smug look on his face, so Graham knew he had some information for him.

"So what did you find out?"

"It took some digging, but I know a lot of people who know other people and ..."

"Get on with it Soro. I don't care who you know," Graham growled, handing the drink to his hired gun.

Momentarily taken aback, Soro continued with an abbreviated narration. "Their names are Edward Kelley and James Lally. They are both former Army Rangers who served in Iraq and re-upped on multiple occasions. And get this. Guess who their immediate superior was over there in Iraq?"

"Ike Eisenhower, how am I supposed to know?"

"The famed Master Sergeant, Elliott Eastman."

"Eastman?"

"Yep, and we have some satellite photos taken a couple of months ago when a pretty large gathering of men was at Mr. Eastman's ranch. Guess who was there?"

"Kelley and Lally?" Graham replied.

"Bingo."

Glancing away Graham said softly, "And that was a few weeks before the 'War on the Deficit' bill was brought to life."

"And we have confirmation that Eastman was in a meeting with the President and General Robert Gates at the White House a few days after that," Soro added.

"And both Gates and the President are strong backers of the bill. Of course, now it all makes sense," Graham breathed. "They needed strong financial backing and someone who knew his way around the Hill."

Soro stared at Graham as the Senator's face grew red. He pounded his fist on his desk.

"Eastman, you bastard!" Graham shouted so loud that dogs started barking nearby. "You've ruined me!"

"Ruined?"

"Yes, he's made the whole nation aware of his damn bill and they know I've opposed it. I'll never get reelected."

Soro watched the man across the desk from him with a measure of apprehension.

"I want him dead," Graham declared with a savage snarl.

Soro was getting a little uncomfortable at the man's demeanor.

"I don't do dead," he said in a hesitant manner.

"You do now," Graham said glaring at him.

"No, no I don't. I'll do drops for you and maybe crack a few heads, but killing is a different ball game. That can get me the chair."

"Do you know someone who does that kind of work?"

Soro thought for a second. "I can locate two or three."

Graham turned and pushed a picture aside and began turning a dial on a small safe built into the wall saying, "I want all three."

"It ain't gonna be cheap. They want $5000 up front and $5000 more when the job is done, plus expenses."

Graham closed the safe and handed Soro three bundles of bills. "Here is fifteen thousand and two grand more for tickets to Colorado. I'll cover any additional expenses and another fifteen thousand when the job is done. My name is not to be mentioned."

Rick glanced at the money in his hands and said, "Colorado? I think Eastman is in D.C."

"I want the job done in Colorado. There it will just be some old man who died in a failed robbery attempt," Graham explained coldly.

"He's a war hero. You don't think the news will get out?"

"Better there than here. He's a damn legend around here. Get going."

# Chapter Fifty-Four

ELLIOTT WAS SITTING up in bed and as usual had multiple newspapers in his lap and the television locked on C-SPAN. He muted the channel and placed a call to Archie.

He got Archie's voicemail and left a message. "Do me a favor Archie. I can't speak very well; I think I'm losing my voice. Please call Stephanie Wells and tell her to mobilize everyone. And get a video out on YouTube about the need for people to contact their senators. And put a full page exposé on the back page of the Wall Street Journal, wait, no scratch that; make it both the Wall Street Journal and the USA Today. I want it to read 'Two senators have put a Secret Hold on 'The War against the Deficit' bill. If two men can control a bill how can we call this a democracy? Contact your senator and find out if he or she put the hold on SB 1190.' And see if you can find some sort of written pledge we can include as a tear out. I want the senators to sign a pledge swearing they are not the ones placing the hold."

Elliott paused for a moment. "And then report it to Politico.com who will publish it on their website. Maybe Citizens Against Government Waste and any others you can think of too. Thanks Arch. Talk to you soon."

After he concluded his message Elliott shut off his phone, leaned back on his pillows and closed his eyes. He was tired of hotel rooms, lying on his backside in some bed, cell phones and most of all radiation treatments that left him sick and weak. He longed for the grand expanse of his Colorado ranch. Was he doing the right thing with his last few weeks of life? Maybe a trip down the Amazon River was in order, or a visit to the Pyramids of Egypt. One last long goodbye to this amazing planet might be in order. Or maybe he could do both; get this damn bill passed and then take a trip. He was planning these implausible possibilities when a polite knock sounded at his door.

"Come in," he said.

Doctor Glynn entered and sat on the edge of the bed.

"How are you feeling?"

"I feel like I'm spending my entire life in bed. I've felt better, but I'm okay. I'm having a little trouble talking."

"You probably have acute mucositis which is very common after an intense exposure to radiation. It's inflammation of the mouth and the GI tract. But I must say you are remarkably strong for your age. The radiation treatment you received is called an ablative procedure, meaning it was very strong which usually leaves most recipients down for a day or two."

"Thanks Doctor Glynn."

"We're approaching zero hour. I've got the bone marrow procedure scheduled to begin in a few hours. I've brought in an expert transplant team. I won't be doing the procedure myself, but I'll be standing by."

"Thank you Doctor. I appreciate your efforts."

"Now, the marrow donor is here. He's been thoroughly tested and the match is perfect. If you would like to meet him you're welcome to do so. He's in the waiting room."

"Yes, that would be a pleasure. I'd like to personally thank him," Elliott said. "Let me throw some clothes on and I'll be out in a minute."

Dr. Glynn smiled. "I wouldn't recommend that. You need every ounce of strength you can muster. I'll contact the nurses' station and ask them to send him in."

"Okay," Elliott agreed, gratefully easing back against the pillows and closing his eyes. He had no wish to be walking anywhere today.

A few minutes later Eddie Kelley silently opened the door and stepped into the room. Instantly he was taken aback by Elliott's appearance. He stopped in his tracks and then turning quietly, closed the door. Elliott was leaning back on his pillows and his eyes were closed. Eddie studied him for a moment and the big man suddenly found his eyes watering. For a moment he thought Elliott was dead. He'd lost much of his hair. His cheeks were hollow and deep dark circles ran under his eyes. He'd lost so much weight there was barely a bulge beneath the blankets. Wiping at his eyes, Eddie sat down on the edge of the bed and Elliott stirred.

"How you doing, boss?" Eddie said in soft tones.

Elliott opened his eyes and sat up in bed. Eddie noted the yellow evidence of jaundice in the former senator's eyes.

"Eddie, what are you doing here?" Elliott croaked.

"I'm your donor."

"You? But how did you know?"

Eddie smiled. "Elliott, you forget we've known you for thirty-five years. Archie was the first one to make the call. He sensed something was wrong and called several of us. He then hacked your phone and that of Doctor Yates."

"Why that sneaky little ... !" Elliott started in, but Eddie held up a hand.

"Don't blame Archie. We pushed him to do the hacking so we'd know what was going on with you. In fact, that's part of the reason I'm here."

"Who else knows?"

"There are only six or seven of us."

"Does Stephanie know?"

"None of us have told her anything."

The two men talked for another hour and a half and then they were called to begin the marrow transplant procedure.

# Chapter Fifty-Five

ARCHIE CALLED STEPHANIE and passed Elliott's words along to her. He then bought the full page advertisements in the newspapers. The banner headline read: "CAN TWO ANONYMOUS SENATORS HOLD UP THE DEMOCRATIC PROCESS?"

The text of the article below the banner explained what had taken place with SB 1190. The bill was passed and sent for typing where the tag team hold was put in place. The article explained what a tag team hold was and explained the need to identify the two perpetrators of this action. Beneath that was an urgent call for action asking the public to contact their senator's office demanding to know if they were the ones placing the hold.

In his next move Archie went a step further and had thousands of flyers printed up with Elliott's message. He asked a dozen of the former Army Rangers in Elliott's employ stationed in the D.C. area to hand deliver them to the masses on the Capitol Mall. Their outrage was immense. A sense of betrayal pervaded the crowd. In one instance they were celebrating the bill's passage and delirious with joy, and the next they were being told it was over. Senator's offices were besieged with calls. Many of the voting public, both young and old, showed up in front of their senator's offices demanding to know if they were placing the secret hold on SB 1190. A second YouTube video was released with split-second images of hundreds of average Americans gazing into the camera and asking one simple question: "Are you the one holding my bill hostage?"

Many of the websites Stephanie contacted instantly expressed outrage at this latest development and sent the information out in mass e-mailings to alert their members.

Within 24 hours the crescendo of anger reached a tipping point and the Senate called an emergency session to deal with it. Several senators stood and read particularly vicious e-mails they had received. Senator after senator stood demanding to know who placed the hold.

Vice President Jackson, the Presiding Officer of the Senate, pounded the gavel and demanded the Senate come to order. Ever the pragmatist and noted for his level headed demeanor, Jackson felt his anger growing and said, "As you know there is no requirement that those senators who placed the hold must reveal their names, so stop asking the question. We will now recess for one hour."

As the senators gathered their files and briefcases, Jackson instructed a Senate page to inform both Coryn and Graham to be in his office in ten minutes. Jackson was considered an easy going giant of a man. A six term senator from Mississippi, his soft southern drawl put people at ease, but could be very misleading. Those who knew him well knew once his feathers were ruffled he had a fearsome side as well.

Under tremendous pressure, Coryn and Graham met privately with Vice President Jackson. He knew they were the ones who were tag teaming the hold because they had to inform the Senate chair first. Initially Jackson had approved the hold, although at the same time he had second thoughts about approving it because there was much to admire about the bill, but he was also reluctant to arbitrarily amend what was a time honored part of Senate procedure. His opinion had since changed. He spoke with the senators at length, but they were adamant that it was a legitimate Senate action and within their rights as senators to continue to keep the hold in place. Vice President Jackson shook his head and simply said, "I don't recommend this course of action. I cannot say what the consequences might be."

The meeting ended in a deadlock. Three hours later, the process of elimination was complete. The torrent of e-mails, phone calls and personal appearances had done the job. With 98 senators pledging they were not the ones who placed the hold, the remaining two were identified. Within minutes the information raced across the Internet. Tens of thousands of protesters appeared at the senator's gated mansions that night. Rocks were thrown, fires were lit, and each senator was burned in effigy. The police were called in with tear gas and the crowds disbursed, but they reassembled later with thousands more showing up and staged a sit-in. The liberal talk shows vilified the two senators as un-American. The conservatives manhandled them as well.

The following morning, looking rather disheveled from a sleepless night, Coryn and Graham, under police escort, returned to the Senate for the morning session and withdrew the hold. C-SPAN covered what looked like a perp walk without the handcuffs for the two men. SB 1190 went to the Government Printing Office.

# Chapter Fifty-Six

SORO STRODE INTO the dark and dingy basement bar and pool hall below a rundown hotel on the edge of Harlem's lower east side. Glancing about the smoke filled room he spied the men he was to meet at a booth along the back wall. Making his way along the bar he crossed between two pool tables and slid into the empty chair beside the booth.

"Reggie," he said shaking hands with a heavy set man in a leather vest and bandanna around his head. "Glad to see you again."

"Same," Reggie replied through a brushy mustache. "This here is Bud and Hulk."

Richard nodded at a wiry man with tattoos up and down his arms and neck. Bud offered a sideways smile revealing a broken row of brown teeth. The aptly named Hulk, a veritable mountain of flesh sitting beside Bud, looked as though he could hold his own single handedly against the entire Green Bay Packers offensive line. The sleeves of his shirt were rolled up and contained a pack of Camel non-filters, but more telling was the fact that he had arms the size of most men's legs and a skull the size of a pumpkin sitting on a massive neck that showed knots of muscles.

Hulk merely grunted his greeting.

Reggie noted the white tape stretched across Richard's nose and the black eyes and asked, "So what happened to you."

"Oh this," Soro said absently reaching for the bandages in the center of his face. "Got jumped in an alleyway by a couple of guys, but I fought them off."

With a skeptical look Reggie demanded, "So gimme the straight scoop on the job again."

"It's an old man who has done something wrong against some very powerful people here in D.C. They want him eliminated as quietly and quickly as possible."

Richard slid an envelope across the table and said in a low tone, "There's three thousand for each of you and an extra two thousand for flights and cars and what not. There's also directions to the ranch in Colorado where the old man lives. When the job is done, and remember they want it done soon, there will be another $9,000 waiting for you."

Richard looked at Reggie's face as the man thumbed through the contents of the envelope. Apparently satisfied, the thug looked up at Soro and said, "I done some work like this a time or two and that second payment is sometimes hard to come by. If we have any trouble getting paid we'll be looking for you."

"I understand, but you don't need to worry about that. I know these people well."

"And we'll do the job our way. I don't like flyin' so we might just drive out there," Reggie explained.

"I don't like planes none at all," Hulk added in a voice that sounded as if it originated at the bottom of a well.

"How you want to do it is your own business. They just want him silenced soon."

"It'll be done inside a week."

"Good."

Richard, with a sigh of relief, left the building and was soon congratulating himself on making a quick six grand by under paying for the job, and another $6000 when the job was done.

A few hours later Reggie and company, armed with maps and high powered rifles, loaded some dirt bikes and a couple of cases of beer in the back of a van and headed for Colorado.

# Chapter Fifty-Seven

ELLIOTT CAME AROUND slowly. He felt as if he had survived a buffalo stampede, barely. Every muscle in his body was aflame. He felt as though he could barely move. For a moment he sensed an urge to call Doctor Glynn demanding to know why he'd downplayed the after effects of a bone marrow transplant. It was an overall downright awful feeling, but he decided he'd not complain. Rolling over on his side, resting his head on a pillow and opening one eye he reached for the television controller. He clicked it on and tuned it to C-SPAN; however they weren't showing the congressional floor activity. Instead the C-SPAN cameras were linked to an outside feed that showed the crowds on the mall. They were strangely silent, but the banners they paraded by with spoke volumes. Elliott hit the Tivo button to record this momentous event.

One read: THANK YOU TO THE FINEST GROUP OF MEN ON THE PLANET!

Another read: THIS IS AMERICA'S FINEST MOMENT. YOU'VE GOT MY VOTE!

And another said: A CONGRESS TO BE REMEMBERED.

The President watched from the Oval Office as he waited for the bill to arrive for signature. Around lunchtime he was called to the Congressional Hall for the official signing.

The crowd on the Capitol Mall had dwindled to approximately two hundred thousand as the days had gone by, but they waited in eager anticipation of the final signing of SB 1190. Many with notebook computers or iPads watched the proceedings on C-SPAN. Cameras flashed and news feeds from around the world followed every motion of President Paul White as he sat down, flanked by the Vice President and congressional leaders and began leafing through the pages of the bill as it lay on the table before him. The congressional secretary held the feather pen in readiness for the President to grasp it and sign. As the President neared the end of the document he suddenly paused and stiffened. The cameras caught him gaze intently at the document for a moment, flip through a few more pages, then stand and say, "I will not sign this bill."

He walked stiffly from the stunned and silent room. Outside, the masses stopped their celebration and questioned each other as to what was going on. The oft asked question was; "What just happened?"

Elliott was staring at the screen, rewound the scene several times and noted it was only when Paul flipped to the pages at the rear of the bill that he tensed and stopped reading. Elliott suspected he knew what it was that Paul had seen that bothered him so much.

A soft knock sounded on the door and Elliott muted the television. It was Doctor Glynn. "How are you feeling?"

"Pretty weak, but doing okay. Thanks for all your hard work, Doc."

"You had a pretty tough four days. Intense radiation and the bone marrow transplant, you may experience a number of different symptoms from these treatments, but one you can almost certainly count on is diarrhea."

"Terrific, you just made my day."

"There's a packet of Depends on your nightstand should you need them. I'll check on you in a couple of hours."

Elliott shook his head.

Chuckling, the doctor stepped out of the room.

# Chapter Fifty-Eight

THE PRESIDENT WALKED past Phoebe, his secretary, barely containing his rage and said, "I don't wish to be disturbed unless there's a nuclear war."

Elliott waited a few minutes for the President to return to the Oval Office and then called his private line. Paul answered on the first ring.

"Elliott, I can't sign that thing. Those bastards air-dropped more earmarks on it than I've ever seen before. It's a deficit reduction bill for God's sake."

"How bad are they?" Elliott asked, not sure he wanted to hear the answer.

"Graham has $21 million for a Gulf Coast Test Center and it doesn't even describe what's to be tested," disgust evident in his voice.

"Bainer has $5 million for a Natural Products Center. What the hell could that be? Coryn has $30 million for a Great Plains Regional Authority. Cardin has $382 million for the Chesapeake Watershed Conservation Program. Whitback has $9.6 million for an Automated Composite Technologies and Manufacturing Center. Doesn't that sound like something, which if it were really needed, private enterprise would have carved out a niche for already? Another similar one is Bond's Nanotechnology Enterprise Consortium for a cost of $15 million. Moran has $4 million for a Proton Therapy Institute. Cochran has $10 million for a Sustainable Energy Research Center. Don't we have a couple dozen of those already? Inhouye has $5.5 million for a Joint Education Center. What or who are they going to educate? Belosi has $5 million for the Presidio Heritage Center. Of course she omitted the fact that her family owns a number of properties in the immediate area. The list goes on and on, Elliott. There are thousands upon thousands of them."

The President fell silent for a moment and then said, "I know what they're up to. I have ten days to sign the bill or it dies forever. They want me to use a pocket veto to make this good bill disappear. They want to make it so onerous that no president in his right mind would sign it," Paul concluded with obvious sadness. "And they have succeeded."

Elliott sensed the President's obvious frustration and gave the situation some thought. They could call on the people again. They could publish the names of the congressperson along with their earmark, but that would be posted on many websites within a few hours anyway.

"What is the final tally of all the earmarks?" Elliott asked.

"Somewhere around 78 billion. It's the proverbial Christmas Tree bill."

Elliott released a low whistle, "They're shooting for a new record."

"By a long shot. I can't sign it, Elliott," the President said wearily. "I simply can't."

"Let me think Paul."

"It may cost me my presidency, but I don't believe a Debt Reduction bill of this magnitude should be treated as business as usual. I thought this was going to be an historic moment."

Elliott remained lost in thought.

"You know, this job ages you quickly," Paul said in a tired and deeply disappointed voice. "You see what goes on behind the scenes. You see how the American people are constantly being cheated by the special interests. All these earmarks are hard earned tax dollars by the American taxpayers, but they're being sent out the door to a favored few businesses and friends of this Congress who then see large portions of it funneled back into their re-election coffers. Elliott, are you there?"

"Yes, I'm thinking. I have an idea. You call for a joint meeting of Congress. We request cameras from every news organization in the world. Then we bring in speakers from the Congressional Budget Office, Tony Lascala from the Treasury, Sam Goldman from the Securities and Exchange Commission, Judith Ross, the Comptroller of Currency and Dick Henghold from the Office of Management and Budget to speak about the dangers to our society from our debt. Then you speak describing the earmark and who submitted it. Maybe even go into greater depth, stating how much the congressperson received in donations back from the company who is the beneficiary of the earmark. It would be like putting them in stocks in the old village square. Everyone in the world will see their faces. We'll embarrass them into withdrawing their earmarks."

"I like it, but I don't think we'll be able to keep their interest with all those speakers. We'll need to pare down the speakers list to three. General Gates would be excellent. He has a commanding presence, is a polished speaker and he believes deeply in the defense cuts we are proposing. Anthony Lascala would be good too. He understands the immensity of the numbers we're dealing with better than anyone and is quite fed up with the congressional shenanigans that have been going on, but I think I'd like another speaker," the President replied.

"Who do you have in mind?"

"You."

Elliott pondered for a moment and then asked, "Do you really think it will help?"

"I do. You've been working on your speech. You're famous for never making an earmark. A lot of these congress people remember you. You were one of them. If we can get half of these earmarks withdrawn I might sign it."

"I did call for one earmark," Elliott said, correcting the President.

"You call that an earmark?" the President retorted. "Two hundred thousand for shipping fifteen hundred wild mustangs slated for slaughter from Nevada to Colorado. The entire bill for that transfer was much higher and you paid for most of it out of your own pocket. You even provided the safe haven for those animals on your ranch property. That's not an earmark. Hell, that's a good day's postage for these guys."

"Okay. You go ahead and call the emergency joint meeting of Congress for two nights from now and I'll be there. But do me a favor, once the seating chart has been arranged can you get a copy to me? I want to be sure we have the proper face on camera when their earmark is announced. And let the bugles blare on this one; loads of fanfare and every news organization we can think of should be there," Elliott added.

"I'll have my Chief of Staff do the scheduling first thing in the morning and the press corps will be alerted as to the date and time."

"Thank you Mr. President. I'll talk with you later."


Elliott studied his haggard face in the mirror and said, "You look like crap."

He placed a call to Eddie.

"Hi Eddie. Can you do me a favor?"

"Sure thing."

"I've been shanghaied into giving a speech to the entire congressional body two nights from now and I was just looking at myself in the mirror. Well, this going to sound a little odd. I'd like to see if you can find somebody that can fix me up a good hairpiece and maybe a makeup artist and a Kevlar vest."

"A Kevlar vest? Do you think someone will try to drop you?"

"No, it's just that I've lost so much weight I feel like I'm a walking skeleton. I'd like to look a little healthier. A couple of shirts or what not won't do, I want something heavier."

"It might be easier to find you a double," Eddie said chuckling.

"I'd accept that too."

"Well, you know we got lots of vests. Let me see what I can do about the makeup and wig, Sarge."

"Thanks Eddie, but don't call it a wig, it's a toupee. And Eddie, thanks for the transplant too. I feel much better."

"I was happy to do it. Think nothing of it."

"How are you feeling?" Elliott asked.

"A little sore, but I'm fine. Don't worry about me."

The two men hung up and Elliott turned for the bathroom for the fifth time that morning. The nausea was almost unbearable. He had lied. He suspected his body was rejecting the marrow.

# Chapter Fifty-Nine

THE FOLLOWING MORNING, as Eddie drove across town to pick up a makeup kit and several styles of hairpieces, he listened to his Sirius XM radio which was tuned to the news and talk shows. It seemed the whole world was abuzz with speculation, first as to what exactly had prompted the President to refuse to sign the controversial bill. Others wondered as to what the emergency joint session was going to accomplish. The prevailing wisdom seemed to believe the two sides were so entrenched little could be accomplished. Eddie's phone call to Stephanie had proved beneficial as the word got out and the crowds on the Capital Mall were growing again.

Elliott sat in his usual spot. In bed with the news channels on and newspapers spread about him. The New York Times lead article announced, "Earmarks Crush Debt Deal" and the Washington Post chimed in, "Government at Standoff over Debt Debate". TIME Magazine rushed out a special edition with the title "Debt Chicanery: A look behind the Battle Lines". The Economist Magazine lit into the fray asking: "Can $78,000,000,000 still be called Earmarks"? The magazine went on to explore the question in greater depth, making note the dollar amount equaled the entire governmental outlays of some countries. The Associated Press ran a lead story, "Pet Projects no longer Out of the Public Eye".

Charlie Rose had as a special guest a former congressman who explained how the earmarking process worked and how it all got started.

"Nice work, guys," Elliott said to himself. "The word has certainly gotten out."


Archie and Goldie flew in the following afternoon a few hours before the joint session was set to begin, and Goldie took command of the hotel room. Once Elliott was showered and shaved, Goldie meticulously applied makeup until the former senator looked thirty years younger. She then selected one of the half dozen hairpieces, glued it in place and trimmed it as she saw fit. Archie and Eddie helped Elliott into his Kevlar vest, then into the tuxedo and finally the three assistants stopped to admire their handiwork.

"I'd say he looks very much like Prince Charming's twin brother. I think I deserve a kiss for all this effort," Goldie announced.

"I must agree, you do look pretty darn good for one of the walking wounded," Archie agreed.

Elliott studied himself in the mirror and agreed, "You know, I don't look half bad."

"Let's make it unanimous. You look one hell of a lot better than me," Eddie chimed in.

This drew laughter from the foursome.

"Shall we?" Elliott asked, picking up his cane and extending an arm towards Goldie who accepted it by circling her arm around his.

A taxi was waiting downstairs which whisked them to the congressional buildings. The entire complex was ablaze with lights. Extra security had been called in. Elliott had arranged for press passes for his three companions. Archie and Eddie were given control over two of the myriad swivel cameras along the walls and also given the seating charts the President had so generously provided. Elliott stood close by as Archie and Eddie took their places along the wall.

They were at their stations as the congress people and various guests began streaming in. Elliott said, "Well I guess I'm off. It's going to be show time in a moment. I don't really feel like doing this."

"Oh, go on Prince Charming. I'm sure you're going to be wonderful," Goldie exclaimed, standing on her tiptoes and giving Elliott a firm kiss on the lips.

"Hmm. Well, with that to fortify me I'll have at it," Elliott said with a smile.

Archie looked over at Eddie and said, "She was my woman once, but now it is over."

They were laughing, thoroughly amused as Elliott, leaning heavily on his cane, walked towards the rear of the stage.

# Chapter Sixty

THE PRESIDENT WAS seated on a raised dais at the back of the stage. The Vice President was seated beside him. Two enormous American flags were draped to either side of them and carved in marble above their heads were the words; 'In God We Trust.'

The Sergeant-at-Arms announced, "Ladies and Gentlemen, the President of the United States."

Applause filled the cavernous room as the President stood and approached the rostrum.

"Good evening ladies and gentlemen. I have asked you here this evening for a very specific purpose. I believe very deeply in the legislation that has recently been the subject of so much controversy, not only here, but in the press as well. I believe this legislation has been given very shoddy treatment in the committees of both Houses and was abused to an even greater degree in the committee conferences. I have invited three very distinguished speakers to lend some clarity to the content of this legislation. I hope you will hear them out and reserve judgment until that time. They are General Robert Gates, a decorated war veteran and former Secretary of Defense, Treasury Secretary Anthony Lascala, a Nobel laureate with a Masters Degree in Economics from Notre Dame, and lastly the former Senator from Colorado, war hero and recipient of the Purple Heart, who many of you know as the 'Master Sergeant', Elliott Eastman. Please give these men a grand welcome."

Applause again exploded around the room.

The Sergeant-at-Arms for the Senate, Terrence W. Garner approached the podium and introduced the first speaker; "Ladies and gentlemen, our first speaker, General Robert Gates."

Former General Gates stepped to the podium. The mass of faces in the main hall and in the galleries up above waited expectantly, cameras flashed by the hundreds, and applause rumbled throughout the building.

"Thank you Mr. President, Vice President and gentlepersons. The President has asked me to join you today. As I drove here I thought about where this great nation is and the course it is taking, the course that will lead to where we will be in the future. The future is defined by the past. I read an article recently about a group of eight or nine Afghan boys who were asked by their parents to go out and collect firewood. There were three brothers and several cousins all between the ages of nine and fourteen. I can imagine the grumbling as the children filed out the door of the hut. Apparently the sticks they were collecting looked vaguely like rifles. One of our gunships opened fire on them and blew them to smithereens. The article showed the weeping parents attempting to clutch to their breasts what remained of them. One was headless. I can only imagine what thoughts must be running through the mother's head. If only she had asked them ten minutes later to collect firewood, our gunship might have missed them."

General Gates paused for a moment, took a deep breath and continued.

"It reminded me of a cover of TIME magazine I remember seeing from 1965. I was growing up and quite impressionable at the time and the image stayed with me. The cover of TIME showed a

little Vietnamese girl whose clothing had been burned away by
napalm. She's running down the street naked and crying in pain.
She's screaming and running for her life. Running for her life, ladies
and gentlemen, running from the great and glorious American Army;
America, the author of peace and tranquility and democratic
principles around the world."

"That was sixty years ago. I ask you what is different between
those little boys gathering wood last week and this little girl so many
years ago. There is no difference; they are dead on the points of
American guns. They didn't know why America was there. They
didn't understand the nebulous reasons we find for war. This is not
World War II, where America stepped forward and saved the world
from true monsters such as Hitler and Mussolini. Vietnam, Laos,
Cambodia along with Iraq and Afghanistan don't have enormous
armies, nor navies or air forces. Those little boys had sticks and that
little girl, she had nothing, not even the clothes on her back. These
countries don't have missiles which can reach our shores. Let's be
honest with each other. These countries offer nothing in the way of a
threat to our country. I ask you, is it not time we think about what we
are doing abroad? Communism is dead. There are scattered bands of
Taliban and Al-Qaeda in far off places, armed in 19th century fashion
and posing little threat to our homeland. We are impoverishing our
people and trying to run the affairs of other countries. Do we need all
those bases around the world? Do we need to continue fooling
ourselves into believing we are the policemen of the world? Do we
need to follow down the same old tired path of empire until we are
bankrupt and simply can no longer support this ridiculous effort?
War is the engine of last resort. Isn't it time for something new in our
approach to the world? Isn't it time we no longer play the role of
bully in the world, shouldering our way into other countries at the
behest of our corporate strongmen? Let's take a moderate path. As
you know, I have been to war and I have sat where you sit now. If I

felt our great nation was under attack, I would be the first to step forward to defend it."

Again General Gates paused.

"Ladies and gentlemen, that's what I am doing right now. I come here to fight for our great nation. The biggest threat to our future is the continuing growth of our vast debt. SB 1190 is a real way to win that war. Cuts in defense spending, especially these useless military bases overseas in Germany, Japan and England, and a reduction in our military footprint around the world is part and parcel of what we need to do to grab the future and mold it into what this country deserves.

"One aircraft carrier battle group and one nuclear sub is more than enough to deal with the miniscule threats we face in the Middle East. So I ask that as you debate this bill, think of that little girl so long ago and those young boys so recently and think about what the future looks like for you and your children if we don't act, and act sensibly now. Thank you very much."

The Sergeant-at-Arms introduced the next speaker.

"Please welcome the distinguished Secretary of the Treasury, Anthony Lascala."

Anthony stood and approached the podium.

"Ladies and Gentlemen, I too thank you for your time and thank you for inviting me to speak to this august body on a matter of concern to all of us; the national debt which stands at over 18 trillion dollars. This is an unimaginable and unsustainable number. It is a number that no nation on earth has had to bear. It is a number that threatens our very existence. It is a number that as the interest payments grow will swallow all government revenue. These are facts. This is truth. Each of you can run the numbers yourself, although you will need a very large calculator."

A ripple of laughter coursed through the room.

"There was a point in time when this number would have left previous generations aghast and asking how on earth we managed to reach this point. We got here the same way we will get out of it; in incremental steps. It is a number that is too high to be paid down in any significant way by raising taxes. The burden is simply too great for our taxpayers to bear. It is too enormous to be done by cuts alone. It will impoverish future generations. At one time I fretted there was simply no way out of this nightmarish situation. I didn't see one. Great nations have been rent asunder by the very problems we now face. But as with the nature of this historically unsustainable number comes an improbable answer. An answer that is truly American in its breadth, scope and ingenuity. An answer that will restore America not to the same pedestal of great nations that have preceded it, but to a rung above them as is befitting our great American spirit and enterprise.

"The idea of a financial transaction tax has been around for some time. The esteemed economist John Maynard Keynes supported it in 1936 as a way to combat the ill of the Great Depression. It was floated as a bill in 2004, but died in the Senate. If only we had enacted it then, but the numbers have changed dramatically since 2004. By way of example, in 2004 the sum of all positions of Options and Futures contracts on the Chicago Mercantile Exchange amounted to $53 trillion. By 2008 they had grown to $81 trillion and today they stand at $115 trillion annually. With trading days per year at just over 200, that's over $750 billion dollars per day. Do you remember the anguish and vitriol accompanying the $780 billion Troubled Asset Relief Program almost a decade ago? The CME moves that much money every day, but that is just a drop in the bucket.

"The Over-the-Counter market which deals with investment banks, hedge funds, and commercial banks and deals in swaps, forward rate agreements, forward contracts, credit derivatives and foreign currency swaps has grown enormously as well. The sum of all trades in 2004 was $220 trillion; in 2009 it was $515 trillion and today stands at $723 trillion. And again, with the number of trading days at just over 200 that's 4.6 trillion trades a day. The New York stock exchange counts 1.8 million daily transactions while the NASDAQ counts 3.2 billion trades per day, and please remember, there are two sides to every trade. So the flat fee aspect on all trades as structured in SB 1190 will amount to approximately 1.5 trillion to 2.5 trillion dollars each year, and that my friends is a very, very conservative number. We can extinguish our national debt in a matter of 4.5 short years, certainly no more than 6.5 years."

A hushed intake of breath gushed from the room followed quickly by a complete and utter silence.

Anthony lowered his voice to a more conspiratorial tone and said, "I'm going to speak very candidly now. In my position as Treasury Secretary I see much of what goes on in these industries. In short, it is gambling on an unbelievable scale. These fund managers and their companies pose a far greater systemic risk than Lehman Brothers could have with their wildest trading schemes. And usually these types of risk end badly. There were banking panics in 1819, 1825, and again in 1837 with many bank failures and a five year depression. Again banking panics struck in 1847, 1857, 1866, 1873 with a four year depression, 1884, 1890 and 1893. I don't want to bore you, but there were banking panics in 1907, and the Great Depression after that and of course the financial meltdown in 2008 that we are still suffering from, but I think you're starting to get the picture.

"Banks and the entire financial industry, time and again has injured the nation and millions of individuals. I look with great favor upon a small fee on their massive profits to help alleviate our dire debt situation and would argue further that the financial industry needs to be heavily regulated so their bad bets don't endanger us all.

"In conclusion, and at first blush this may sound a little odd, I would like to acknowledge and thank all those financiers the world over, past and present, who had a hand in creating the behemoth that is our national and world wide financial system. I know they have been vilified over the years for many past indiscretions; however it has grown so huge, especially over the past few years, that it is now suited perfectly to fit our needs. In what amounts to a pin prick of cash each day from this beast, we can face down financial Armageddon with a brand new weapon and, I believe, in a few short years we will have paid down our debts to zero. We will fund Social Security and provide a true golden era for our retirees and relieve future generations of the burden they now face. We will be here to witness the rebirth of a nation. Ladies and Gentlemen, please join together for the sake of your parents' generation, your generation and that of your children and create a world far better than we could have hoped for by making SB 1190 a reality. Thank you very much."

A thunderous ovation thanked Treasury Secretary Lascala as he turned from the rostrum.

Elliott felt deeply moved by the speech. He studied the faces of the congress people and those of the audience in the gallery and found he was surprised at what he saw. There was joy in the faces of the members of Congress. Perhaps, he thought, they really are good people. As often happens, people are deeply swayed by those around them. A mob mentality sets in, where what once might have been unthinkable slowly becomes widely accepted. Seventy years ago a vote for a large sum of money to be sent to a major supporter under the guise of some lofty sounding title would have been grounds for an instantaneous ethics committee investigation, but it had slowly become a standard operating procedure called earmarking. Today earmarks were second nature.

'Perhaps,' he thought, 'these congress people, who had busy lives themselves, had been misled by a nefarious few in congress and self serving lobbyists into believing the bill would indeed have an adverse impact on the nation. The truth could be easily twisted. Perhaps the vast majority of congress had not heard much of the debate in committee about the details included in this momentous bill and were simply not aware of the ramifications of SB 1190, but Tony Lascala's speech had reached them. The idea of such a vast new source of revenue brought joy to their faces. They did indeed love this country and were just now realizing the ugly and brutal cuts on the elderly, the middle class and those most in need were no longer required. Suddenly, there was a bright light showing them the way.'

These thoughts made what Elliott was about to do all the more onerous, but it still needed to be said. Every last one of these congress people had placed earmarks in the bill. It was a task long overdue. Elliott heard his name called and stood up. Once again thunderous applause deafened those in the room.


Elliott approached the podium with a minor degree of difficulty, leaning heavily on his cane. Cameras flashed like a mass of shooting stars, and the complete alphabet soup of news companies with shoulder-held units and some tri-pod mounted units followed his every move.

"Thank you Mr. President, Vice president, Mr. Speaker and Chair, members of Congress and those in the galleries. It is my pleasure to be here today. I have been asked to speak regarding our defense department budget and our state of readiness, but no one can do that better than General Robert Gates has just done, so with your permission I'd like to speak a little bit about our place in history. And, I might add, I hope I don't put you to sleep."

Laughter coursed across the room.

"Before we begin, I'd like to acknowledge the bankers I see in the gallery. Mr. Blankenship of Bank of America, Mr. Hearthstone of Capital One and Mr. Borel of Sallie Mae, these fine men have all stepped up and voluntarily led the way in one of the most generous acts of corporate social responsibility I have ever had the pleasure to witness. These fine men lowered the rates they were charging and spearheaded a move that brought numerous other lenders in line which instantly gave the people more purchasing power. The upward movement of GDP to over 5.5% in the last quarter is ample proof of the enormity of their generosity. Thank you, gentlemen."

The three men seated not far from one another in the gallery stood and waved, each bearing long practiced beaming smiles.

"They stand shoulder to shoulder with the American people," Elliott continued, "bringing about change and bettering the lives of millions."

Polite applause greeted the men and then they sat down.

"There comes a time in the life of a nation when it faces a crossroads. Our great nation has faced them before at Valley Forge, Gettysburg and again at Pear Harbor. Each time we rose up and persevered in the face of long odds. At this moment our great nation faces a crisis of greater magnitude than any of those I have just mentioned. We are at a crossroads once again."

Elliott took a sip of water.

"In a few short years we will face a National Debt of twenty six trillion dollars. The interest on this debt will consume seventy percent of our national income at that time. Civilizations fall for a combination of various reasons, but the surest way to fail is the burden of empire and an impoverished citizenry. Take a quick look at our debt and you will realize we are running out of time."

Elliott paused briefly and collected his thoughts.

"I ask you, what is life? Life in the simplest of terms is merely a measure of time. Each one of us is given a finite length of time on this beautiful planet. When I look at these earmarks I am reminded that each and every dollar is from a hard working American taxpayer. Each dollar represents a length of time in that individual's life.

"Right now, somewhere in America, a hard working mother of three is living in fear of losing her job, a job that pays her $22,500 a year. That's about $1900 a month. From that sum she pays $1100 a month in rent, her heat and electricity run about $170 a month, she has a car payment of $150, auto insurance of another $110, and credit card payments of $300 which leaves $70 for food and clothing for her children. She gets by on help from the church and if she is lucky a stipend from her family. The story is repeated time and time again across our nation. And from that meager paycheck she pays $2,935 in federal taxes.

"I think of that young woman each time I see earmarks of these sorts and I wonder what she must think of us. As hard as she works and pinches pennies to make ends meet we, a millionaire's club, will take her tax dollars and waste them in the frivolous manner exhibited by the earmarks we see attached to this bill today. An earmark is effectively stealing from each and every American taxpayer."

Elliott paused for a moment and studied the sea of faces before him.

"I ask you, what is a nation? Is it the magnificent buildings, the great highway systems, or even the thousands of great cities? No, it is none of these. It is the people. The people built it all. From this grand structure over our heads to the very chairs in which we now sit, the people built them all. How do we thank them? We allow corporations to have their way with them. We allow school book publishers to charge hundreds of dollars for a single book and then we allow those publishers to alter a few words each year so our children must buy them anew. Enormous profits for a few by imposing an unnecessary financial burden on others. Meanwhile, a decent education has become so expensive that student loans are required, but those loans are granted at exorbitant rates and we changed the laws so these students cannot bankrupt themselves out from under this onerous debt when they can't get a job. There was a time when we could not charge each other more than 10% interest because it was considered usurious, but we allow banks to charge 18, 20, 27 percent on their credit cards until our friends in the gallery stepped up."

Again Elliott nodded in the direction of the bankers.

"Our home-grown corporations like GE and Exxon-Mobil, built by the hands of these very same people, have become huge multi-national profit machines. How do we thank those people? We pass laws, often written with the help of the lobbyists for these huge corporations, to reduce or eliminate taxes so when these same corporations have found cheaper labor overseas and laid off thousands of people here at home want to ship their goods back to America they can do so without paying tariffs, insuring unfettered access to the American consumer. We then allow these corporations tax havens overseas so they can avoid paying taxes to the America they owe so much to. They pay less tax than the poor woman I spoke of a moment ago. But it goes a step further; these untaxed corporations, awash in untaxed cash, can turn around and shower you, the elected official, with cash to further bend the laws in their favor. How is loyalty defined? One definition might be to look at the behavior of the parties. That poor woman I mentioned dutifully pays her taxes, while the corporations pay none. Which citizen is more loyal? At some point we must acknowledge this is not right. When does it end?"

Elliott paused and took a sip of water.

"We then require these very same people to pay a portion of their paycheck towards their Social Security so they can have a stipend to live on in their golden years. Then, every year that money is taken from them, put in the general fund, and they are told that Social Security is bankrupt. Does that sound right to you?"

"In short, those of you in Congress do your best to insure these citizens, who you are sworn to represent, are given the grimmest of futures, and yet you vote yourselves and your families and your corporate benefactors the best medical care available and a king's ransom in additional benefits."

Elliott paused to let the words sink in. He felt his anger growing.

"Ladies and gentlemen, this is shameful treatment of the American people, the very people who are this nation. When did it become commonplace to treat these good people in such shameful fashion? Where did we go so wrong? How morally bankrupt are we?"

Elliot paused and directed his hard gaze at the faces before him.

"And yet it continues as we, a room full of multi-millionaires, sit here today and attempt to destroy a piece of legislation, one that could be the very path to salvation for a nation in grave danger and a path to salvation for these good people, by loading it up with billions of dollars in earmarks for your friends and supporters. When are we going to acknowledge the accomplishments of these great people and do right by them? When are these ghastly crimes against the American people going to cease? When?"

Elliott shouted and slammed the podium with the open palm of his hand with such force it sounded like a gunshot in the stillness of the room.

"I'll tell you when. It ends right here. It ends now. Is Representative Clapo here?"

A heavy set white haired man stood and waved. His fellow representatives clapped their hands politely. All the cameras in the vast room swiveled to capture Clapo before he sat back down.

"$1.75 million for animal waste research for University of Missouri? Really, Mr. Clapo? Are you sure that's enough?"

"Is Senator Bucas here?" Elliott asked.

A lanky man in a dark suit, Senator Bucas stood briefly.

"$2 million to refurbish the Vulcan Statue in Birmingham, Alabama? Can you tell me what a Vulcan Statue is made of? And $413,000 for peanut research for the great state of Alabama, as well? You must really enjoy those peanuts, Senator."

Thoroughly embarrassed, the Senator quickly sat down.

"Is Representative Stevens here?"

Stevens started to stand up, but was pulled down by the representative sitting beside him. Still the cameras found him.

"$2.2 million for projects to benefit North Pole, Alaska? Mr. Stevens, do you know what the population of North Pole, Alaska is? I'll tell you it's 1,750. That's over ten thousand dollars a head, Mr. Stevens. I assume you'll win the vote there next year."

Laughter erupted briefly at this comment.

The cameras caught Representative Stevens glancing at those sitting about him with a foolish grin.

"$208,000 for Beaver Management in North Carolina, Mr. Coryn?"

Again a titter of laughter rippled through the room.

"Representative Waters, I assume is here. $25 million for the International Fund for Ireland? If it's an international fund why are you requiring so much from the American people? I mean, I like the Irish, but not that much."

"Is Senator Belosi here?" Elliott asked.

The members of Congress had quickly gotten wise to what was taking place and now did not stand to be recognized. Eddie studied the seating chart and quickly moved the camera across the crowd while Archie and his spotlight followed. Not a soul moved as the cameras panned across the crowd until Belosi was found in the back of the room and stopped there, pinning her in the bright light. Her plastic smile belied a stone faced mask of anger that lay underneath.

"$250,000 for a National Preschool Anger Management Project? I would argue these children have a right to be angry, I know I am."

Again nervous laughter sounded and then quickly petered out.

"I could go on with what has been earmarked in SB 1190, and I remind you these dollars are appropriated without so much as a vote, a thank you or a by-your-leave to the American people. $150 million for Rural Business Loans and Grants, $176 million for the Agricultural Research Service, $50 million for Watershed Rehabilitation, $290 million for Watershed and Flood Prevention Operations. Watershed seems to be a popular one, isn't it?" Elliott's voice trailed away. He felt faint for a moment and then he spoke again with renewed strength.

"This is not a democracy. At the very least it is a cruel hoax on the American people and at its worst, with no debate or vote on these earmarks, it is a breach of the democratic process and the public trust. It is thievery."

Elliott paused and glanced about. For a moment the faces swam before his eyes.

He began speaking again in a very firm voice, but softly as he said. "No, that is not true, that is not the worst of it. What I believe is the worst of it is the proof here in this very room that money is God. Proof right here that money rules with pitiless sway in the affairs of mankind. It saddens me greatly, and it is not right."

He cleared his throat.

"I'm sure you're all familiar with the Teapot Dome Scandal of the 1920's. Did you know that Senator Albert B. Fall received approximately $404,000 illegally and was sentenced to prison for it?"

Elliott took another sip of water from the glass resting on the podium.

"I have been told the earmarks in this bill total $78 billion. I repeat, $78 billion. For his measly $404,000 Fall spent a year in prison. His crime pales when compared to yours. And make no mistake about it, what we are witnessing with these earmarks is also a crime.

"Perhaps it would be wise to revisit the definition of graft, a uniquely American word. Webster's dictionary defines it as the acquisition of money, gain or advantage by dishonest, unfair or illegal means, especially through the abuse of one's position of influence in politics or business."

At that moment Senator Curt Graham, who sat in the third row, stood and made as if to leave saying, "I don't need a civics lesson."

Instantly Elliott exploded. With eyes blazing and lips peeled back he snarled. "Stand where you are Senator!"

The Senator froze and turned to face the furious wide eyed look that flashed fleetingly across Elliott's face.

"I would expect nothing less from you, Graham. Our nation stands on the brink and you would turn your back on her. You will turn and take your seat!"

Retreating a step, the Senator sat back down.

Elliott smoothed his coat and said softly, "There was a time when I too sat in this room with great pride. There was a time when I greatly admired the men and women of this institution. We were the standard bearers of this great nation vowing to uphold a lofty set of principals. We were attempting, in noble fashion, to guide this nation on a wise and prudent course. In the past thirty years I've seen us descend into petty squabbles over dollars, shirk our moral duties and lay down in adoration before the corporate money barons. When I look at these earmarks, I ask what will be our legacy? These types of actions have become so commonplace, the easy callousness of these thefts reflects the complete moral disregard for the pledge we have all taken to uphold the Constitution. I find it truly frightening. Personally I feel it is not only disgusting, it is disheartening. A bill that provides the greatest hope in generations is going to fail because of the level of greed of a few citizens. And ultimately that's what you are; citizens."

Again Elliott took a sip of water. His legs were beginning to tremble.

"What will history write of us? What will those future generations see when they look upon the decisions made here today? I'll tell you what they will conclude. They will say you held the future in your hands and threw it away. When the right and true path stood before you, you chose instead to succumb to hubris and self-serving activities. Putting it bluntly, you decided to line your pockets at the expense of the loyal citizens you are sworn to represent."

The Kevlar vest he was wearing suddenly seemed to grow heavier. It was warm in the room.

"Ladies and Gentlemen, we have once again reached a point where we face the crisis of a lifetime and yet precious little is being done about it. Our course of action is clear and our response must be decisive, bold and proportional. What I am about to say I believe very deeply and believe it to be an undeniable truth. We are all shareholders in this great nation. We are all stakeholders in the future of this great nation. Let us join together and face the challenges and persevere once again. Let us move beyond this pettiness and once again stand together against a common enemy as we have done so many times in the past."

Elliott coughed and a moment's dizziness claimed him. He was immensely tired and began to wonder if he could finish the speech. Clutching the edges of the podium he steadied himself. He spoke so softly that some in the back rows leaned forward to hear him.

"I love this country. America is a grand experiment, but the American dream is a simple one. Each of us wants freedom to work and earn enough to bring food home to our families, a roof over our heads and maybe a little time off to enjoy the fruits of our labor with our loved ones. It doesn't seem like too much to ask, but the dream is imperiled and if we stay the current course in a few short years the American dream, our dreams, will be dashed forever."

Falling silent Elliott let these words sink in. Again a wave of dizziness assailed him and he clutched the sides of the rostrum. As he did so, the 3 x 5 cards he was using slid onto the floor. He didn't trust his legs or the vertigo he was experiencing to allow him to reach down and collect the cards. He risked falling from the stage, but in a moment of foresight he remembered he'd tucked the rough draft of the speech in his coat pocket. Pulling the folded pages from his pocket he quickly opened them. Only then did he realize he'd written several different conclusions to the speech and failed to indicate which one was the final draft. He simply began with the last one on the second page. The entire switch from note cards to pages had only taken a few seconds. Those gathered didn't realize anything was amiss. Elliott could only hope he wasn't about to repeat himself.

"This is a very thoughtful and compassionate piece of legislation. I see this bill as tantamount to a second Declaration of Independence. It strikes a blow for freedom from massive and impoverishing debt. It provides us with an opportunity today that may not be available to us a few years from now. You can hear the millions of people outside these hallowed halls. The people have spoken. I urge you to remove these earmarks and allow the President to sign this marvelous bill into law. In so doing you will change the course of our nation and leave your legacy as the authors of one of the greatest pieces of legislation the world has ever seen. History is watching. This is your moment. Do what your moral duty requires of you. Remove these earmarks, and America once again will be a land of limitless horizons. Generations for years to come will sing your praises."

Elliott took a sip of water and then continued in a very solemn tone.

"Ladies and Gentlemen, I will close with one last simple truth. Please listen to me. Must the lives of most Americans be an unceasing struggle from birth to death? The answer is no. Now the answer lies in your hands. The American people who courageously created this country are powerless in the face of the moneyed interests except when, by virtue of their vote, they are represented by the honest, just and compassionate people cloistered here in this room. They rely on you. They have placed their faith in you. You are their hope. You are their prayers. Remove these onerous earmarks and you change the course of this nation. I urge you to do what you know in your hearts is the right thing to do. Thank you very much."

Elliott turned and made his way slowly and painfully between the raised daises which seated the President, Vice President, members of the cabinet and their wives to the curtains at the rear of the stage. They stood to clap as he passed. Several of the reporters began to clap as well. Other people stood and the ovation gained strength. The chamber reverberated as the standing ovation crashed over it. News cameras panned across the room and found many a woman and man as well, brushing tears from their eyes.

But Elliott heard none of it. Once the curtain closed behind him the cane slipped from his hand and he collapsed to the floor.

Stephanie, seated in rapt attention in front of her big screen, stood and applauded as well. But as she watched him walk slowly and woodenly from the stage, tears welled in her eyes. She noted how his coat hung from his shoulders. Something was wrong. "Oh Elliott, my beautiful Elliott what has happened to you?"

She knew there was something more than the results of a few years of aging going on with her former lover. She yearned to be by his side, to hold his face in her hands and kiss him. Then her anger grew. "You promised to call me when you were going to be in the Capitol and you didn't!"

Throwing on her coat she dashed out the door and a few minutes later she was winding her way through heavy traffic towards the Capitol Mall. It took two hours of searching and finally a call to Capital Security to find that Elliott had taken Air Force One back to Colorado shortly after his speech. She booked a flight for the following morning and went back to her condo to pack and get a few hours sleep.

# Chapter Sixty-One

THE FAINT DRONE of airplane engines brought Elliott back from the edge of darkness. He was lying in a double bed, but noted the Seal of the President of the United States on the door. He was aboard Air Force One again. Glancing at a port window he saw it was dark outside. Dr. Yates sat snoring in a well cushioned chair at the foot of the bed. A single light glowed overhead.

He coughed and Yates was instantly awake.

"Elliott, how are you feeling?"

"I'm not sure, a little groggy and really quite thirsty."

"Let me get you a glass of water."

"Sure, thanks Doc."

Elliott failed to tell the good doctor that his side ached terribly and both his knees hurt while there was also a singular pain in his chest.

The doctor returned with a small glass of water. Elliott finished it in three hefty gulps.

"Would you like another?"

"If you wouldn't mind."

Doctor Yates returned with another glass which Elliott drank down.

"One more for the road?"

"No. Not right now. By the way, where are we?"

"You don't know?"

"Not really."

"We're probably over southern Indiana on board Air Force One headed back to Colorado which, I might add, you adamantly insisted on once you'd been brought around after your fall."

"I fell?"

"Yes, and your cane hit you square in the chest on the way down."

"That's why my chest hurts."

"You came around and insisted on leaving for Colorado immediately."

"I don't remember any of it."

"I think it was dehydration, the medication and the strain of the speech."

"That's right, the speech. It came off okay?"

"Okay? The President said to tell you it was one of the most moving speeches he'd ever heard."

"That's good."

"Good? You should hear some of the news pundits. I recorded several of them."

Yates hit the power button on the flat screen TV built into the wall and said, "Let me take the intravenous tube out of your arm while you check out the news. I inserted it to ease the dehydration."

MSNBC showed an announcer running through the numbers. "It appears that immediately after the speech over two hundred members of Congress withdrew their earmarks. When news of Mr. Eastman's collapse after the speech and the filming of the event by a newswoman who just happened to be backstage reached the news wires, another one hundred and seventy five congressmen and woman withdrew their earmarks. We'll be airing the speech again in its entirety on the morning program, but at this time we'll show the events that transpired backstage once more."

The screen went black and then it showed Elliott stumbling from the stage, clutching a curtain as he released his cane and for a brief instant managing to hold himself up. The cane stood on end as one of the security guards attempted to catch the former senator. The guard missed with his lunge and Elliott plunged face first catching the cane in the center of his chest, and then fell heavily to the floor. Women screamed and people rushed towards him.

The screen went black and the announcer appeared again.

"The latest information we have is that Mr. Eastman is headed home and said to be recovering from his fall quite satisfactorily."

Dr. Yates muted the television. "So there you have it; the grand exit."

Elliott groaned. "I can't believe that was shown on national television."

"I can't believe you don't have cracked ribs," Yates responded.

"There is a significant degree of pain near my sternum," admitted Elliott.

Doctor Yates said in low ones. "I took the liberty of probing about while you were out and I believe you are still in one piece. I also took the liberty of doing a few blood tests when you were out. I have some more bad news. It seems all I do is give you bad news, but I don't think the bone marrow transplant is taking the way we had hoped. The t-cells are not multiplying as they should."

"What does that mean?"

"It means that we're losing the fight. The bone marrow was going to buy us some time and slow the pace of degeneration of your overall health and the bone cancer. It's not like it wasn't worth it, it's just that the antigen it was supposed to support is not going to get the level of help we estimated."

"English Doc."

"You're going to deteriorate much faster from here on out."

"Which means?"

"You're weakness will grow worse. Your incontinence will get worse. Pain will increase. You may experience some respiratory distress."

"Meaning?"

"Your lungs may develop fluid in them making it harder to breath."

"Go on."

"There may be some organ damage."

"Meaning?"

"Heart and liver damage. Blood flow will lessen and your liver will not process things as well. In fact, you probably should consider abstaining from alcohol."

"Paul," Elliott said, feigning being taken aback by the suggestion. "I've got three weeks to live and you'll deny me my scotch?"

"I'm just saying …"

"Go on."

"Eventually you'll lose your clarity of thought. Most of your sight and hearing will blur and muscle control will lessen. You will lose the ability to speak. Then it might be a few days or a week at the most before you lose complete motor control. You won't be able to stand or eat. Eventually you'll be placed on a breathing apparatus. That's about the time we call for the morphine drip. Finally you'll be in a complete vegetative state, except there will be some brain activity."

The doctor was sniffling now and struggling to retain his composure.

"And that's when … that's when we increase the morphine dose and you slowly go to sleep."

"Hell Doc, it doesn't sound that bad. It can't be a whole lot worse than falling on my cane."

"Don't make jokes Elliott. I've seen it before and it's not pretty. It's not noble. It's just ugly, sad and ignoble. I'm having a hard time with this. I don't like seeing you this way."

The two men sat quietly for a moment pondering what the immediate future held for each of them.

"I've got some morphine pills. They aren't as strong as the drip, but they may help your chest injury," Doctor Yates said putting a rather large bottle of pills on the nightstand while giving Elliott a knowing look. He stepped back and said, "The speech was very good, Elliott."

"It would seem to have done the job."

"That's right, I almost forgot. The President called about an hour ago to check on you and said he'll probably sign the bill tomorrow evening. It looks like 410 members of the House have withdrawn their earmarks and 92 of the 100 Senators have withdrawn theirs."

"That's good," Elliott said in a soft and very quiet tone.

"I want you to get some rest. We still have a long road ahead of us. We'll be landing about three hours from now at about four in the morning and then we have a three hour ride to the ranch."

"Okay. Thanks Doc."


They landed in the private area of Colorado Springs Municipal Airport and Elliott walked painfully from the plane towards the Cadillac limousine waiting not far away. Dr. Yates helped Greer carry the bags from the plane to the car. Once they were seated in the limo with Greer in front and both the doctor and Elliott in back, Greer reached back and handed a bundle of newspapers to them saying, "I thought you might enjoy a little light reading."

As Greer pulled out of the airport Elliott opened the first newspaper, The New York Times. The headlines screamed at the reader; "Smack down on Capitol Hill". The Washington Post chimed in; "The Speech that Changed a Nation." The local Denver Post carried the headline, "Mr. Eastman Goes to Washington" and carried the sub-heading; "Straight talk may bring end to era of pork."

"Hmm," Elliott mused. "It would seem we raised a ruckus."

Dr. Yates chuckled. "Here's your phone. I answered it a couple of times while you were resting and explained to two gentlemen, one Eddie and another Archie that you were okay. Stephanie called to see how you were doing. I explained you were resting and should be fine. By the way, I also checked my Yahoo account when we were on the plane and their lead story asked, 'Who is Elliott Eastman?' with a short bio, but I read the thread of comments. Apparently you have over 1000 marriage proposals."

It was Elliott's turn to chuckle and then he asked in all seriousness, "They didn't include my home address in the article did they?"

"No, but it did mention you live in Colorado."

Elliott sighed.

Doctor Yates yawned and said, "You know, I'm feeling pretty whipped. Would you mind if Greer drops me at my place and then I'll come out to check on you in a day or two?"

"That's fine," Elliott said and passed the word to Greer. "I'm pretty worn too. I feel like I could sleep for days."

"Sleep would do you some good."

After dropping the good doctor off at his home they pulled into the ranch compound and Greer said, "I'll carry your bags in Mr. E. and then I need to repair some fencing over by the buttes. Something punched through the barb wire. Is there anything you need me to help you with?"

"No, I'm going to say hello to Dusty and then lie down for awhile."

"Why don't you get some rest and then I'll burn us a couple of steaks."

"That sounds nice Greer," Elliott said.

As he made his way for the barn his cell phone rang. It was the President.

"Elliott here."

"Elliott, how are you feeling?"

"A little beat up, but better than a few hours ago."

"Glad to hear it. Well I thought you'd want to know, SB 1190 is signed."

His elation carried through the phone and Elliott smiled.

"That's great news," Elliott said in a tired voice.

"It was your speech that shook them up. I had a gut feeling having someone like you, with your resume, would be able to tip the scales in our favor."

"That's very kind of you, but it was a team effort. There were a number of other speakers. I think Tony's speech was spot on."

"Agreed. Have you seen the news? It's all they're talking about. Even Belosi admitted she had to withdraw her earmarks after your speech. She said she always thought of it as business as usual, but when you illustrated how grossly unfair it was to the American people she had to vote her conscience."

"So I can imagine who the hold outs were who wouldn't remove their earmarks."

"The usual suspects. It was rumored Senator Graham tried to increase his earmarks."

"We know some folks are never going to change."

"Anyway, I wanted to pass along the good news. You sound tired so I'll let you go."

"Thanks Paul. We'll talk in the next few days."

Elliott spoke in low tones to Dusty, gave him a cube of sugar and then made his way to the house where he stripped off his clothes and curled up under the quilt on his bed.


Elliott slept for fourteen hours with Greer checking on him occasionally. Finally he got up around 8:00 pm, ate a few bites and went back to bed.

# Chapter Sixty-Two

GREER SAT BOLT upright in his bunk. The fire in the potbelly stove had burned down to embers. A slight whiff of a breeze moved the curtains on either side of the window on the far wall. They brushed the wood siding of the bunkhouse with a very faint wisp of sound. A night bird called in the distance. These were all familiar sounds. Something else had brought the long time ranch hand out of a deep sleep. There it was again. He recognized the sound as that of the slow creak of a deck board bending under weight. Someone, or something, was over at the main house moving across the wrap around deck. Quietly Greer pulled on his boots over his long johns, lifted the double barreled .20 gauge shotgun from where it rested by the door and quietly stepped outside. A sliver of moon provided scant light, but Greer could still make out two figures in the deep shadows beside the house. As he watched, they rounded the corner of the house heading for the bedroom wing. Greer crept forward. The shadows stopped and one raised his right leg and planted a boot right in the middle of the French doors that led to the master bedroom. With the sound of splintering wood and shattered glass the door exploded inwards. The two men stepped inside and unloaded three shots each at the lump in the center of the bed. A split second later, from behind the two men, a bright flashlight burst to life spraying the two startled men with a halo of luminescence.

Elliott, seated in chair in the far corner of the room with a rifle leveled at them said, "I believe you owe me some new French doors and a mattress."

"What the hell?" Bud mumbled, squinting into the blinding light.

"I suppose you were never taught when you mount an attack you should already have plotted your route of retreat," Elliott advised.

Greer stepped into the room with glass crunching beneath his boots and the shotgun trained on the intruders saying, "You alright boss?"

"I'm fine. I've been listening to their slow progress around the house for the last ten minutes."

"Drop yer guns," Greer demanded.

The guns clattered to the floor.

"Who are you?" Elliott asked.

A voice spoke from the darkness. "It don't matter who they are. Walk out here with your hands held high or one of you is gonna die in the next few seconds."

Greer held the rifle above his head and stepped outside the door with Elliott not far behind.

"Set your guns at your feet and head for the road that leads outta here," Reggie ordered. "Bud, Hulk, let's get moving before someone else shows up. After all the racket you knuckleheads made I'm hoping this old guy is the only dude around here."

The men walked about one hundred yards up the road with the two prisoners in the lead, Reggie behind them with Bud and Hulk bringing up the rear. Then Reggie said, "Turn right along this game trail."

They covered about a quarter mile over uneven terrain and were nearing the forested hills south of the house when Elliott saw a slight movement off to his right in a low area. A brief high-pitched whistle sounded in the night similar to a night thrush's cries. A response came from a short distance away. To the uninitiated ear it merely sounded like a winged creature of the night, but Elliott instantly recognized it as a cry he and his men had used many times in Afghanistan. Elliott slowed and finally stopped walking.

"Keep moving," Reggie ordered.

"I can't. I've got one titanium leg and the other one is in a cast. Look, we know where this is headed. Let the old man go. It's me you want. He's not important to you."

"He's seen our faces. He ain't going nowhere and I ain't carrying your dead bodies for a couple hundred yards into the trees. It ain't much further and then we'll plug you and bury your bodies in the brush."

"Look, God damn you. He's just a lonely old man. He's half blind and probably couldn't pick you out of a lineup if his life depended on it!" Elliott shouted.

The captor's eyes locked for a moment on Elliott's raging display in the glow of the flashlight when a dull thud sounded close by and Hulk fell to the ground. As Bud looked around a rifle butt crashed into the side of his head and he fell to the ground also. Alerted by the noise behind him Reggie turned, but just as he did so a cold metal blade touched the side of his neck and a low voice said, "One sound and I slit your throat. Drop the rifle."

The rifle clattered to the ground and then another sharp blow sounded and Reggie crumpled down beside his rifle.

Two figures materialized out of the night. Dressed in complete black with darkened faces and stocking caps, Jim Buckner and Gordon Harrison stepped forward asking, "You guys okay?"

"Yeah," Elliott replied. "Where did you come from?"

"Once we were done interviewing Soro, Archie had him followed. Soro met with these jokers and Archie had a feeling they might try something. He figured it would be here at the ranch rather than in D.C. so he gave us some time off for camping nearby. We heard the gun shots at the house and then heard you guys marching along the road and just trailed along waiting for a chance to get close."

"I'm glad you're here. You probably just saved our lives."

"What do you want to do with these three?" Jim asked.

"Get their wallets so we'll be able to identify them in the future, if need be. And then have them take their boots off and walk out of here," Elliott ordered.

"You don't want to turn them in?"

"Nope, that'll just be more unwanted publicity."

Gordon poured a little water from his canteen on the faces of the prone men and nudged them with the toe of his boot. They slowly came around.

"Greer, you alright?" Elliott asked.

"Aside from being lonely and half blind, I'm fine."

Elliott laughed out loud. "Sorry, Greer, I beg your forgiveness."

"You're forgiven. I'll head back to the ranch and get the Jeep to pick you up, Mr. E."

"Thank you Greer."

Elliott watched as the three assassins removed their boots and began to hobble away through the dirt.

"Do you gents want to come back to the house for a drink?" Elliott asked.

"That sounds downright outstanding," Jim responded instantly.

The four men had several nightcaps and then Jim said, "We'd better get moving. We're gonna break camp and be out of here tomorrow. We're heading back to the big city. I can't imagine they'll try anything else."

"I doubt it," Elliott said and shook hands with both men. "Have a safe trip and thanks again. Greer and I owe you. See you later."

# Chapter Sixty-Three

EXASPERATION DIDN'T DESCRIBE half of what Stephanie was feeling. First her flight was delayed six hours and then after they were in flight they were diverted around a sizable storm cell and landed in Akron, Ohio to wait it out. Ten hours later they were finally in the air again. She tried to read her book, but couldn't focus. Her thoughts kept returning to Elliott. She knew something was terribly wrong. He was one of the most honest and honorable men she'd ever known and yet he had lied to her. He'd promised to call when he was in DC and hadn't. And if he was giving a speech of that magnitude, one witnessed by millions across the nation and around the globe, he had to have known weeks in advance and could have called her if he wished to do so. She knew he still loved her. A woman sensed these things. His voice softened noticeably when he spoke to her and he would listen intently to the least important little thing she might have to say. Smiling she folded the page in her book, closed it and set it in her lap thinking back on their first night together. They'd eaten dinner and were working late at his office on the first draft of a bill when she reached across the table and squeezed his hand. He looked up and she said, "I'm pretty tired. I think I'll call it a night, but it's snowing quite heavily out there. Would you mind giving me a ride home?"

"No problem," Elliott said.

The drive was difficult with a number of cars spun out along the road. When they finally reached her condo he walked her to the door, shook her hand and was turning to go when she said, "Elliott?"

He turned back to face her and she boldly stepped closer to him, took his face in her hands and kissed him full on the mouth. It was a long kiss and she pressed her body against his. When the kiss ended both of them were breathing heavily. She said breathlessly, "I like that."

Elliott replied, "Me too."

She leaned forward and kissed him again, but this time she slipped a hand behind his head and he wrapped his arms around her waist. When they separated she'd said, "You must come in."

"Are you sure?" he asked.

Stephanie merely laughed, took his hand and led him into the condo.

The plane hit some turbulence and woke her from her reveries. She read a bit more and dozed fitfully until the aircraft landed at 3:00 in the afternoon. After arranging for a car, Stephanie found herself at the sprawling ranch house shortly before six o'clock. She pulled to a stop and climbed out, put a hand over her eyes shielding her view against the setting sun and studied the house. Not a sound issued from the enormous river rock building. The barn and corrals off to her left looked deserted, and the eight car garage to her right looked just the same. A dust devil formed and swirled across the vast expanse of the graveled parking area and then petered out. Scanning her surroundings she made her way across the gravel drive, up the front porch steps and rang the doorbell. There was no response. She rang the bell several more times and finally circled around to the rear of the house. The French doors to the master bedroom were slightly ajar. Stephanie noted the damage to the doors and the missing glass panes and her pulse quickened. After hesitating a moment she pushed the doors open and stepped inside.

"Elliott, Greer?" she said softly. As her eyes grew accustomed to the darkened room she saw a body sized lump on the bed. Stepping closer she made out Elliott's pained features.

"Elliott?" she said softly.

There was no response.

"Elliott?" she said again a little louder and he stirred slightly.

She noted a glistening sheen of sweat on his forehead, reached over and pressed a hand against his cheek. He was burning up with fever.

"Elliott," she said louder now and he opened his eyes. "You've got a very high fever."

Even though he appeared to be disoriented he said, "Stephanie, what are you doing here? I don't want you to see me like this."

"I'll see a lot more of you in a minute. You get out of those clothes while I fill the tub with cool water. We need to get your core body temperature down."

She filled the tub and came back out to find him just as she had left him.

"Okay big fella, we're going to wrestle you out of those clothes."

She pulled off his shoes and pants and was working on his shirt when she noticed the plastic bag hanging at his waist. Retreating to the bath she gathered a wad of toilet paper together and removing the bag applied the paper over the wound.

'Here's the hard part' she said to herself as she hauled off and slapped him across the face as hard as she could.

"Hey, what ... ?" Elliott mumbled.

"Sorry honey, but we need to get you up," Stephanie said pulling on his arms for all she was worth.

Elliott slid around in bed until his feet hit the floor.

"Okay, okay, I'm up."

She managed to guide him to the bath where she maneuvered him into the tub. Elliott sighed as the lukewarm waters closed over him.

With loving hands Stephanie applied a washcloth to his fevered brow and gently washed the wound in his side.

While he rested in the cooling waters Stephanie went in search of aspirin, a proven fever reducer.

An hour later they were sitting on the back porch, Elliott in a white cotton robe and Stephanie in blue jean cut offs and a tee shirt. The sun was going down and a cool breeze wafted across the deck. Elliott was feeling much better sipping a scotch and water and Stephanie was enjoying a glass of white wine.

"It was a marvelous speech, Elliott."

"Thanks, it seems to have created quite a stir."

Stephanie laughed. "That's the understatement of the year. This morning's Wall Street Journal called it a long overdue tongue lashing."

Elliott smiled. "I did get a little carried away at times and strayed from the material I had prepared."

"It worked. You do know that the bill was signed by the President this morning?"

"Yes, he called me shortly after he signed it and seemed, in a word, ecstatic."

"I should think he would be overjoyed. It virtually guarantees him a second term. His approval rating is in the high 80's."

"He's a good man in a tough job. I hope he wins."

Stephanie studied Elliott's face. He had aged greatly in the five years since she'd last seen him. It saddened her and she turned away to take in the panoramic view. Swallows dipped over the pond catching insects and cattle grazed in the meadow beyond. The sun was slowly setting behind the snow clad crags of Mount Lincoln which dominated the horizon. It is so peaceful, she thought.

"I love it here," she said suddenly.

"Me too," Elliott agreed.

"Why did you not tell me you were coming to DC to give the speech? You had to know weeks in advance. Do you not want to see me?" Stephanie asked, unable to keep the hurt from her voice.

"No, it's not that. It's not that at all."

"Then what is it?"

"I didn't want you to see me like this."

"Like what? You look fine. I'm sure we have both aged a bit."

Elliott glanced over at her and their eyes met and then his gaze hardened and he pulled the toupee from his head.

Stephanie attempted to stifle a sudden intake of breathe.

"What's wrong?"

"Cancer."

"What kind? What are they doing for it?"

"It's lymphoma and bone cancer. Dr. Yates has done all he can."

For a moment Stephanie was speechless and then she felt hot tears rolling down her cheeks as she whispered, "How long do you have?"

"Dr. Yates gave me maybe two weeks. He's says I'll go downhill very fast towards the end," Elliott answered in a leaden tone.

With a sob Stephanie stood and crossed the space between them in two strides and began kissing his face, cheeks, neck and lips.

"Whoa, whoa there woman, I'm not dead yet," Elliott said chuckling, grasping her shoulders and holding her at arms length.

At that moment Greer stepped out on the deck and caught the last of the exchange between the two. He could readily see that Stephanie had been crying.

"Oh, I beg your pardon, Miss Wells. I saw the car in the yard and thought I should check on Mr. E."

"I understand Greer. Now get over here and give me a hug."

Greer embraced her briefly and then continued, "I was going to run into town and get some supplies and I thought I might stop in at the Rawhide Saloon and tip a few with the other wranglers. I might not be back tonight if that's okay with you boss."

"As you wish, Greer."

The ranch hand tipped his hat to the two of them and said, "I'll be seeing you."

Once Greer departed Stephanie chose willfully to ignore the topic of the previous conversation and simply live in the here and now as she said, "I don't know about you, but I'm starved."

"Now that you mention it, I am pretty hungry."

"I'll rustle up some steaks, mashed potatoes and salad. Sound good?"

"Perfect."

"Do you need a refresh of your drink?"

"I'll get it, you tend to the food."

"You stay right where you are mister, or I'll fill you full of lead," Stephanie said forming her hand into the shape of a gun with her forefinger pointing at him and trying to muster a scowl on her face.

Elliott smiled, "Whatever you say, Marshall Wells."

After dinner Stephanie lit a fire in the fireplace and they talked softly into the wee hours of the night. Finally she said, "I'm going to make the remaining time we have together as wonderful as it can be."

She stood and pulled her tee shirt off and began to slip out of her bra.

"I should tell you right now that I have a colostomy bag."

"I know that. Take it off and give it to me. I'll take it to the bathroom and clean it out."

Her frankness startled Elliott a bit, but he began unfastening the straps and tubing.

"You know Steph. I'm taking a lot of different medications. I might not be able to, you know …"

"Do you still have the Viagra in your nightstand?"

"There should be some. I haven't used it since you were last here."

"I'll be right back. Don't go anywhere."

A short while later, completely satiated, they fell asleep in each others arms on the bearskin rug in front of the fire.

Greer arrived the following morning with a bundle of newspapers and a special edition of Time Magazine. Elliott's face graced the cover and the caption read: "Hands Down Man-of-the-Year."

Elliott blushed.

"That's a little bit much."

"I object, Mr. Senator. It's perfectly reasonable after all you've done."

The articles inside included a bio on Elliott and a blow-by-blow of how the bill was maneuvered through Congress which it described as part arm twisting, part artful dodging and part alchemy. However, the article Elliott enjoyed the most was a projection of what the world might look like ten years hence. It was titled, "A far better place."

Greer held up the front page of the Financial Times which had one word splashed across the top: "FINALLY!"

It went on to talk about the financial fee structure as one being fair and reasonable and sparing the little fellow.

"I'm going to feed the horses, slop the hogs and then take the ATV on a run around the eastern perimeter fencing. Is there anything you need done before I go?" Greer announced.

"You could saddle Dusty and Lady. Would you like to go for a ride, Elliott?" Stephanie asked.

"I can try."

Elliott made it a mile before the pain was too great. The jostling bounced his insides around too much. His bone mass had diminished so much so that at one point he felt as though his spine might snap.

"We have to go back," he managed to utter while gritting his teeth against the pain.

# Chapter Sixty-Four

THEY SPENT THE next three days together reminiscing and just enjoying each other's company, but each morning Elliott was forcing down more pain pills and the burning sensation throughout his body had grown more intense, just as Dr. Yates said it would. He could sense his overall weakness growing more and more each day.

The morning of the fourth day, as they were sitting on the deck sipping coffee, Elliott broached a topic he'd been dreading to bring up.

"You know, I could use some time to finalize my arrangements. I want to be sure I leave some dough to the guys from Iraq and some other last touches. You should probably be packing up your things and heading back."

"I'm not leaving," Stephanie stated firmly.

"Look Steph. I love you and I think you love me, but it is best ..."

"You think I love you? Is that all you can say, you THINK I love you?"

"Well, I mean ..."

"And BEST? What is best about this situation? I'm going to lose you in a short while and yet you would deny me the last few days of happiness with you?"

"It is going to get pretty ugly at the end, at least so I'm told."

"I don't care about that. I want you for every minute I can have. Let me be the judge of when it gets ugly. In the meantime, these have been the happiest days, well the happiest days I can remember in a long, long time. Please don't cut them short."

They gazed quietly at each other for a moment and then Stephanie stepped closer, sat on the edge of the lounge and rested her head on his chest and offered, "I can help you with your final papers. I can type."

Elliott didn't respond. She leaned more heavily against him and said, "Don't do this Elliott. I love you so much."

Elliott lifted her face until it was a few inches from his and saw the tears brimming in her eyes. After a short moment he smiled and said, "You know, you wield those tears like a weapon."

She smiled. "So it's settled then?"

"It seems I don't have much choice."

She looked up and kissed him suggesting, "You are such a good man Elliott Eastman. For lunch let's picnic over on the meadow beyond the pond."

Elliott nodded agreement, but he had already made up his mind. No one, not even his beloved Stephanie was going to see him as a helpless bag of bones. Helpless was something Elliott had never done well. It had never been Elliott's way and he certainly wasn't going to change now. Unfortunately what he had in mind had to be done soon, while he still had the strength.

# Chapter Sixty-Five

THE FOLLOWING MORNING, while it was still quite dark, he leaned over and kissed Stephanie on the cheek. She murmured something and rolled on her side pulling the covers over her bare shoulder. Elliott eased from under the covers, gathered his clothes in his arms and made for the stables. There he checked the saddlebags to make sure the tequila and morphine pills that Dr. Yates had provided were still there and struggled mightily to get the saddle on Dusty's back. He took a note he'd written the night before and stuck it on a nail near the door. The note was brief. They had already said their good byes. It read: "Steph, I love you with all my heart. Greer, take care of the graves." Mr. E.

Elliott tried several times to pull himself into the saddle. He was weak, weaker than he could have ever imagined he might be.

'Perhaps I've deluded myself into thinking I can do this. Perhaps I've waited too long', he thought.

With sweat beading his brow and his arms quaking from the effort, he finally managed to gain the saddle. A few hundred yards down the road they cut left. Dusty knew where they were going the moment they turned off the main trail. Despite the number of pain pills Elliott had taken he still gritted his teeth and tried to keep from teetering from the saddle. The sun was just coming up over the eastern peaks when they spied the narrow trace that wound through the rocks towards the hanging valley. Picking their way along the steep parts of the trail Elliott tugged back on the reins hoping to slow Dusty down. Even the most gentle of steps from the big horse drove spikes of pain through his body. He clung desperately to the pommel with both hands, gasping in pain with each lunging step. Horse and rider were just rounding the pond when a sharp whinny sounded in the distance. Dusty's ears perked up and his gait quickened. Elliott grimaced and once again gripped the pommel for the last two hundred feet until they reached the fallen log. With great care he dismounted stiffly, pulled the saddle bags loose and let them fall on the ground and clutched his side. The whinny sounded again and Dusty pawed the earth. Elliott looked up and saw the mare. There she was, just fifty yards away across the pond. The mare stood with ears trained forward and nostrils flared.

"She is beautiful isn't she?" Elliott breathed.

As if he understood Dusty snorted and nodded his head up and down. The pure white mare merely stood there staring at them for a moment and then she pawed the ground as if to say, "What are you waiting for?"

"She's pretty and demanding, sort of reminds me of Steph," Elliott observed with a grin. "Do you want to go Dusty old boy?"

The big horse snorted again and swiveled his head around to look at Elliott as if to say, "Are you sure?"

"She's probably half your age," Elliott reminded him.

The mare merely stared, as if daring them.

Elliott slipped his arms around the big stallion's neck and held him close for a long while knowing what he should do. With conflicting thoughts clouding his emotions he loosened the bridle of the horse he loved so much and took it off. Slowly he did the same with the straps for the saddle and let it fall to the ground. He pulled the saddle blanket away and Dusty was free. Sensing his release the stallion bounded away, crossed to the other side of the pond to within a few yards of the white horse where he stopped, raised his tail, stood at full height and gracefully side stepped a little closer. Suddenly the mare wheeled and dashed away through the trees. Dusty instantly gave chase, then spun and stared back to where Elliott sat on the log. It was as if the beautiful stallion knew he was seeing his friend for the last time. Dusty lingered a moment longer, his brown eyes locked on Elliott's face. It seemed as though Dusty was committing to memory this last image of Elliott sitting in the shade near the pond.

"Better move Dusty or you'll never catch her," Elliott said softly with a wave of his hand.

The stallion whinnied and gave chase.

And the reverse was true. Elliott committed to memory that last moment when Dusty was so alive, when the hunt was on, love was in the air and the excitement of the chase was on. This was how he wanted to remember the great horse.

The stallion disappeared. Elliott succumbed to a coughing fit and sat down heavily beside the log.

For a moment he stared at the point where Dusty had vanished through the trees. Suddenly he was struck by whispers of doubt running through his mind, second guessing his supposedly well laid plans. Perhaps he was wrong. Maybe just another day or two were his to cherish. All he wished to ask for was a little more time, a few more precious hours until he could agree it was the end. He wanted to spend another day or two with Stephanie, of that he was sure. There was still time, he thought. For a moment he considered calling out for Dusty to return. Then glancing down he noted the saddle lying on the ground and smiled. Ruefully, he told himself it was too late! He'd never get the saddle back on the big horse and he wouldn't survive the ride without it. Besides, he thought, Dusty wasn't returning. With a sad smile he studied the cast on one foot and the titanium stump resting in the other boot. There was no way he could walk all the way back to the ranch.

The saddlebags were close by. Elliott settled in with his back against the granite boulder. Pulling the saddlebags close he opened one side saying, "It is a far, far better thing I do today …"

His thoughts were jumbled. His thinking confused. He couldn't remember how the saying went exactly and couldn't finish it, but it seemed appropriate. Pulling the plastic bottle of morphine pills from the bag he set them beside his right leg and then pulled the quart bottle of tequila from the bag along with a shot glass.

After he tugged the jar open and popped three pills in his mouth he poured a healthy shot in the glass and raised it to his lips where he stopped for a moment and said, "Here's to you Greer. It's a tequila morning."

With the next few pills he said, "Stephanie, my love, thank God you came into my life. I'll miss you."

The third batch of pills and shot of tequila went down smoothly and Elliott said out loud, "Here's to you Father Time, thank you for the years you gave me."

He was beginning to feel a bit woozy already.

As he poured another shot and dug another few pills from the bottle his thoughts meandered. He recalled an article he'd read years ago about ancient Mount Vesuvius erupting and Pompeii being buried in ash. Archeologists discovered a building where one man, trapped in a room, had escaped the gas and lahars only to succumb to suffocation. That man had taken the time to write his last words in his own blood on the wall of his prison. He wrote on the wall, 'Nothing lasts forever!'

"And so it would seem," Elliott said aloud as he downed another shot. "Here's to you, nameless philosopher."

It seemed fitting for all the places of the world he had visited that here, beside a pond in the high lonesome he would find his final moments. The warm sun beat down across the pond. Dragonflies buzzed about, birds sung and darted through the trees. A gentle breeze carrying the scent of sweet grass and sage caressed his face and lifted the leaves which danced across the ground.

His thoughts drifted to Eddie and James, Rick and Gordon, Paul White and Doctor Yates, Jim and Mike, Archie and Goldie, Bruce Bennett and Rosa Sparks, and he raised his glass once more.

"To all of you and to the good people of America," he murmured. "We did it."

He gazed out across the sprawling vastness before him. The earth fell away towards the green fields of the valley below and then above it all Mount Lincoln basked in the rays of early morning sunlight.

'It is indeed a beautiful land,' he thought, 'a beautiful land once more.'

Suddenly his entire body shuddered and he clutched his chest. His heartbeat began slowing and he blinked several times. He took a deep breath. Slowly he slid across the face of the rock until his cheek gently touched the earth. He whispered once more, "To all of you."

And closed his eyes.

# EPILOGUE
## THREE MONTHS LATER

GRAHAM LOST HIS seat.

Bainer resigned in disgrace.

Cobbings did not run for another term.

Whitback quit his post midterm.

Coryn lost his bid for re-election.

Paul White won re-election in a landslide.

Each of Elliott's men received a check for $250,000.

John Bainer's secretary received a check for $100,000.

The nurse walked into the room with the ultrasound in hand. She pointed out various tell tale signs and then announced, "I can say with absolute certainty that you have a healthy little boy on the way."

Stephanie, smiling through her tears said, "His name shall be Elliott."

Greer tended the graves.